IN REAL LIFE

Also by Chris Killen

The Bird Room

IN REAL LIFE

CHRIS KILLEN

CANONGATE
Edinburgh · London

Published in Great Britain in 2015 by Canongate Books Ltd,
14 High Street, Edinburgh EH1 1TE

www.canongate.tv

1

British Library Cataloguing-in-Publication Data
A catalogue record for this book is available on
request from the British Library

ISBN 978 1 84767 262 9

Typeset in Sabon LT Std by Palimpsest Book Production Ltd,
Falkirk, Stirlingshire

Printed and bound in Great Britain by
Clays Ltd, St Ives plc.

This novel was written with assistance from
a grant from Arts Council England.

for Jessica

part one
age sex location

LAUREN
2004

One night, while Paul was at work, Lauren turned to a blank page in her notebook and drew a line down the middle. PROS, she wrote, on the left side of the page, then CONS on the right. And then she stared at the empty PROS column, hovering the nib of her biro above it. After a couple of minutes, she shifted her attention across to CONS.

Anxious/paranoid, she wrote, almost immediately.

Bad breath

Never plans ahead

Pretentious

Unimaginative

Works in a bar

Has never given me an orgasm

And then she stopped, feeling a sudden lurching guilt, as if Paul was right there in the room with her, looking over her shoulder. She turned back to PROS. She stared at the empty rectangle. She tapped the bitten end of the biro against her front teeth and looked around the tiny living room of their rented two-bed terrace for inspiration: at Paul's framed *Breathless* poster, at the unhooverable red Ikea rug beneath it, at a giant cream candle that had never been lit.

Would never cheat, she wrote, eventually.

Lauren woke a few hours later to the sound of the bedroom door slamming against the wall. The main light went on and there was Paul in the doorway, his mouth all sour-looking and his cheeks flushed like someone had slapped them.

'What the fuck!' he shouted, flapping something at her.

The thing he was flapping, Lauren realised, was her notebook.

(Occasionally, in the ensuing weeks, she would wonder if she left it lying open on the coffee table on purpose, subconsciously, for Paul to discover at three in the morning when he got in from work.)

'Oh shit. I'm sorry . . .' she began.

'Anxious,' Paul interrupted, his voice quavering as he read. 'Paranoid . . . Bad breath. *Bad breath*? Fucking hell. Couldn't you have just *said* something. Told me to get some mints or something?'

'I'm sorry,' she whispered into her hands, which

smelled of Kiehl's moisturiser (a birthday present from his parents), too afraid now to look into his slapped, miserable face.

'Fuck's *sake*,' he spat.

And then he groaned, as if a plug had been pulled somewhere inside him, all the anger gurgling away as he collapsed onto the edge of the bed.

Lauren felt herself resisting the urge to get out from under the covers and put her arm around him, maybe kiss him on the neck.

'I didn't mean for you to find it,' she said, not moving, not doing anything.

'Then why did you leave it out like that on the fucking coffee table?'

'I don't know,' she said.

Which was the truth.

That night Paul slept on the sofa and Lauren didn't sleep at all, and as soon as it was even slightly light outside she got out of bed again and began padding around the bedroom in wonky circles, opening the wardrobe doors in horror-film slow motion in case they made the slightest creak. She slipped her gigantic green-and-brown wheeled suitcase from beneath a pile of coats she now hated and began emptying her chest of drawers into it: knickers, teenage love letters, a pair of Mickey Mouse socks with a hole in the heel.

What exactly am I doing? she wondered a few hours later as she wheeled the squeaking suitcase past the lump of Paul's body, rising and falling beneath his dark blue parka. Over by the front door, she got the distinct feeling that he wasn't actually asleep. To test this theory out, she stood there for a bit, one hand on her suitcase, the other on the front-door handle, like an advert for someone leaving a relationship.

She was waiting, she realised with a kind of foggy embarrassment, for Paul to leap up and plead with her not to go.

But Paul was not that kind of person.

Paul was quiet and bitter and calculating – *add those to the list!* – and exactly the kind of person who would just stay there beneath a coat, pretending.

Lauren waited a full five minutes, counting down the seconds like a game of hide-and-seek, and then she let herself out into the street, which was a luminous milky blue and completely deserted, birds chirping madly in the trees, full milk bottles standing on the doorsteps.

'I think I'm breaking up with Paul,' she told her mum, as soon as it reached a suitable time in the morning to make a phone call. There was an especially long pause on the other end of the line, during which Lauren listened to a boiled sweet clacking against her mum's teeth as – Lauren imagined – she tried to wrestle the smile off her face. Lauren's mum had never really liked Paul.

'Oh dear,' she said finally. 'Oh love, I'm sorry to hear that. Has he done something? He's *done* something, hasn't he?'

'No,' said Lauren quickly, feeling that same tight,

choking, collar-y feeling she got whenever they tried to talk about Paul. 'It's me. I just . . . I don't know, I don't think I'm happy any more.'

'Well, you can always come and stay with me if you need a little time to think things over. Or you know, just for a break.'

'That's what I was hoping you'd say,' Lauren said.

She was calling from the train station.

She'd already bought her ticket.

IAN
2014

Carol isn't there to meet me at the platform, so I drag my things through the busy departures hall and down a not-working escalator. Outside it's pissing down. I roll a fag beneath the glass lip of the entrance and watch the black cabs pulling in and out of the rank as I smoke it.

This is the first time I've come to visit since she moved here for university, over ten years ago. I'm sorry, Carol, I think. I'm sorry it's taken me so long. I'm sorry for being such a selfish dickhead all the time. Now please let me come and live in your spare room for a while.

On the phone, we didn't talk about how long I might be staying.

I'm hoping for a month or two.

Just as I'm stubbing my fag out, a faded red Corsa pulls into one of the slots in the short-stay car park, just a few metres away. The door yawns open and there she is: Carol, except with weird glasses and shorter hair.

'Ian!' she calls, waving at me even though I've already spotted her.

I wave back, feeling my mouth pull itself into a grin.

I begin carrying things over from the pile on the kerb, slinging them two at a time into the boot. First my rucksack and holdall. Then my guitar case and a bin bag. Then my taped-up cardboard box and another, smaller rucksack.

'Is that everything?' Carol asks.

Yep, I nod.

It's everything I own in the world.

There's no radio playing in the car so I listen instead to the sound of an empty Fanta Zero can rattling around in my footwell as we drive out of the city centre, past boarded-up shop fronts with bits of unimaginative graffiti sprayed on them. For some reason, I'd imagined things would look different here. I want to touch the buttons on the stereo, but I must be careful not to piss Carol off. I must remain on my best behaviour.

'What's with the beard?' she says, not taking her eyes off the road. 'Makes you look about fifty.'

'I've just . . . not shaved,' I say.

'You need a haircut, too.'

'I know,' I say.

I hold myself back from saying how strange her new short hair looks.

'Thanks for all this, by the way,' I say, just as she flicks the indicator and we turn a sharp left.

'Don't mention it,' she says.

So I don't. I rest my forehead against the window and watch the wet black streets flick past as we drive in the direction of her flat, wherever it is, somewhere on the outskirts of Manchester.

'It's not the Hilton,' she says outside the front door, up on the third floor of a converted redbrick house. The winding communal staircase smells of damp and take-away dinners, and the light above my head is fluttering like a moth. From somewhere down the hall comes the muffled hum of Sunday night telly.

'I'm sure it's great,' I say, as she turns the key and then leads me down a grim once-white corridor with institutional carpet and no pictures on the walls. There's an odd, sour smell coming from somewhere, too.

'Have you got a cat?' I ask.

'No,' she says. 'How come?'

'Never mind.'

She pushes open the door to a box room at the far end of the corridor.

'Wow,' I say. 'It's perfect.'

It looks like the kind of room you might decide to end your life in. Blank white walls, threadbare carpet, a tiny, steel-framed single bed. I drop my bags in the doorway and walk towards the single-glazed window on the wall opposite. A view of the car park and the recycling bins and, beyond that, another large redbrick house. From where I'm standing I can see all the way in: into its brightly lit, expensive-looking living room. I try to will my body out through the window and over the car park towards it.

'Are you sure it's okay?' Carol asks from the hallway. 'I've not really got round to doing it up yet.'

'It's great,' I say.

The only other thing in the room is a large brown wardrobe, the gloss flaking off it in long translucent splinters. As I touch it with my finger, I feel something like a candle go out inside me.

A little later, we sit facing each other at the two-seater kitchen table. Carol watches me eat my beans on toast like I might try and spoon it out the window if she left me alone. It's only just gone ten in the evening but my eyes have already started to buzz and sting at the edges.

The salt shaker in the middle of the table is in the shape of a little white ghost-person, its arms outstretched, but the pepper is just a thing from Morrisons.

'What happened to his friend?' I ask, pointing at the shaker person with my knife.

'They must've had an argument,' Carol says, 'because one night she jumped off the table and committed suicide.'

'Oh dear,' I say.

I try to think of something else to say.

'How's Martin?' I say.

Martin is Carol's boyfriend. They've been together for years now, but he still refuses to move in with her. I only ever see Martin occasionally, at Christmases and family parties, but I really don't like him. Martin makes me feel uncomfortable and useless and like I'll never quite fully grow up; he's physically bigger and makes lots of money and speaks, sometimes, in a fake Cockney accent.

'He's alright,' Carol says, picking at a bobble of cotton on her cardigan. There are small creases around the edges of her mouth when she talks; little lines I've not seen before. 'He's on a lads' holiday at the moment, actually.'

'Nice,' I say.

'So what's the plan, then?'

'I don't know. Find a job? I shouldn't need to stay here too long.'

Please don't make me pay rent, I think.

'I could ask Martin if there's anything going at the call centre,' she says. 'He gets back next week.'

'Yeah, maybe.'

(I can think of almost nothing worse than working at a call centre with Martin as my boss.)

'Have you spoken to Mum yet?' she says.

'Yep,' I say quietly.

'Well, you haven't, because I called her just before I came to collect you and she knew nothing about all this.'

'I'll give her a ring later on.'

'You're going to have to help with rent and bills, you know.'

'I know.'

'And if you want to smoke, you'll have to do it outside.'

I can hear it in her voice, just how much she's enjoying telling me what to do. I keep quiet and nod my head as she continues, listing all the rules of the flat: how I have to try to keep all the doors closed to save the heat, and how I can't have baths, just showers, and how I mustn't run the taps unnecessarily while cleaning my teeth.

She is only six and a half minutes older than me but she's always been the one in charge.

'Is there internet?' I say.

'No.'

This takes a few seconds to fully sink in.

Who doesn't have the internet? I think.

'Who doesn't have the internet?' I say out loud.

'I don't,' Carol says. 'It's a waste of money,' and the way she says it reminds me of Dad.

I'm about to tell her, then stop myself.

I get in under the blankets, still in all my clothes, and curl myself into a ball. I close my eyes but suddenly I'm not tired any more.

I've unpacked most of my things – my two pairs of jeans and my three jumpers and my one smart shirt and trousers – into the wardrobe, and I'm using the taped-up cardboard box as a makeshift bedside table. There's nothing useful inside it, anyway. It's just full of sentimental things that I can't quite bring myself to throw away: an envelope of letters, a collection of worn-down plectrums, a printed-out photo of a person holding a birthday cake, about a thousand gig tickets.

I've stuffed my guitar case as far as I can beneath the bed and set the alarm on my shitty Nokia for half-seven in the morning, and my plan is to find somewhere in the city first thing to print out copies of my CV and then spend the rest of the day walking around, handing them out.

I stretch my legs, and my feet touch a cold patch of blanket.

I turn onto my back.

I feel an email-shaped ache appear inside me, somewhere around my stomach.

It begins flashing on and off, but I ignore it as best I can.

Please leave me alone, I tell it.

All you've ever done is make me unhappy.

Earlier on, when I first unpacked and opened my laptop, a dialogue box popped up in the corner of the screen, asking if I wanted to view available wireless networks.

So I clicked OK and scanned down the list, and they all appeared to be locked and I was about to give up when I noticed one right at the bottom, open to anyone, called 'Rosemary's Wireless'.

As I watched my cursor begin to float towards it, I made my decision:

No more internet for a while.

And then, very quickly, before I could change my mind, I closed my laptop and put it away, right up on top of the wardrobe.

PAUL
2014

Somehow Paul finds himself teaching creative writing. He is thirty-one years old. He is going bald. He is wearing black skinny jeans and a pale blue shirt and a pair of smart, real-leather shoes. He is standing in a large room on the first floor of a university building, holding a marker pen, about to write something on a whiteboard. There are nineteen students in Paul's class, a mixture of second- and third-year undergraduates, and as they all look up from their horseshoe of desks, waiting for him to speak, whatever it was that Paul had planned on saying disappears completely from his head.

It's like *Quantum Leap*. He feels beamed-in. He feels like a stranger, suddenly, in his own body. He takes his hand away from the whiteboard and slips the marker back into his jeans pocket, as if that was what he'd meant to do with it all along.

'Okay,' he says, turning to face the class. 'Let's have a look at, um, at Rachel's story. Did everyone print out Rachel's story and read it through, yeah?'

The class give no indication that they've heard him.

'Okay, who wants to go first?' Paul says.

Nothing.

Each week, after about twenty minutes of Paul's stuttering and mumbling on an aspect of creative writing, they will critique the first draft of a short story by someone in the group, and no one will ever say anything much about it except, 'I liked it, I guess.'

This week it's Rachel's turn.

Rachel's story is called 'The House'.

Nothing happens in it.

There are no characters.

It's just this three-page description of a house.

Paul glances across at Rachel, who's looking down at her desk, puffing out her cheeks in mock embarrassment, her scrappy, disorganised ring binder spilling open in front of her.

'Alison?' Paul asks the girl with the pale moon face and thick black eyeliner, seated directly to Rachel's left. 'Do you want to start us off? What did you think of Rachel's story, Alison? Alison? *Alison*?'

Alison looks up from her iPhone, startled, then opens her plastic folder and takes out the three sheets of paper that Paul had asked them to print out and gives them a once-over.

'I liked it, I guess,' she says.

Eventually, class finishes and everyone closes their folders and puts away their tablets and laptops and zips up their rucksacks and starts drifting out of the room. It's protocol for the person whose story has just been workshopped to have an extra ten minutes alone with the tutor afterwards, in case there's anything else they need to go over in private. So as the class disperse, Rachel hangs around by Paul's desk, chatting to Alison.

'Right, let's head down to my office,' Paul says, once they're the last three in the room.

'Is it alright if Alison comes, too?' says Rachel.

'Well, she'll have to wait outside,' Paul says.

They're both looking at him now: Rachel in her unflattering Rip Curl hoodie and baggy jeans, Alison in a translucent whitish T-shirt that hangs off her shoulder and a pair of those shiny black leggings.

They're so *young*, Paul thinks. They can only be nineteen, if that.

Don't look at Alison's bra, he tells himself, as his eyes drift down towards it, completely visible beneath her T-shirt.

He still can't work out if she's a goth or not. Do you even get goths any more? Her hair is dyed black and her fingernails are painted black and her eyes are always heavily made up in thick black eyeliner, but unlike the goth girls Paul knew as a teenager, she's always wearing these aggressively tight clothes, and whenever she walks around, at the start and end of class, she causes something to coil, a little inappropriately, in Paul's stomach. There's a small tattoo on her forearm, a black triangle which – for the first few weeks of class – he thought was drawn on, and another (a rose? a snake? a rose *and* a snake?) curling mysteriously in the hair behind her left ear.

'Alright, let's go,' Paul says, bundling up his notes and pens and nodding towards the door. Rachel exits first, then Alison, then Paul. He feels himself hanging back a little in order to sneak a quick glance at the smooth round curves of Alison's buttocks beneath her shiny leggings as she swishes along the corridor ahead of him.

Jesus, he thinks, stop being such a cliché.

Outside the door to 'his' office (which is actually just a spare office room that Paul and all the creative writing PhDs have been sharing this semester) Alison announces that she's gonna go downstairs and get a coffee actually, and that she'll wait for Rachel in the café bit.

As she turns to leave, she catches Paul's eye and says, 'I read your book at the weekend, btw.'

'Oh . . . right,' Paul says, taken aback, wanting to carry on speaking but not quite sure what to say.

'See ya,' she says, possibly to Paul but much more probably to Rachel, spinning on the rubber heel of her low-rise Converse and heading off down the corridor, her leggings stretched so tight that Paul can just about make out the tiny strips of her knicker elastic beneath them, digging into her hips.

And then he and poor old dowdy Rachel Steed go into the office, a cramped grey room with an old computer desk in the far corner and a couple of brown plastic chairs which Paul sets out for them.

'How do you feel that went?' he says.

Rachel examines the end of her stubby fingernail, picks at it, then looks up at him with an intensity he wasn't expecting. 'My story's *shit*, isn't it?' she says. 'Admit it.'

Paul glances at the printout on the desk in front of him, at the parts he's underlined, his handwritten notes in the margins, things like: *Where are the characters?* and *What's this about, exactly?*

He looks back up at her and she's still staring at him.

'Oh, I wouldn't say *that* exactly,' he says, feeling a bit scared of her all of a sudden.

'It's good,' he hears himself say, which was definitely not what he'd planned on saying last night as he read it over for the first time and groaned, inwardly, not just about how shit Rachel's story was but about almost everything in his life: his writing, his flat, his relationship, his diet, his bank account, his baldness . . .

'I mean, it needs more work,' he says, 'but as a first draft, it's actually kind of great.'

LAUREN
2004

Lauren woke in her old pyjamas, in her old bed, in her old room, and felt a frustration so acute it was like a needle jabbing at her heart. She lifted her phone from the bedside table, brought it to her face, and squinted at the display, where a tiny envelope symbol flashed on and off. Paul, she guessed, correctly, before clicking through to her messages. Without opening it she held down a button on the phone, until it asked her if she wanted to delete this message.

Yes, she selected.

Oh, if only she could also delete the memory of the one time he came here, and slept in this bed with her, his bony elbows digging in her back. And then, the next morning, he'd crouched down by her bookcase and slid her battered copy of *Ariel* off the shelf (the one with all her embarrassing, well-intentioned A-level annotations in it), even though she'd already told him she didn't want him looking through her things. And then, that same night, he'd fallen out with her mum over seemingly nothing, maybe it was for smoking in the garden, and the whole time he'd had that same dazzled, gawping face on him which was the face almost everyone made the first time they came here and saw her mum's house and commented on how *big* it was, and realised just how well off they must be.

Halfway down the stairs, Lauren heard the sizzle of bacon.

Don't be argumentative, she told herself as she entered the kitchen and took a seat (the nearest to the door) at the gigantic wooden table – a new addition to the room. Just say nice things. Do whatever your mum wants. Tell her about yourself. Don't act like a stroppy teenager for once. Finally become a grown-up.

'You are eating meat at the moment, aren't you?' Lauren's mum said.

'I've stopped again,' Lauren lied.

Why did you say that?

Lauren's mum turned off the hob and ran her fingers through her newly cut hair (a shiny, dyed-gold bob, the kind of thing you might see on daytime TV), then scratched at a fleck of burnt lasagne on the counter top. 'What's your plan, then?' she said in a different, colder voice.

'Dunno,' Lauren said.

'Planning on getting dressed at all?'

Lauren pulled her dressing gown a little tighter around her waist, brought her feet up off the cold tiles and onto the chair.

'I *am* dressed,' she said.

Her mum scraped the half-fried rashers of bacon into the pedal bin, then stuck the pan into the sink. It hissed like a cat.

Start again.

Try to be nice this time.

'I guess I *could* have some bacon, actually?' Lauren said.

Her mum just sighed.

'Look, I don't know what I'm doing yet, alright?' Lauren said. 'With my life. Okay? And anyway, it's not as if . . .'

Oh dear.

What are you about to say now?

There's still time not to say it, you know, to say something else.

'As if what?' her mum asked, plunging her hand into the sink, angrily rummaging around beneath the frying pan in the suds.

Say something else!

Anything!

Tell her how nice her new haircut is!

Ask her where she got the kitchen table from!

'Well, it's not exactly as if *you* work either,' Lauren said, watching her mum's face twitch and flicker.

'Fuck!' her mum cried – a strange thing to cry, Lauren thought, until her hand emerged from beneath the suds, and Lauren saw the dark flower of blood pumping out from her clenched fist, curling quickly around her wrist, then beginning to drip from her elbow and spatter on the floor.

'Shit, keep still, put your hand up,' Lauren instructed, trying to lift herself up out of her seat but feeling pinned by a woozy gravity, her own head spinning as the blood landed, too loudly, on the kitchen tiles. 'I'll get a towel,' Lauren said, but she didn't. She couldn't get up.

Lauren hated anything at all to do with blood.

When she was little she threw a tantrum in the doctor's, during her one and only blood test.

She'd screwed her eyes shut and gripped her mum's hand, squealing just from the feel of the cold, wet swab of cotton wool, before the needle even went in, and then, when it did, she couldn't help herself: she opened her eyes and looked, even though it was the thing she was scared of most of all, and she saw the cylinder filling with bright red liquid and almost fainted.

'We'd better call a taxi,' Lauren's mum said, holding her dripping elbow over the sink. 'This is going to need stitches.'

'Right,' Lauren murmured, still unable to stand.

She pushed out her chair and sat forward, resting her elbows on her knees and her head in her hands, closing her eyes, taking deep breaths, fighting back the nausea, as her mum took the large cordless phone from the table with her good hand and calmly thumbed through for the taxi number.

* * *

While Lauren was out walking around the village a few nights later, just as she used to do when she was a stroppy fifteen-year-old – just to the post box on the green and back – her phone began buzzing in her pocket.

Paul, she thought, but the display read EMILY T. Emily was a large, hippyish girl from her third-year post-colonial literature and theory module, who was always up for going for a drink afterwards, and who always wore bags and headbands with little circles of mirror sewn into them, and who Lauren could never quite work out if she was actually friends with.

'Hello?' Lauren answered cautiously, one quarter of her suspecting that this was an accidental call, that all she'd hear on the other end of the line were the muffled swishes of the inside of Emily's mirrored handbag, full of joss sticks and tobacco-free cigarettes and dream catchers.

'Hey,' Emily said, happily, friendlily, as if she was carrying on a conversation from last week. This, Lauren remembered, was one of the things that had annoyed her about Emily: a general lack of self-awareness. 'I was just calling to say goodbye.'

'Goodbye?'

When Lauren reached the post box, she stopped walking and touched the cold, dimpled top of it with her palm.

'Yeah, I'm leaving Nottingham,' Emily said. 'I'm going to Canada.'

'Oh, wow, um, great,' Lauren replied.

'Yeah, I got a year's working visa sorted out,' Emily

continued. 'It just came through. Only applied last month.'

Why is she telling me? Lauren wondered. Is she just doing it to show off?

'Great,' Lauren said again, as she looked at the sooty little houses hunched around the edge of the green, then back down the lane towards her mum's. The sun was dipping behind the trees and this view should be pretty and tranquil, but instead it just looked so miserably *small*, so depressingly *English*, so un-Canadian, where things would be large and spacious and new-built, probably.

'How about you?' Emily asked. 'What are you up to? How's Paul?'

'I thought you might've heard,' Lauren said. 'We broke up.'

'Oh, so what are you doing now?' Emily asked.

Emily was like Lauren; her parents were rich, she didn't need a job. At uni, between semesters, she'd disappear off to places like Goa and Bali and Fiji and always come back with a dusty-looking tan and braids in her hair and anecdotes about bonking – who the fuck called it 'bonking' in 2004? – boys in teepees.

'I'm living at my mum's for a bit. Just until I know what I'm doing next.'

'Oh shit,' Emily said. 'Sorry, Lozza.' (She was the only person who ever called Lauren that.) 'That's rubbish.'

'Yep.'

'So what *are* you doing next?'

'All I've got pencilled in,' Lauren said, 'are a few more

weeks of moping around in my dressing gown and a few more arguments with my mum.' She was hoping it would sound funny, but it didn't. It just sounded depressing.

'Come to Canada, then.'

'What?'

'Come with me. Why not?'

Lauren ran her hand back and forth over the cold dimpled top of the post box and tried to come up with a good reason.

Three weeks later, Lauren showed her mum how to use the computer, the once-top-of-the-range Dell that had been sat yellowing in the study, gathering dust and static, for the past three and a bit years, ever since she'd insisted on keeping it during the divorce. It creaked and groaned like an old person when they turned it on.

'Does it *always* make noises like that?' Anne asked.

Ignore her, Lauren told herself.

She's just playing up her uselessness, her fear of technology.

Lauren told her to sit down, in Dad's old office chair.

'I'm warning you, by tomorrow I won't remember any of this,' Anne muttered as she slid into the creaky Aeron chair and Lauren stood behind her.

Once the computer had finished booting up, Lauren guided her, step by step, through the process of connecting to the internet, ignoring her when she winced at the dial-up noises, then showed her which icon to click on (which she insisted on calling 'The Earth' even though it clearly said Internet Explorer beneath it), her still-bandaged right hand pushing the mouse cautiously around its mat, as she navigated herself awkwardly towards the Hotmail sign-up page.

To reach this point took almost half an hour.

Everything about it was a struggle.

It was like some sort of awful failed sitcom pilot (*Net Mums*: 'Mothers and Daughters Attempt to Surf the Web Together with Hilarious Consequences').

'I really don't see the point of all this,' Anne muttered as she filled in her personal details.

'The point,' Lauren said, 'is that in a few weeks' time I will be on the other side of the world, where it will be too expensive and too late at night to just phone you all the time, and at least this way we'll be able to keep in touch. Alright?'

Anne just nodded and clicked submit.

IAN
2014

My alarm goes off and I press snooze, then snooze again, and then, finally, I just turn it off and lie on my back, unable to get out of bed. I hear Carol go into the bathroom. I hear the flush of the toilet and the buzz of her electric toothbrush and the hum of her hairdryer, and then, a little later, the slam of the front door.

On my way to the bathroom, I stick my head into the living room, which I didn't really get a chance to look at properly last night. It's just a small cream-coloured room with a leatherette sofa and an Ikea coffee table and a non-flatscreen TV in it.

I squat down in front of the little bookcase in the corner. There's a shelf of DVDs (*Along Came Polly*, *When Harry Met Sally*, *Bridesmaids*) and below that, a shelf of self-help books (*The Alchemist*, *Ways to Happiness*, *The Secret*, etc.).

When we were teenagers, Carol used to listen to Sonic Youth and Nirvana. She used to read William Burroughs and have her nose pierced.

When did she get into all this shit? I wonder, sliding out one of the books and reading the back cover.

Are you lost? it says.

(Yep, I think.)

Are you seeking more purpose and direction in your life?

(Yep.)

Do you sometimes feel that you have perhaps strayed from your original path?

(Yep.)

If you have answered 'yes' to any of the above questions, then this book is for you! Simply carry on reading and let Jennifer McVirtue (PhD) be your guide on the path back to happiness.

I turn the book over and look at the front cover, a badly photoshopped image of a garden path with wispy fairies dancing up and down it.

I want to go home now, I think, not knowing quite where that is any more.

Before I leave the flat, I look at myself for a long time in the bathroom mirror, wondering what to do about my beard. Should I just trim it a bit with Carol's nail scissors, or shave it off completely using the purple ladies' razor on the side of the bath?

I make a growling face at myself and think: Would you employ this person?

(Probably not.)

So I pick up the nail scissors and start snipping.

As I'm doing my chin, I find six bright white hairs hiding amongst the black ones.

I keep thinking about what Carol said in the car: 'Makes you look about fifty.'

I'm thirty.

I feel about a hundred.

In the city centre, there's an even bigger HMV than the one I used to work for. Its shutters are down and there's a big red 'RETAIL UNIT TO LET' poster tacked in the window. I stand outside it for a long time, smoking roll-ups and pretending to be waiting for someone.

When our branch closed, it was chaos.

On the last day, everyone left with handfuls of CDs and DVDs stuffed in their backpacks. I got home with mine and looked them up on eBay. Even brand new they were only worth about a penny each.

A little further down the street, a crowd has gathered round a small break-dancing boy. They clap and cheer as he spins on his head, then pops himself back up onto his feet. Still in time to the beat, he flips the baseball cap off his head and moonwalks around the front row of the crowd with it, flashing a gappy, milk-toothed grin as the hat fills with change.

I try to imagine myself busking: standing in the middle of this street, playing 'Wonderwall' or 'Hey Jude' or whatever it is the people of Manchester might want to listen to, and just the idea of it makes a queasy knot appear in my stomach. My guitar hasn't been out of its case in almost two years. It's been even longer since I actually played it and sang in front of anyone.

I start walking back towards the bus stops in Piccadilly Gardens. I dodge past the charity muggers and the phone-card people, pretending I don't see them waving at me, almost all the CVs I printed out this morning still sitting at the bottom of my rucksack.

'You sound tired,' Mum says, on the phone that afternoon. 'Are you sure you're okay?'

I'm back in the spare room again, sitting on the bed, feeling sorry for myself. Earlier on, I tried to start *Ways to Happiness*, but I felt too sad to concentrate properly.

'Don't worry about me,' I say, as not-tired sounding as I can. 'I'm fine.'

'Are you sure?'

'I'm good. I feel good about things.'

Maybe it's a bad connection, but Mum sounds older than normal on the phone today. She sounds like she's made from bits of cobweb and flannel, and as I speak I can feel my throat swelling painfully.

'Well, take care of yourself,' she says.

I'm sorry, Mum, I think. I'm sorry I've not yet done anything in my life to make you proud of me. I'm sorry I've never been able to see anything through to the end. Don't worry. Hopefully this is just a phase I'm going through and soon I'll be absolutely fine, honestly. I really and truly feel like I'm right on the cusp of finding something good and rewarding that I want to do with the rest of my life, and right now is just a strange blip that we'll soon be able to look back on and laugh about, or better still forget about completely, just you wait . . .

'I'd better go,' I say.

'Make sure you're eating well,' she says.

'Love you,' I say, quickly hanging up the phone before she can say anything else.

'Can I have a quick word?' Carol asks, appearing so suddenly in the kitchen doorway that it makes me jump.

I'm halfway through the washing up. I've been trying my best to be helpful around the house, to not do anything to piss her off. I turn around and she's holding the carrier bag we use as a bin in one hand and what looks like a food-stained till receipt in the other.

'What's up?' I say.

'Twelve mini chocolate croissants,' she reads from the receipt. 'Six raspberry jam doughnuts, one packet of Jaffa Cakes, three *The Best* ready meals, one bottle of Heinz brand tomato sauce, *squeezy* style . . .'

'So?' I say.

She raises an eyebrow.

'What?' I say, honestly confused.

'*So*, do you know how much all this came to?'

I have no idea.

'Twenty quid?' I guess.

'It came to *thirty-six* pounds sixty-eight.'

'I don't quite see what your point is,' I say.

I've stopped doing the washing up now.

I'm just standing there with my hands in the water.

I imagine myself taking a plate out of the sink and smashing it against the counter top.

'My *point*,' Carol says, 'is that you need to start saving money and stop buying brand names like a dickhead. How much do you have left in the bank, in total? Three hundred quid?'

'Something like that.'

(It's actually closer to thirty, but I don't know the exact figure because I've been too scared to check my balance.)

'You really need to start being more careful,' she says.

'I'm sorry,' I say. 'I'm just a bit of a mess at the moment. I'm not really thinking straight.'

I can feel my eyes becoming blurry and a buzzing warmth creeping up from my collar, so I turn back to the sink and pretend to do more washing up, but really I'm just putting my hands in the water and swishing them around to make noises.

I hear her screw up the receipt and stuff it back in the bin bag, then walk across the kitchen towards me. She rubs my arm and rests her head gently against my shoulder and I remain very still, like a rabbit. Beneath the water, I press my fingertip against the ridged blade of a bread knife.

'You'll be okay, you wally,' she whispers.

PAUL
2014

Paul spends two distracted hours, wandering around the university library, unable to find a suitable table to work at. Then he sits, finally, in the Herbivores vegetarian café and doesn't write anything anyway, just sips a cup of tea and attempts – vaguely, frantically, unsuccessfully – to come up with a better idea for a novel than the one he's currently writing. Then he takes the bus home, to the one-bed flat in Didsbury, South Manchester, which he shares with his girlfriend Sarah.

During the journey, he takes his phone out of his jacket pocket and looks at his emails. There's two: one from LinkedIn, telling him a person whose name he doesn't recognise wants to connect with him, and one from his agent Julian:

From: Julian Miechowicz <julian.miechowicz@conwinblackagency.co.uk>
To: 'Paul Saunders' (paul_saunders@gmail.com) paul_saunders@gmail.com
Date: 06 Oct 2014 16:57pm
Subject: Novel

?

Sent from my iPhone
Julian Miechowicz | Conwin Black Associates
julian.miechowicz@conwinblackagency.co.uk

Julian is a transplanted American, a few years older than Paul, with a thick black beard and a pained, disinterested way of speaking. Every time Paul's met Julian, Julian has at some point or other touched his beard and squinted and said a variation of the statement, 'The publishing industry is a sinking ship; in ten years' time people won't be reading books any more.' At their last meeting, which took place in the back room of a small pub in Soho, Paul promised Julian that he'd start a Twitter account, even though, deep down, he suspects that Twitter is for arseholes. He also promised that he'd have a draft of his novel ready for Julian to read 'very, very soon'. That was almost two months ago, and Paul's getting worried that Julian might drop him if he doesn't deliver soon.

Paul stares at the floating question mark.

He begins to compose a reply on his phone – *Sorry.*

Almost there. Just a few more – then gives up and exits Gmail, and taps his Facebook app instead, scrolling down the feed for something to distract him. He scrolls past a post about someone losing weight, a post about executions in Iran, a post about what film someone should stream tonight, and then taps, finally, on a shared link to an old *Guardian* interview with Jonathan Franzen about his writing method.

When you get home, Paul thinks as he begins to scan through the article, you are going to develop a new writing method, which is where you just sit down and actually write. No more dicking around on the internet. No more watching *Come Dine With Me* in the living room. Not until you have a full novel draft to show for yourself. When you get home, Paul, you are going to shut yourself away in the bedroom and work hard, for the first time in your life.

He stops reading the Jonathan Franzen article – turns out he's read it before – and puts his phone back in his pocket and looks out of the window at a kid on a bike/a woman tying a dog up outside a cornershop/a man closing the boot of a Ford Fiesta/a plastic bag floating around in the wind like that bit in *American Beauty*.

Alison Whistler, Paul thinks.

In his head, she's sat in class again, not paying attention to him, tapping away at her iPhone. She had a 5, which is two models up from Paul's. She's . . . what? Thirteen years younger than me? He wonders what she's up to tonight. Whether she goes to those Vodka Island foam parties that he always sees the flyers for, littered up and down Oxford Road. He wonders whether she has a boyfriend.

(*'I read your book at the weekend, btw.'*)

Paul's book is called *Human Animus.*

It's the reason he got the job at the uni in the first place, the reason he's not working in a bar any more.

When Paul thinks about the Paul who wrote it: a thin, single man in his mid twenties, who still had all his hair and smoked twenty-five to thirty cigarettes a day, it's as if he's remembering someone else, a character in a film, maybe.

He removes a stale piece of nicotine gum from his mouth and rummages around in his coat pocket for a bit of paper to wrap it in. He takes out a small Moleskine notebook (which he paid over a tenner for at the university shop, and which he has decided to carry around with him, since about three weeks ago, in order to reignite his creativity), tears out the first page (still blank) and wraps up the gum. Then he takes a packet of Wrigley's Extra from his other coat pocket and pops a pellet into his mouth. Since Paul gave up smoking almost eight months ago, at Sarah's strong insistence, he's been chewing gum – both nicotine and regular – like a maniac. He's on about two packs a day.

Is Jonathan Franzen on Twitter? Paul wonders, remembering hazily that in another interview he had possibly spoken out against it.

As the bus creeps home, Paul imagines Franzen standing in a gigantic, air-conditioned kitchen, stretching his back a couple of times (it's morning, he's just woken up), then cracking the top on a bottle of ice-cold Perrier and walking with it, barefoot on cool blue tiles, down a long white corridor, through a set of sliding glass doors and out onto a warm green lawn, somewhere in America, where the sky above him is bright and still and endless and he is able to lie down gently beneath it and concern himself only with matters relating to the creation of Art.

'Good day?' Sarah asks, when Paul gets in.

Paul stands in the doorway to the living room and thinks about his day: the hours spent preparing his creative writing mini lecture in the morning, almost all of which evaporated from his head the moment he actually needed to say it, his shitty overpriced chicken tikka sandwich for lunch, his class in the afternoon, then Alison's 'I read your book at the weekend, btw', his complete inability to tell Rachel her story was dreadful, the wasted hours wandering around Blue 2 with his head swimming and buzzing, for some reason unable to just choose a table and sit at it, and then this: coming home to a small, damp living room and the smell of drying washing and not even feeling bad or angry or fucked off about it, just *nothing*, absolutely nothing, like he's trapped in a Paul-sized envelope of fog, maybe, and thinks: no, I've not had a good day.

'Yeah, pretty good,' he says. 'You?'

'Not bad,' Sarah says. 'There's some soup in the freezer if you like. I'm not eating anything this week.'

So Paul walks into the kitchen, takes an ice cream

tub from the freezer, opens it, and tips the contents – a speckled orange brick of frozen carrot soup – into a pot on the hob. As it begins to hiss, he turns on the little radio on the countertop.

'We live in a culture now,' an angry-sounding person says, 'where people simply don't want to pay for and support the arts any more.'

Paul nudges the sizzling brick of soup around the pan with a stained wooden spoon.

'I'm sorry but that's rubbish,' another angry-sounding person on the radio says. 'People always shared things. They lent each other books, records, CDs. Digital piracy is just a new form of borrowing. We have more access to culture than ever. And I think people are still willing to pay for that culture, if it's something they really—'

Paul turns off the radio.

According to his last royalty statement, only four hundred and twenty-one people were willing to pay for his novel in paperback.

He thinks again about his new thing, whatever it is, about how impossible it seems to just decide on a single idea and see it through to a satisfying, meaningful conclusion. He doesn't seem to have a brain that can think in a straight line any more. In its current incarnation, Paul's new 'novel' is actually just a straight retelling of his first serious relationship at university. Oh dear, he thinks. Who the fuck would want to read that?

He feels sick suddenly. A spinning, dizzying sickness, like the one he gets whenever he tries to smoke weed. He turns off the hob and tips the mostly-still-frozen brick of soup back into its ice cream tub and returns it to the freezer. He takes a few deep breaths – in, *hold*, maybe I should start a Twitter account, *release* – and waits for the panic to subside. Then he goes and stands in the doorway, looking at the back of Sarah's head.

'I'm going to do some writing in the bedroom for a bit,' he says.

'Okay,' Sarah says, not taking her eyes off the TV.

On his way to the bedroom, Paul passes the BT wireless router. I should just turn it off, he thinks. I should just unplug it and ask Sarah to hide it somewhere.

He doesn't, though.

He carries on down the hall to the bedroom and climbs onto the bed. No slacking off tonight, he thinks as the laptop boots up. Once it's running, Paul just sits looking at his desktop for a long time. He feels completely numb. He thinks about Alison Whistler. He thinks about Jonathan Franzen. He thinks about a person called Lauren Cross who was his first ever girlfriend and who is one of the two main characters in his latest novel (the other being himself).

No slacking off tonight, he thinks again.

He looks at the icon for Word.

He looks at the icon for Chrome, sitting just to the right of it, like Alison Whistler sitting just to the right of dowdy Rachel Steed in class.

He double clicks on Chrome and it opens on the Google homepage. Paul types 'Twitter' into Google. He clicks the link to Twitter. On the homepage, he begins filling in the sign-up form, wondering what shitty username he's going to choose. Even just writing 'Paul Saunders' makes him feel a little depressed. If I had a better name, Paul thinks, a more interesting, unusual name, like 'Franzen' for instance, then all the other things in my life would probably be more interesting, too, as a consequence.

Paul fills in his email address and types in a password (Lauren500, the password he *still*, automatically, unthinkingly types for everything), and then, wearily, hits return.

On the next page, Twitter has suggested his username for him: paulsan62904936.

He selects and deletes paulsan62904936 and enters PaulSaunders.

This username is already taken! it says.

He tries 'PaulSaundersNovelist' but it only lets him type as far as PaulSaundersNove.

He types 'Iamadickhead'.

This username is already taken! Twitter tells him.

A few hours later, Sarah comes into the bedroom. It's half-ten, which is her usual bedtime on a weeknight. She has to get up at six in the morning, to commute an hour and a half on public transport to an admin job in Liverpool. Paul wonders why she never complains, about anything, even though, for the last year or so, since Paul's royalties dried up, she's been covering almost all of their rent and bills, never quite leaving enough money remaining to go out or buy anything other than 'essentials' (toilet paper, rice, etc.). She's had to cancel her Virgin Active membership and her subscription to

Marie Claire. ('It's fine,' she said. 'I'll just read things on my phone.')

This teaching job is a positive new development; it might only be a single-semester contract right now, but Paul's hoping it will lead to other similar work, because it's not like he's about to finish his novel anytime soon, despite what he's been telling everyone.

'What's the matter?' Sarah says.

'Nothing's the matter,' Paul says, quickly closing Chrome.

'You just looked all . . . shifty.'

'Shifty how?'

'Just *shifty*,' she grins. 'Like you were doing something you shouldn't be doing. Were you writing another sex scene?'

He knows she's just trying to joke around with him, but he can't join in.

'No,' he says, slamming the lid of his laptop. 'I mean, I was writing but it was just . . . you know, *writing*. Nothing sexy, I'm afraid.'

Paul and Sarah have not had sex in almost four months. At moments like this, it dangles between them like a cobweb. Sarah takes off her shirt and reaches behind her back to unclasp her bra and the no-sex cobweb flutters a little in the breeze.

'Carry on writing if you want,' she says. 'You don't need to stop just because I'm here.'

'It's fine,' Paul says. 'I think I'm done for the evening, anyway.'

His heart's pounding and his hands are trembling as

he puts the laptop on the floor next to his side of the bed.

He gets up and starts undressing, too.

'You sure you're okay?' Sarah asks.

'I'm fine,' Paul says, a little too quickly, as he fumbles with the clasp of his belt.

About half an hour before Sarah came in, he'd received a Facebook notification – a friend request from Alison Whistler (0 mutual friends) – and he had stared at it, at Alison Whistler's thumbnail photograph, feeling confusion and disbelief and perhaps a little too much excitement, as he debated whether or not to accept it. There were probably rules at the university about lecturers being Facebook friends with students, even part-time, single-semester-contract lecturers, and so he'd just sat there, staring at Alison's picture and conducting a daydream about the two of them sitting on the warm, digitally green grass outside Jonathan Franzen's house and passing a bottle of ice-cold Perrier back and forth as the smell of Johnny's barbecue (he was cooking them all some low-fat turkey steaks for lunch; 'Mama's secret recipe!') drifted over gently on the breeze – the dream shattered, suddenly, by Sarah's appearance in their bedroom.

Sarah carefully lays out her outfit for tomorrow on the little chair by her dresser, then gets into bed.

Paul sits on the edge of it, peeling off his grey M&S socks and throwing them, one by one, into the gloomy corner of the bedroom. Before getting into bed, he quickly goes back into the corridor and rattles the bolt on the front door to their flat, just to make sure that nobody is able to burst in during the night and attack them. Then Paul gets into bed, imagining actually talking about their relationship; asking Sarah if she's really happy, hinting abstractly towards the possibility of them breaking up.

How can she be happy? he wonders. This is awful.

'Can you put the light out?' she says.

'Sure,' Paul says.

I'll say it tomorrow night, he thinks. Sarah needs her sleep.

She turns her back to him and curls herself into a ball at the edge of the mattress, which is the only position she can ever get to sleep in.

Paul reaches over and puts the light out, then lies on his back for a long time in the dark with his eyes open.

LAUREN
2004

On the aeroplane, Lauren closed her eyes and pressed her balled hands into her lap and waited for the noisy, shuddering part to finish. As she waited, she tried not to think about Paul. She tried not to feel guilty about The Notebook Incident, or to picture him shuffling around sadly in his BHS dressing gown, left like an abandoned pet in the house which, she guessed, her mum was still paying half the rent on.

As the screeching got louder instead of quieter, she began to convince herself that the plane was going to crash. She began to imagine – as the cabin lights flickered and the plane's body dipped very slightly and a lady a few rows behind made a small *oh* sound – one of the engines exploding in a shitty, mid 90s *Die*

Hard-style flash of superimposed flames and sparks. What a corny way to die, she thought as her heart began to thump.

Then, very suddenly, all the screeching stopped, and Lauren trained her vision on a small hinged rectangle of the plane's wing, flapping away above other larger rectangles of boring brown field, before everything tilted and span, and then was hidden beneath a solid-looking layer of cloud.

The seatbelt lights blinked out.

The captain made a crackly announcement about cabin pressure and altitude.

The pastel-pink old lady in the next seat over smoothed a few invisible creases from her trousers, and then turned and gave Lauren such a forlorn, biscuit-yellow grin it forced Lauren's heart to break just a tiny bit.

When the drinks trolley finally appeared, Lauren asked in her most grown-up voice for a vodka and Coke, please, even though it said six a.m. on the clock inside her body. (She'd planned to ask for a double, but chickened out at the last minute.)

And then, once she'd had a few sips, she began an argument with Paul in her head:

I'm not just doing all this to bum you out, she told him sulkily. *I was feeling miserable, too. It just wasn't working, and deep down you know that.*

Things sometimes just don't work.

People don't work together.

And you and I were two of those people, okay?

Okay?

Paul?

But he didn't reply.

She put down her drink and rummaged through her hand luggage, amongst the lipsticks, ChapSticks, boiled sweets, and *The Rough Guide to Vancouver*, for *The Second Sex*, which she'd been intending to read for the past year and a half, and opened it, finally, at page one.

She forced her eyes along the sentences, even though she knew nothing was going in. And eventually – a whole three pages later; *good going!* – closed the book again and rested it on the tray next to her drink, unable to remember a word.

She looked out of the window.

She drummed her fingers against the grey plastic armrest.

Finally, she unwrapped her complimentary headphones, plugged them in, turned on the little seat-mounted TV and, from everything on offer, selected *Legally Blonde 2: Red, White and Blonde*.

In Vancouver International Airport, she attempted to feel excited, reminding herself that this was a Once In A Lifetime Experience. A few feet ahead, a group of tanned-legged, overly giggly female backpackers were all snapping away at the large Native Canadian totem pole at the bottom of the escalator, and when Lauren passed it, she forced herself to stop and take out the brand new Pentax her mum had bought her and do the same.

During a long, shuffling wait at passport control, she considered listening to her iPod, but realised that all the music loaded onto it was music that *Paul* had loaded onto it.

Paul, she thought.

Paul would recover.

Paul would be fine.

Paul would write a short story about this.

Paul would write a whole novel, probably.

Paul would sit for hours in the Broadway café and smoke a million roll-ups and drink pints of continental lager in funny-shaped glasses and write copious notes about what a total fucking bitch she was in one of his pretentious little Moleskine notebooks.

Oh Paul, I'm sorry, she thought just as the man in the passport booth beckoned her forward with a small wave.

I wonder how many miles apart we are, right at this exact moment.

IAN
2014

In the Jobcentre, an extremely tall man in a shiny grey suit tells me that his name is Rick and shakes my hand and smiles at me. There's something wrong with his skin. Little bits of his face look so dry that they might flake off at any moment. It's especially bad around his mouth. He gestures me into the seat opposite, then starts typing on his computer. Occasionally he stops to glance up at me. I wonder how old he is. It's impossible to tell.

'Right, then,' Rick says, finishing his typing. 'It says here that you worked in a music shop for the last six years, yeah? Can you tell me a little bit more about that?'

'We sold CDs and DVDs and games and books,' I

say. 'I just worked behind the till. I wasn't a manager or anything.'

Rick nods and types a few words.

I don't feel like I'm selling myself particularly well.

'Then it closed down,' I say.

'Oh dear,' he says. 'And why was that? Nothing to do with you, I hope?'

He smiles at me.

I can't quite bring myself to join in.

Maybe his mouth might heal up quicker if he stopped smiling quite so much.

'Things were cheaper online,' I say.

'Right, right, of course,' he says, nodding so vigorously that a little flake of his cheek detaches from his face and flutters, snowflake-like, towards the desk. It lands on a leaflet about depression counselling. 'Amazon?' he says.

Amazon, I nod.

He clicks his mouse a couple of times, then frowns at his screen, fiddling with a small patch of stubble on his chin and making a soft clacking noise with his tongue.

If I had to guess, I'd say he was in his mid thirties, about three school years above me.

'And what were you doing before that job?' he says.

'Just bar work.'

'No other skills?'

'Not really.'

'And you've got a degree in . . . in media studies, is that right?'

'Yep. A two-one.'

'Alright,' he says. 'I've got a bakery here. In Sale. Think you could handle working in a bakery?'

I try hard to imagine myself working in a bakery: I'm wearing an apron and one of those net hat things, and I'm carrying a tray of sickly, uncooked sausage rolls towards an industrial-sized oven.

'I'm not sure,' I say.

'I'll print it out anyway,' Rick says.

He clicks his mouse and the printer begins to whirr and it sounds, very slightly, like the end of the world.

In the music shop, I spend a long time by the door, reading all the adverts on the Musicians Wanted notice board: *Bass player needed for funk/soul/rock combo. Drummer required to complete British r'n'r/blues band. Energetic frontman/lyricist seeks full backing band. Influences: COUNTING CROWS, BLACK CROWES, BLACK SABBATH, ROLLING STONES, STONE ROSES, STONE TEMPLE PILOTS, OASIS, COLDPLAY, KEANE . . .*

Eventually, I shuffle over to the plectrums and maracas at the counter.

'Need any help there, mate?' a large bearded man with a deep voice asks when he notices me.

You don't need to do this, I tell myself. There's still time to change your mind. You could just say, 'No thanks,' and smile and walk away.

'I was just wondering how much I might get for a guitar, second-hand?' I say, nodding down at the case in my hand.

'Follow me.'

He leads me towards the back of the shop, past the bass guitars and the P.A. systems and a teenage boy playing a Queens of the Stone Age song on one of the Gibsons.

'Right, let's have a look then,' he says, dragging up a couple of stools.

His beard is big and black and greasy-looking with grey and white bits in it, and, just like mine, the fingertips of his strumming hand are nicotine-yellowed, the nails bitten back to the quick. I hand him my guitar case, feeling a twinge of embarrassment at the large black-and-white Postcards sticker on it, and he lays it on the floor in front of him, pops the locks, lifts the lid.

'Very nice,' he says, his tongue doing a quick, slimy swoop of his chapped bottom lip.

Then he lifts my guitar out of the case and up onto his lap.

'You in a band?' he says.

'Not any more,' I say.

He plugs the guitar into one of the practice amps, adjusts a few knobs, then strums some clean-tone blues riffs. I watch his stubby fingers go up and down the fretboard. He plays in a very different way to how I play. To how I *used* to play. He changes channels on the amp and starts doing some technical, widdly, Steve Vai-y stuff, the tip of his tongue peeping out from between his lips as he does a few bends and hammer-ons.

I feel sick.

I want to go home.

I want to get into bed and pull the covers over my head and never come out again.

'Nice axe,' he says, lifting my guitar up to his face to inspect the pick-ups, then the bridge. He rests it against the amp and rests his hands in his lap and looks at me sternly.

'I'll give you four twenty for it.'

On eBay, on a good day, it could fetch double that.

I take a deep breath.

'So?' Carol asks when she gets in from work. 'How's it going, jobseeker? Any luck?'

She's dressed in the kind of smart black clothes you might wear to an office. I still don't know what she does, and it's gone on too long now to just straight-out ask her. All I know is that it probably has something to do with accounting, because accounting was what she studied at uni.

'Oh, you know,' I say. 'Went into town again, handed out a few more CVs.'

She takes off her coat and kicks off her shoes and sits down next to me on the sofa. I'm watching a programme about a middle-aged couple renovating their house. They keep complaining about things and then spending too much money and then complaining about things and then spending too much money. I'm waiting for them to have an argument or start crying.

'I've got your rent money, by the way,' I say.

'You don't have to give it to me now,' she says.

'I'll just spend it, otherwise,' I say.

I go back to my room and count out two hundred and twenty pounds (which is how much we've agreed for a month's rent, including bills) from the four hundred and twenty in the envelope.

My plan is not to tell Carol I sold my guitar.

She'll just freak out.

And anyway, I'm planning to buy it back again as soon as I get a job.

'Want me to ask Martin if there's anything going at the call centre?' she says as I hand her the roll of notes.

I look over at the mantelpiece, at a framed picture of her and Martin together. I look at his piggy, too-close-together eyes and his thick red lips, his ruddy pink cheeks and Neanderthal brow, and try to imagine him as my boss.

(It still seems like the worst thing ever.)

'Alright, yeah,' I say, unable to hurt her feelings. 'That'd be great, thanks.'

PAUL
2014

In bed one night, on his own, Paul closes Chrome, and hiding behind it is a pop-up window. *Meet horny local single girls online for sexy camchats in your area*, it urges him. It's sometime in the early hours of the morning and Sarah has taken a week off work to visit her parents in Surrey and Paul has finally managed to get up off the sofa and climb into bed with his laptop, where he's spent the last hour and a half poring through Alison Whistler's Facebook photos (he accepted her friend request), then watched pornography.

Would any horny local single girls really be online at three thirty-eight a.m. on a Wednesday? Paul wonders. In the bottom right-hand corner of the screen is a live feed of a thin, pale woman in a bright blue bikini. She stares blankly from her little window, then smiles and waves in Paul's general direction. There's a glistening pink dildo and a bottle of lube on the bed next to her. She doesn't look local to Paul. She looks Eastern European, maybe. She's blue-eyed and bleached-haired and scarily, skeletally thin. Paul closes the pop-up, shuts the lid of his laptop and puts it on the floor next to the bed.

He removes a tasteless wad of nicotine gum from his mouth and places it on the bedside table next to his charging iPhone, a sticky clump of toilet roll, and a paperback copy of his own first novel.

He's been flipping through it, trying to remember what was in it, trying to look at it from the imagined perspective of Alison Whistler.

There's a slightly miserable scene in it where a couple try to have sex in a train toilet, and another, a little later, which is supposed to be erotic, where a girl describes an awkward threesome in minute detail while her boyfriend masturbates.

He wondered, as he read back over these scenes, what Alison thought when she reached them, whether they changed her opinion of him at all, whether they turned her on or just made her think he was creepy . . .

He picks up the phone and wipes his thumb across the screen.

No new texts, or emails, or anything.

He types 'Goodnight x' in a message to Sarah and hits send.

Then he turns off the light, takes a pillow from the empty side of the bed and starts to spoon it.

When Paul closes his eyes, he finds himself looking once again at that glossy, harshly lit webcam cabinet. The thin, pale girl in her tiny blue bikini smiles and waves at him. Jesus. Paul swipes her away to the back of his brain with a big, imaginary thumb. And now, instead, sitting a little awkwardly at the other end of the webcam chat is Alison Whistler. 'Take off your top,' Paul commands in a computery Stephen Hawking voice. But Alison Whistler gives him the finger, then lifts a bottle of Jägermeister to her lips and chugs it, just like she did in that Facebook video from a student house party in Fallowfield. She pulls the bottle away, wipes her mouth with the back of her hand and says, 'I read your book this weekend, btw.'

Paul's phone buzzes and he picks it up and looks at it.

'Goodnight x,' Sarah's message says.

We really need to break up, Paul thinks, shifting onto his other side and throwing his leg over the pillow now, too, sort of dry-humping it in an effort to get comfortable. Sarah can move back in with her parents and I can stay here, or maybe I'll get the deposit back from the flat and go travelling instead; India, or Australia, or somewhere warm anyway, where I can grow a massive beard and walk around barefoot and not talk to anyone about writing for a wh—

He moves his tongue to brush what feels like a small bit of food away from his gum, but it's not food, Paul realises, as his tongue continues to scrub across it. It's a lump. Maybe I burned my mouth earlier on, he thinks, hopefully. Except Paul can't remember burning his mouth on anything and anyway, the more he tongues it, the less it feels like a burn and more just like a hard, scary, not-going-anywhere lump. Oh shit. It feels massive against his tongue, sitting there on the inside of his lower gum on the right-hand side of his mouth. Paul worries it with his tongue, flicking the tip against it, then pressing his whole tongue against it, as hard as he can, in an attempt to make it go away or soften. Which it doesn't.

His heart's thudding now and a cold sweat is prickling out all over his body.

Mouth cancer, a voice whispers inside him.

Fucking hell.

This is the result of all those years smoking, from when you were fifteen years old until about eight months ago.

Fucking hell.

You were a smoker, a full-time, twenty-a-day smoker for close to sixteen years. Of course this has happened. Mouth cancer at thirty-one.

Fucking hell.

His T-shirt becomes damp at the armpits as he reaches into his mouth and touches the lump with his fingertip.

What will he tell his parents?

They're getting old, they've just retired; the last thing they need is their only son phoning them up to announce that he has mouth cancer.

He presses the lump hard with his fingertip but it doesn't go away, and as he tongues it, he makes an involuntary whimpering sound. The bed sheets twist around him, pinning him, and he wrestles himself free and props himself upright, gasping, yanking at the neck of his T-shirt.

He grabs his phone and swipes his thumb across the screen. It illuminates the room like a cold blue candle. He checks his emails, his messages, his Facebook, but there's absolutely nothing online – not even a folder of Alison Whistler's photos from three years ago titled 'Pyjama Lolz' – that can distract him now.

He opens the Google app, types 'mouth ca', then stops.

Because if I write it down, Paul thinks, then it becomes real.

LAUREN
2004

At the baggage claim, as Lauren waited for her gigantic suitcase to pop from the flapping mouth of the carousel, she felt a gentle tap on the shoulder. She turned and looked up into the bright, tanned face of a tall blond boy. He looked German, possibly, or Scandinavian.

'Are you going on to Whistler? For snowboarding?' he asked in a hesitant Swedish(?) accent. His teeth were extremely square and white, and he had one of those ridiculous little triangular patches of hair beneath his bottom lip, which waved at her as he spoke.

Be nice, Lauren told herself.

It took almost every single fibre of her being not to just tell him to fuck off.

Instead, she politely shook her head and said, 'Just Vancouver. Sorry.'

'Hey, me too,' he said, smiling and nodding too excitedly as he flashed his ridiculously white teeth at her again.

I bet nothing bad has ever happened to him in his entire life, Lauren thought, before remembering that nothing bad had ever really happened in her life, either.

'Are you taking a taxi, yes?'

'I guess so.'

'And you already have a hostel booked, yes?'

Lauren considered lying, then shook her head.

'Then you should come with us,' he said, turning and gesturing to another two identical, possible-Germans who were both smiling and waving at her, looking full of energy and not like they'd just come out of a nine-and-a-half-hour Reese-Witherspoon/feminist essay marathon.

Is this actually what happens in other countries? Lauren wondered. Is everyone else really just as friendly as those cartoon teenagers in foreign language text-books, as soon as you step outside England?

Just then the familiar brown and green of Lauren's suitcase caught her eye, about to sail past them on the conveyor belt.

'That's my . . .' she said, pointing it out but making no real effort to move towards it, instead feeling an immobilising tiredness sweep through her.

The blond boy smiled and bounded towards it, plucking it off the belt with one hand.

'Okay, great,' he said breathlessly as he placed it at her feet, as if something had been decided.

The boy, it turned out, was called Per (pronounced 'pear'). He was Norwegian, and so were his two friends, Leif (like 'leaf') and Knut ('nut'). As in salad, thought Lauren, as they crammed themselves into the back of a rattling, synthetic-pine-smelling taxi. She stayed quiet and let the three of them do the talking, pretending to be Norwegian too.

As they drove towards the city, the Rocky Mountains rose up from behind the concrete loops of the highway, and the Norwegians gasped and pointed them out, and one of them even tapped her on the shoulder, trying to jog her into excitement, too.

Be happy, she told herself.

The clock on the dashboard said 3:56, late afternoon, but it felt like no time at all.

The hostel Per had earmarked (The Flying Dog) looked, from the outside, more like a nightclub: just a large entranceway, set between a shuttered-up sports bar and a shuttered-up bookstore in what, Lauren guessed, was a slightly seedy, possible red-light area, just past the bridge into downtown. She kept her hands in the pouch of her hoodie, letting Per lift her bag from the taxi's boot and carry it, along with his, up the sticky, glittery stairs and into the large, brightly painted, blue and white, first-floor reception area, where the Red Hot Chili Peppers' *Californication* album was playing in full on the stereo and groups of backpackers were lounging around the edges of the room on beanbags and the floor.

They trudged slowly towards the reception desk, and Lauren hung back, again letting the Norwegians do the talking. When it was finally her turn to check in, she showed the girl her passport, filled out her form and paid for a week's stay using stiff, sharp new fifties, still in the Post Office wallet her mum had pressed into her hand at Milton Keynes. She felt a ripple of surprise flutter around the Norwegians *re* the amount of money she was carrying. Then each of them received a tight roll of hard, starchy sheets and a room key with a grubby, green plastic handle.

Here were a few questions that Lauren asked herself as she climbed the much less glittery, much more piss-smelling concrete stairs at the back of the hostel, up past the vending machines and the shared toilets and a row of industrial laundry baskets, to room 464:

Am I really doing this?

Am I enjoying myself?

Is this an exciting and valuable new life experience?

Am I making a massive mistake?

Are the Norwegian boys all staring at my arse?

She could, she knew, just get a real hotel room: a clean one, with just her in it.

The fourth-floor corridor smelled of a mixture of rotting vegetables, dirty washing and – possibly – marijuana. Their room was even worse; a wave of warm, rancid air attacked Lauren the moment she opened the door.

The others didn't seem to mind or notice it, claiming their beds and talking in Norwegian. They laughed loudly in unison, then turned to look at her, grinning.

'What?' Lauren said.

But they just carried on chattering, and she felt her cheeks begin to burn.

There were three bunks in the room – six mattresses in total – two of which had already been claimed by strangers; by their stained hiking rucksacks and their balls of dirty socks and their damp, dangling sports towels.

Lauren held her breath and wished she'd never agreed to this.

She wished again that she was in a hotel room instead, a proper one.

You could do it, you know.

You have the money.

You could say, 'Fuck this,' and leave, right this second.

'You smoke? Drink?' Per asked softly, tapping her on the arm, miming taking a swig from a bottle with one hand and then puffing on something with the other.

She looked down at her horrible bottom bunk, at the thin roll of bluey-grey sheets that she couldn't quite bring herself to fit onto it, and nodded.

IAN
2004

As I wait for my name to be called, I have a go on one of the Jobsearch machines. I tap through the listings on the greasy, smudgy touchscreen, but there's almost nothing that I can realistically see myself doing. Either you have to already have a specific qualification like animal care or a foreign language or a PGCE, or else you have to be prepared to do something really, really awful, like harass people in the street or clean their offices at five in the morning. I print out only two listings: one seeking someone willing to dress up as a large top hat to advertise a city-centre printing company, and the other for a part-time general assistant in a funeral home. I fold the long waxy printouts and put them in my jacket pocket, making sure to leave the edges poking out far enough so that Rick will see them. Then I wander back over to the seating area.

The Jobcentre is open plan, and from where I'm sitting I can see Rick chatting enthusiastically to a woman in a burka. He's leaning across his desk and smiling at her, occasionally tonguing the sore red corners of his mouth. The whole place is heaving. It's like a really depressing Argos. There must be over a hundred people milling around this large grey-and-red room.

Eventually I hear my name ('Ian Wilson?') and I look up, and there's Rick waving me over.

'So how are we doing today then, mate?' he says once I'm sat down.

Up close, his mouth looks even worse than before. I almost want to ask him about it.

'Not bad,' I say.

'Any luck on the old job front?'

'Not really,' I say, feeling my mind suddenly shed itself of all the fake information I'd stuffed it with. I'd spent all morning going over my story, making sure I'd filled in a decent number of boxes on the What I've Been Doing To Look For Work booklet and then memorising all the things I'd made up.

'O–kay,' Rick says, peering at his computer screen, double-clicking his mouse. 'Call centre. I've got a call centre here.'

'Alright,' I say.

'We need dynamic, self-motivated individuals to work in this unique and exciting new business opportunity,' he reads, not very dynamically, off the screen. 'Sound any good?'

'What would I be selling exactly?'

He rests his chin on his hand. His little finger dabs at the blistered corners of his mouth as his eyes dart hopelessly round the screen.

'It doesn't say,' he says.

'I don't know,' I say.

'I'll print it out,' he says.

PAUL

2014

On Saturday night, Paul goes for a pint with his friend Damon at the bar down the road. They sit at one of the small circular tables in the busy pavement seating area, where the air is thick with cigarette smoke and baking hot from the overhead heaters.

'It's this bloke, right,' Damon says, 'and he's shouting at this busker, this trumpet player, telling him how shit he is. But he's, like, really, really intelligent.'

'I've definitely not seen it,' Paul says.

'It's great,' Damon says, trying to find the YouTube clip on his phone. 'Fuck. It's not buffering. I'll send it to you when I get in.'

'Cheers,' Paul says.

Damon is one of Paul's only friends in Manchester.

They met six years ago, when they were both working on the fiction desk in Waterstone's, while Paul was still writing his first novel. And now Paul's teaching and writing full time and Damon is working in telesales. Sometimes Paul can tell how envious Damon is of his lifestyle – how, from the outside, it must look to everyone like he's just swanning around in his own clothes, making things up all day – and as such Paul finds it almost impossible to ever really complain, at all, about anything: about how he wasted the whole of today watching videos of Jonathan Franzen interviews, for instance, or how yesterday he wrote two and a half thousand words of seemingly good prose, only to come back to it this morning to discover it had transformed into a fucking piece of shit overnight. And so whenever Paul hangs out with Damon, Paul has to just pretend that everything is completely, totally fine.

'I almost handed in my notice the other day,' Damon says. 'I wrote it in between calls and printed it out on my morning break. And then I carried it round in my pocket, you know, waiting for the right time to give it to my manager. But I found that, just by having it on me like that, I felt a bit better, you know? A bit more in control of things . . .'

'Right,' says Paul, not really listening.

'. . . so I've decided to just carry on like that for a while and see how it goes . . .'

Paul tongues the lump in his mouth.

'. . . I'm not like you. I don't have a *thing* that I'm good at . . .'

Paul moves his tongue backwards and forwards over the lump, wishing it would go away. The skin around it has become sore and rough, due to all his recent tonguing. It has the same kind of sting as an ulcer, and as he tongues it, his mouth fills with a thin, sour fluid.

He considers telling Damon about the lump, but he doesn't know quite how to phrase it. Also, he doesn't want to say it out loud. He's very nearly Googled 'lump on inside lower gum' six or seven times now. He's stood in front of the bathroom mirror with his mouth open, peering inside it at the visible pinky-white bump, feeling his heart quicken and needle-pricks of cold sweat break out on his skin.

It's nothing, he's told himself.

It will go away.

It's just . . . *mouth cancer.*

'I think I'm dying, Damon,' Paul (almost) says, there at the wobbly little outdoor table. And he knows what Damon would say, too, if he *did* actually tell him. He'd say what anyone in their right mind would say: 'Go and get it checked out at the doctor's, you fucking idiot.'

But the thing is, as long as Paul *doesn't* get it checked out, it could still be benign.

He watches Damon chugging away on a full-strength B&H, complaining about how much he hates his job but doesn't know quite what he wants to do instead, his lips all chapped, his huge forehead beaded with sweat, his ginger hair sticking up in brittle tufts, his eyes small and round and angry, and thinks: You lucky, lucky bastard.

Take a big swig of your pint, Paul. It's Friday night. You should be enjoying yourself. Relax. Take a few deep breaths. Just focus on what Damon is saying.

Paul's gaze drifts to the twenty-pack of B&H on the table between them.

He takes his phone out of his pocket, checks it, puts it back, then looks at the fag packet again.

'Can I have a cig?' he says.

'Is that really a good idea, mate?'

But before Damon can stop him, Paul opens the pack, sticks one in his mouth and lights it.

A little later, Paul stumbles up the stairs to his flat, fumbles with the key, gets the door open after three attempts, stumbles inside. He's bought a pack of ten Marlboro Lights from the garage on the way home. Sarah's not back until Sunday evening, he reminds himself as he forces the living-room windows open as wide as they'll go, then heads into the kitchen for something to use as an ashtray.

He comes back in with an old saucer and a fridge-cold can of lager and sits down on the sofa, turns on his laptop, lifts it onto his knees. He lights a Marlboro Light and sucks deeply, then exhales a plume of smoke towards the ceiling.

Sarah would go mental if she saw him.

Her uncle died of emphysema.

Her whole family are extremely anti-smoking.

That was one of the things that got Paul off on the wrong foot with her mum in the first place: he'd sneaked downstairs to have a roll-up in her back garden and then left the stub in one of her plant pots.

The whole family went nuts at him.

On the train back afterwards, he'd promised Sarah he would give up, right there and then.

He opens Facebook, ignoring the 'Trumpet Fight' video that Damon has already posted on his timeline, instead going straight to Alison Whistler's profile.

She's changed her profile pic to a photo of a cat wearing sunglasses, and her cover photo is now a neon-pink, galactic-looking background.

The first post on her wall is a rant about how the server in Starbucks was rude to her this morning:

Idgi, it concluded. *Why do ppl think it's alright to treat you that way? 0_o*

Paul types 'what does idgi mean' into Google.

Takes another swig of his lager.

Lights a cigarette.

Tabs back to Facebook.

He turns on chat, not actually intending to *chat* to her, let's get this clear, just to see if she's online, and looks down the list of names (mostly people he went to school with, who he never really talks to any more), and when he sees her name with a small green circle next to it, his heart does a little cartwheel.

He swigs his lager and chain-smokes three more cigarettes, all the while looking at Alison Whistler's name, wondering what would happen if he just clicked on it.

I could do it, he thinks.

It would be so easy.

I could just type 'hi'.

'Hi,' he types.

But I'm not actually going to press return, he thinks, taking a deep drag on his cigarette, feeling drunk and dizzy and for one brief moment like the Paul he used to remember being: the Paul who wrote that novel, mostly very late at night and a bit drunk, pretending he was Charles Bukowski, the Paul who didn't have mouth ca—

He presses return.

Oh shit, he thinks, as soon as he's done it.

Oh shit, oh fuck. What have I done?

'hi' Alison messages back, almost instantaneously.

Oh god, Paul thinks. Oh shit. Oh fuck. Oh shit.

He considers just quickly closing the chat box, shutting the laptop down, going straight to bed. Instead he takes a big swig of his can, then a long drag on his cigarette.

'Hi,' he types again.

'how are you?' Alison messages back, almost instantaneously.

'OK,' Paul types. 'You?'

'cant sleep,' Alison types.

'Me neither,' Paul types.

There's a pause.

What the fuck am I doing? Paul thinks.

'I'd better go to sleep,' he types, but doesn't send.

'theres a lot of sex in your book lol,' Alison types.

A moment later a little picture appears, of a blushing cartoon face.

Paul deletes 'I'd better go to sleep' and types 'What did you think?'

He is about to send it when his mobile buzzes.

It's Sarah.

'Missing you. Can't sleep. You still awake? xxx,' it says.

Fucking hell.

Paul deletes 'What did you think?' and retypes 'I'd better go to sleep', quickly hitting send before he can change his mind.

'lol,' Alison Whistler types.

'Bye,' Paul types.

'see you monday,' Alison types.

Paul doesn't reply.

He waits.

A winking cartoon face appears.

Alison Whistler has gone offline, the chat box tells him.

LAUREN
2004

They ended up on a small roof terrace, which was still part of the hostel. One of the Norwegians went off somewhere and came back a few minutes later with ice-cold cans of beer. They were small, like Coke cans, and Lauren felt dreamy and spaced out as she sipped from hers. It was not unpleasant, this feeling, and she finally felt herself unwind and begin to have a good time.

You are here in Canada, finally.

The Norwegians were laughing and talking amongst themselves, and there were other groups up on the roof, too: a tanned kissing couple in the corner nearest to them, both with ratty white-person dreadlocks; and she could hear other voices behind her, English accents and Canadian accents and maybe French ones.

'Smoke? Smoke?' Per was saying.

He'd snaked himself right in close on the low wooden bench that ran around the edges of the terrace. Down below, she could hear cars beeping and swishing along the street, headed, she assumed, into downtown Vancouver. It was dark but not cold – she was only wearing a T-shirt – and the lights of the nearby buildings glittered and twinkled. How pretty, she thought as she took a large gulp of beer then accepted the joint from Per.

She took a long blast, held it in.

She passed it along to the stranger on her left.

'So how long you here for?' Per asked.

'I'm on a working visa. So . . . a year, I guess? You?'

'We are just here as tourists,' he said, smiling. 'Just one week here. Then America. Seattle. You like Seattle?'

'I don't know. I've never been.'

'You like grunge music?' he said, miming playing a guitar.

'It's okay.'

Pretty much all music made Lauren think of Paul now; of his meticulous, tiny handwriting on the compilation tapes he used to make her, of the way he would very seriously put on a CD in his room and then quickly pad back to the bed and just sit there in silence next to her, listening to it, wanting desperately for her to hear whatever it was he was hearing in it.

'What were you doing back in England?' Per said, and as he spoke, his Adam's apple bobbed wildly in his throat. His voice was soft, but it was also deeper, more manly than Paul's, and Lauren wondered if, perhaps, she fancied him. Not really, she decided, but there was definitely something very clean and pure about him, if only he'd shave that bit of hair beneath his lip.

What did they call it? A soul patch?

'Sorry, what did you say again?' she said, lurching back into the present, realising that Per was staring at her, waiting for an answer.

'What were you doing?' he repeated. 'Back home?'

'Oh, nothing much.' She could feel her scalp tingling, just from that single toke, and her head tugged at her neck as if it wanted to float off her body and up into the sky. 'I just graduated from university.'

'You have a boyfriend back home?'

'Yep,' she lied.

She could feel his arm moving in behind her, his hand gently brushing that tingly inch of bare skin between her jeans and top.

'If you have a boyfriend,' Per said, enunciating each word in his soft, slow way, 'then why have you come away from him for a year?'

'I don't know.'

'I don't think you have a boyfriend,' he continued, smiling broadly like he'd just solved a cryptic crossword. 'I think you're lying.'

'Maybe,' Lauren said, feeling herself smile too, against her control. 'Maybe I am.'

'And maybe then I could be your boyfriend?'

The sheer brazenness and absurdity of the idea made her laugh out loud, laugh so hard in fact that she began coughing violently. Per laughed, too, but when she didn't stop he began patting her back, and when she sat back up again he didn't move his hand away. He left it there, his fingers tracing up and down the bumps of her spine, scooting back and forth over the clasp of her bra, and Lauren discovered that she was completely unable to say anything about this or attempt to move his hand, or herself, away.

I'm on holiday, she thought fuzzily.

I'm single.

I can do what I want.

IAN
2014

I look in at the contents of my kitchen cupboard: three Jaffa Cakes, one jar of Marmite, two thirds of a bottle of squeezy ketchup. Carol's right. I'm bad at shopping. I need to start saving money. There's a pot of stew bubbling on the hob, filling the kitchen with a warm, hearty smell. Oh god, I think, my stomach growling. If I could just eat a bowl of Carol's stew, just one small bowl of it, then I might finally gain the necessary energy to turn my life around.

I head down the hall to the living room, to ask her. I can hear *Bargain Hunt* on the TV.

'What?' she says, when she notices me hovering in the doorway. She looks different somehow. She's done her hair up and she isn't in her normal work clothes.

Instead she's wearing a floral-print dress and a fancy necklace and there's a strong smell of perfume hanging in the air.

'We gave this couple two hundred pounds to spend on antiques,' the man on *Bargain Hunt* says. 'Let's see how they got on.'

'*What?*' Carol says again, just as I realise who the stew and the clothes and the hair and the necklace are for.

'Nothing,' I say. 'I'm just off to the shops. See you in a bit.'

I make the mistake of pausing on the front steps of the building to roll a fag, and before I can safely make it out of the car park and onto the street, Martin's black Audi is pulling in through the entrance. He flashes his lights and beeps his horn and I can hear the muffled wub of house music.

I light my roll-up and walk over.

He gets out and locks the car with a big black key fob. He's wearing a tight-fitting pinstripe suit and his hair looks rock-solid with gel.

'How we doing then, me old tiger?' he says in his fake Cockney accent. He slaps me hard on the shoulder. 'So, how's things?' he says in his real voice.

'Oh, you know.'

I wonder how much Carol's already told him about my current situation.

(Absolutely nothing, I hope.)

'Any luck finding a job yet?' he says.

'Not yet,' I say.

'Fucking dead out there, right? Well, if you get really stuck, I could always use you at my place, yeah? It's not rocket science. Sure a bright lad like you could handle it.'

'Cheers, Martin. I'll keep that in mind.'

'Nice one,' he says, kicking an invisible football into the darkness of the car park. He turns to head up the front steps. 'You going in too, yeah?'

'Just popping to the shops.'

I drop my roll-up on the tarmac and grind it out with my trainer.

I will give up smoking on my thirty-first birthday, I tell myself.

'See you in a bit,' I say to Martin.

'Nice one,' Martin says, in his fake Cockney accent.

In Morrisons, nobody seems happy. A baby is screaming its head off and a tired-looking woman is having an argument on her phone and someone's knocked over a whole display of pasta sauce and left it there, a dangerous puddle of tomatoes and glass. Shania Twain is playing on the stereo. The bananas all have bruises on them. A woman at the cheese counter offers me a tiny cube of Cornish pasty on a cocktail stick.

I walk up and down the aisles very carefully, trying to pay attention to everything, trying not to make any mistakes with my shopping this time.

At the damaged items display, an old lady is attempting to get a box of teabags down from the top shelf, and when I step in to help her, placing the dented box in her gnarled purple hands, the way she nods her head and says, 'Thank you very much,' makes me want to put my arms around her and sob into her woolly hat.

In the tinned soup and vegetables aisle, I slow right down, lifting items carefully into my basket, as if I'm on a hidden camera game show and Carol is watching from a back room. I'm sure she'd be proud of my selection: I make no rash purchases, instead choosing only the absolute necessities and nearly all from the economy range. Chopped tomatoes, baked beans, soup. I add it up as I go along and so far I've still not quite spent a quid.

I'm trying desperately to feel good about the idea of saving money but it's hard to do.

For starters, my basket looks like a selection of things you might find in a nuclear fallout shelter.

Also, I'm worried that it's all going to taste like shit.

I turn the corner and walk down the meat and cheese aisle, mainly just to punish myself. I stop in the beef section and force myself to look at the biggest, juiciest sirloin steak on the shelf. I force myself to imagine frying it and then sticking a fork in it and lifting it to my mouth, whole.

Right now it feels like I'll never have enough money to buy anything nice, ever again.

By the time I reach the cheese, I'm about ready to faint.

My thoughts are swirling.

I'm not making much sense.

For some reason, I'm thinking about Rosemary again, patron saint of free wireless internet. I wonder what sort of person she is, and why she doesn't encrypt her network.

Maybe she's just really kind.

Maybe she's my age and one day we'll meet and fall in love and move in together.

As if in answer to this last thought, an insanely pretty girl turns the corner and begins walking down the aisle towards me. She's like someone from an American indie film: her hair is dyed black and shiny with a severe fringe and she's wearing big black glasses and a bright red duffel coat and listening to music on white Apple earbuds.

Rosemary, could this be you?

As she approaches, I look down at my shitty economy items and feel a deep wave of shame wash over me. I grab a large bag of Babybels off the shelf and drape them over the things in my basket like a camouflage net, just before she walks past.

Then I turn and follow her to the self-checkouts.

I join the queue directly behind her, feeling my heart thudding against my ribs, listening to the whispering tick of her iPod, wondering what she's listening to, and hoping pathetically that something miraculous will happen – that she will drop her shopping, perhaps, and I will have to help her pick it up – that in some way the elements of our lives will contrive themselves into a scenario where we will start talking and discover that we have loads in common and exchange phone numbers and fall in love, just like in the movies.

500 Days of Rosemary, I think as the basket queue shuffles forwards.

I can't take my eyes off her.

Her hair's so black and shiny.

In fact I'm so busy watching her scan her shopping through the machine, I forget it's my turn next and the man behind me has to tap me on the shoulder and point out a machine that's become available.

'*This summer*,' a gravelly American movie trailer voice announces inside me, '*the unexpected item in the bagging area turns out to be . . . LOVE*.'

I scan my items and bag them up and stuff my pocketfuls of change into the plastic mouth of the self-service machine as quickly as I can. Then I snatch my receipt and grab my bags and dash out through the exit.

I look all around me, but Rosemary's long gone.

I'm already halfway home before I realise. I open my carrier bag and peer inside it. Sure enough, there they are staring back up at me: one large net bag of Babybels.

Fuck's sake.

I can't take them back into the flat.

If I put them in the fridge and Carol sees them, she'll have another go at me about wasting money. She'll think I'm taking the piss, directly challenging her after our talk the other night.

I could return them to the supermarket, but it seems so far away all of a sudden.

So I tear a hole in the netting and take out a Babybel,

peel off the wax coating, and stuff it whole into my mouth. As I'm chewing the first one, I peel open a second and force that in, too. By the time I reach the car park again, I've eaten almost half the bag. I want to throw the rest away but I think again about how much they cost. (*Two hundredths of my guitar!*) So instead I crouch by the bins, out of view of the windows to our flat, out of view of the house next door, and stuff the remaining Babybels into my mouth, one by one, until they're finished.

PAUL
2014

Paul wakes up with a foggy, throbbing head and a dry, sour mouth. Last night I smoked, he thinks. And then he remembers chatting with Alison and feels even worse. And then he tongues his gum hopefully, but the lump is still there. It's grown, too, or else he's just made it more prominent with all the fiddling he's been doing. Either way, it's still there.

He takes his phone off the bedside table, wipes his thumb across the screen, and looks at his text messages, at 'Missing you. Can't sleep. You still awake? xxx' that Sarah sent him, which he's still not replied to. 'Sorry I didn't reply,' he types. 'Had an early night. Missing you too. Love you x,' and presses send.

He checks his inbox.

Three new emails. The first is from one of his undergraduate students, Craig (a shy bespectacled boy with a soft Birmingham accent), who is submitting his story for Monday's workshop, a Word doc with the file name 'Guardian of the Tombs.docx', the second is a notification telling him that a person called @sexwand52 is now following him on Twitter, and the third is an email from his agent, Julian, a follow-up to his question mark of a few days ago. This time there's a full sentence:

Anything to show me yet?

Why did I ever tell him it was almost finished? Paul thinks, remembering their last meeting, in that pub, The Dog and Something-or-Other in Soho.

The truth of it was that Paul had written one-and-a-half chapters and a few scattered, semi-legible notes about the rest, and he was still in that precarious first flush of excitement, when the enthusiasm for an idea could run cold at any moment, the way it had for all Paul's previous second novel ideas, and – oh god – he should've just kept his mouth shut, but instead he'd drunk one too many exotic lagers on the Conwin & Black expense account and attempted to convince Julian that he wasn't a failure, that all that hard work that Julian and everyone else had put into establishing Paul as an 'extraordinary new voice' a couple of years ago hadn't gone completely to shit.

Paul reads 'Anything to show me yet?' again, then flips off the covers, gets out of bed, and scuttles into the living room, where it still reeks of smoke even though the windows are jammed open, cold air whistling into the room.

I don't *have* to write, he tells himself.

I could just work in a bar again. Or a shop.

At least when I was working in a bar there was no real pressure to do anything I didn't want to.

Maybe I was just a person with one novel inside them.

I should just stop.

Do something else.

Go to Australia.

Grow a beard.

Buy a car and crash it into the sea.

He picks up the packet of fags on the coffee table and shakes it, feeling the last three or four rattle inside.

He sits down on the sofa, teeth chattering, and picks up his laptop.

'Hi Julian,' he types. 'Almost there! I should have a pretty decent first draft to show you in, say, another week or two? Maybe a month, tops. Sorry for the delay but I just want to make sure it's all perfect. Sound okay?'

What the fuck am I doing? Paul thinks as he clicks send.

'It's freezing in here.'

This is the first thing Sarah says when she gets in that evening. Then she sniffs the air and her face darkens.

'Before you say anything,' Paul whimpers, 'I haven't been smoking. It was Damon. Damon came round last night and we got drunk and he ended up smoking in here before I could stop him.'

'I thought you said you had an early night.'

'I did. I mean, he came round and we got drunk, but it was still early when he left. I just went to bed at, like, ten. That's how drunk I was.'

'Great,' Sarah says.

'Hey,' Paul says. 'Don't be like that.'

'Like what?' Sarah says.

'How were your parents?' Paul says.

Sarah leaves the room. Paul hears her stomp down the corridor and into the bedroom, slamming the door behind her.

He knows he should go after her.

He sits down on the sofa instead.

We should just break up, he thinks.

He stands, heads down the corridor, gingerly opens the bedroom door, and looks in at Sarah who is now untangling a huge black ball of tights.

'I love you,' he says from the doorway.

Sarah doesn't reply.

'How were your parents?'

'Fine.'

'What's the matter?'

Sarah turns to look at him.

'Nothing's the matter.'

Something is definitely the matter. Her face is crumpled and sad-looking in a way that Paul hasn't seen before.

'Have you eaten anything apart from pasties and

doughnuts and peanut butter on toast while I've been away?' she says.

'I had some pizza too,' Paul says, wandering over to her, not really sure what he'll do when he gets there.

He stands behind her and slips his arms round her waist in a loose, awkward hug.

'I love you,' he says again.

'I'll do you a curry later.'

He wonders if her face is still all crumpled.

Why is she still going out with him?

'You're too nice to me,' he says into her clean, pale neck.

LAUREN
2004

Lauren woke with a thick, sour taste in her mouth and an arm that wasn't hers hanging heavily against her hip. The air in the room was stale and clammy and when Lauren tried to slip herself out of the bunk and away from Per, she found that her ankles were tangled in her underwear and she had to cling to the bedframe to stop herself falling, face first, onto the floor.

She could only remember some of what happened last night, and she winced at what she did remember.

Fucking idiot, she chided.

Her head was throbbing and she needed water. Water, and a nice clean hotel bed.

Canada. You are in Canada now and you are a

fucking idiot and you are dehydrated and last night you did something incredibly stupid. You sat on the roof terrace of a hostel with a group of strangers and drank strange lagers and smoked some of an extremely strong joint that might have had something else in it too, and then you let a Norwegian boy fuck you.

Did you use a condom at least?

Lauren stuck her fingers between her legs, lifted them to her nose, and smelled the sharp tang of rubber and not washing.

The five other bodies in the room – all men – were snoring softly in their bunks as she padded around the sticky, horrible-smelling room, collecting her things, fastening her bra, pulling up her jeans, and when she squatted to tie her shoelaces, her knees cracked so loudly it made her heart flip.

Down in the lobby there were only a couple of sleepy, stoned backpackers sprawled on beanbags. The music was quieter too. It must be very early in the morning, she guessed, looking around for a clock and not finding one. The girl at the desk – a different girl from the one who checked her in, thank god – didn't look up from her Sophie Kinsella paperback when Lauren left her room key on the counter, then turned and walked, as straight-backed as she could manage, the wheels of her suitcase catching and squeaking, as she went out of the door and down the glittery, sticky steps towards the street.

* * *

The man in the internet café let her leave her suitcase behind the counter.

'Just got here, eh?' he asked, grinning, his face large and round and stubbly.

Lauren nodded.

'Australian, right?' he said, trying to catch her eye.

'English,' she mumbled, wishing she was back in England, where no one talked to anyone unless it was absolutely necessary.

She was unable to look him directly in the eye as she placed a warm dollar coin in his palm then took the stub of paper from his other hand. She headed quickly towards the PCs, set out in two long rows at the back of the café, sat down and logged on, feeling a little queasy at how tacky and stiff and dirt-encrusted the keyboard was as she typed in the passcode. The tiredness was almost like mania now. It howled through her like wind in a tunnel.

What are you doing?

Why are you checking your emails?

You need to find another hostel to sleep in. Or a hotel. A cool, dark hotel room. A bed with clean white sheets. Go on. You could check in for one night, just to get some sleep. And then stick to hostels after that. Emily isn't here for another week yet. You could check into hotels, until just before she arrives, and no one would ever know about it.

She opened Internet Explorer and typed 'www.hotmail.com' into the address bar. Her cutesy, Paul-related password made her cringe whenever she entered it, but she was too tired right now to change it.

As she waited for her inbox to load, she listened to whatever music was playing on the radio in the café; a song she didn't recognise, with soft, dreamy female vocals, and there was a warm, sweet smell of biscuits drifting in the air, too.

Canada.

You are in Canada now.

Everything is going to be okay from now on, possibly, in Canada.

Three new emails, her inbox interrupted.

The first, the newest, was from Paul.

'Things we still really need to talk about' read the subject line.

Really? Lauren thought. Because as far as she was concerned, there was nothing left to discuss. It was over. It'd been over for weeks. Boo hoo. She opened the email, but couldn't quite bring herself to read through it properly.

She just let her eyes scan over it, immediately able to pick up the general tone: hurt, bitter, possibly drunk. There was tons of it, too. Angry paragraphs spilling down the page. She scrolled through them, feeling so tired, so completely drained, that she might burst into tears.

She clicked delete.

The next email was from her mum.

'Just a quick note,' it said, 'to wish you a safe flight! And don't forget, if you need anything I'm only a phone call away! Be safe now and call me once you're all settled! Lots of love, Mum xxx'

She felt too tired to reply to that one either.

The final email of the three was completely unexpected.

It was from Ian, one of Paul's ex-flatmates from university.

Date: Tue, 21 Sep 2004 19:44:32 +0000
From: fiveleavesleft@hotmail.com
To: lauren_cross83@hotmail.com
Subject: Hello

Dear Lauren,
Ian here (Paul's ex-flatmate). this is just a very quick email to say hi and i hope you are okay and have a brilliant time in Canada. (have you moved there permanently??)

i hope this isn't too weird, emailing you out of the blue like this. (i found your address from a group email thing Paul sent last year.) i guess i also wanted to say that i hope you'll consider me your friend, too, as i always felt we got along well.

right, anyway, hope you're having a good day, doing whatever it is people do in Canada. here in Nottingham i'm about to eat a plate of beans on toast and then go to a pub quiz. (exciting.)

all the best,
your friend,
Ian

What a sweetheart, Lauren thought once she'd finished reading it.

She felt weirdly flattered, too.

And as she thought about Ian, the howl died down a little inside her.

They'd only ever really spoken a handful of times – mostly late at night in the kitchen of the house, at the pub a few times, and once for about an hour at a party – but yeah, she'd always felt like they'd got on well, too, and that whenever they'd talked, they'd *really talked*, whatever that meant.

She tried to remember the last time she saw him. It was just before the break-up. They'd all met in that new fake goth pub that had just opened in the city centre and he'd wanted to tell her and Paul some good news; that he was having a demo recorded with his band, and someone from a record label (was it Sony?) was even *paying* for it. And as he'd told them, shyly fiddling with his sleeve, pulling it down over his knuckles so just the ends of his fingertips poked out, and speaking in his soft, sweet voice, she could feel Paul bristle and stiffen in his stupid, throne-like chair beside her. She could actually feel the jealousy coiling within him; not jealousy about the demo per se (Paul couldn't play a musical instrument) but jealousy simply that *something was going right for someone else.*

The howling started up once more inside her.

A hotel room, just for one night!

Before logging out, though, she clicked reply.

Date: Sun, 26 Sep 2004 09:22:09 +0000
From: lauren_cross83@hotmail.com
To: fiveleavesleft@hotmail.com
Subject: Re: Hello

Ian,
Thanks so much for your sweet email, it really means a lot. I felt we got on too, the few times we talked, and I'm glad that you consider me a friend. I know things didn't end that amicably between P and I, and I don't know exactly what or how much he's told you, but anyway, thank you very much.

No, it's not permanent! I'm here for a year on a working visa. A friend of mine (Did you ever meet Emily? Tall girl? Always wears things with mirrors on them?) was going already and said come along, and slightly unimaginatively I thought, fuck it, why not?

I've only been here for a day or so (I'm still recovering from the jetlag; it feels a bit like someone's injected me with soup) and this is the first time I've stumbled into an internet cafe so apologies if I veer into incoherence at any point, but yes, it's been really, really ace so far! Thank you for asking! Everything is so much cleaner and nicer and brighter and happier here, which is exactly what I was hoping for. A new start and all that. And I've even made a few friends, too – some impossibly blond Norwegian boys that I tagged along with at the airport.

Anyway, enough about me. HOW ARE YOU??? Please tell me that you're dating Avril Lavigne and riding around everywhere in stretch limos by now? (Also, how did the pub quiz go?)

Again, I can't say enough how nice it was to hear from you and how much your email meant to me. It's really cheered me up! So, um, thanks. And please stay in touch, you.

Also your friend,
L xx

Lauren clicked send, logged out, then wandered groggily towards the man at the counter, with his big, wet, stubbly smile.

As she stumbled out of the café into the hot white light of Monday morning, people bustling past her on the pavement, clutching cups of coffee, she thought: Maybe I should've gone out with Ian instead.

IAN
2014

Is three floors enough of a drop to kill you, I wonder as I dangle myself out a bit further over the banister. I look down into the shadowy darkness at the centre of the stairwell. At ground level are three locked bikes and an abandoned, shelfless bookcase, which is what I would land on, I guess, if I just let myself fall over the edge.

I relax my grip and the thick wooden banister digs into my stomach.

And then a new feeling churns in there, too; a sudden, worrying, puke-or-shit-myself feeling, and I pull myself away from the edge and pick up my shopping bags and hurry back into the flat.

* * *

After I've puked up most of the Babybels, I go and lie down very still on top of the covers and plead with my stomach not to do it again.

I lift *Ways to Happiness* to my face.

I look at the back cover, at Dr Jennifer McVirtue's photo. She's a blonde-haired American lady with kindly-looking wrinkles around her eyes and a fluffy white cat on her lap.

I turn to page one, Introduction.

You've probably picked up this book because something in your life is not quite the way you would like it to be.

In the living room, I hear the TV click off and then the sound of Carol and Martin walking slowly down the hall towards the bedroom next to mine.

Maybe you don't even know what's wrong, only that SOMETHING BIG needs to change.

'We'll have to be quiet,' Carol whispers.

'Don't worry, babe,' Martin says at full volume.

Well, do not fear, for in this book I will equip you with all the tools you will ever need to find – and maintain – the pathways that will lead you towards a tranquil garden of happiness within your own life.

Carol's bedroom door opens then closes.

I flick forward through the book, trying not to listen to Carol asking Martin to unzip her dress or to Martin grunting his reply, and I try not to think about my queasy, churning stomach. I scan through the book, but I can't seem to locate the exact sentence or paragraph in *Ways to Happiness* where Jennifer McVirtue (PhD) explains in clear, concrete terms *exactly what you have to do to feel better*.

The words begin to swim around the page, so I close the book and drop it on the floor.

I'm never going to meet someone.

I'm never going to have sex again.

I'm never going to stop feeling sick.

When did I even last *have* sex?

I count backwards.

Was it two years ago? Three?

Nope.

It was four years ago, with an angry girl I met at a house party in Forest Fields.

And when it was over, I apologised and she got up almost immediately and just before she pulled her jeans on I saw the condom stuck to her bum cheek and didn't even say anything.

Just then, as if on cue, I hear Carol and Martin begin to shag.

This is a new low.

I am having the worst time out of anyone in the world, ever.

PAUL
2014

On the bench outside the brick and glass structure of the New Writing Centre, Paul smokes one of his remaining Marlboro Lights, assuring himself that once the packet's finished he'll go straight back to nicotine gum. Sarah doesn't ever need to know. He'll wash his hands and clean his teeth and have a shower before she gets home this evening.

Each time Paul allows his mind to wander in the direction of Alison Whistler, he feels a small twinge in his stomach.

What will happen next?

Will she mention their chat?

He drags on his cigarette. Tongues the lump. Drags on his cigarette. Tongues the lump.

At about five to one, people from class start drifting past him into the building. 'Hi,' he says as each one passes. No Alison, though. He drops the cigarette onto the tarmac, grinds it out with his shoe, looks at the time on his phone. Three minutes to go. He takes another cigarette from the pack and lights it.

At one minute past, Paul heads up the stairs and into the seminar room. They're all there, waiting, everyone except her.

He walks around to his table at the front, drapes his blazer on the back of his chair, and looks across at the one empty seat where Alison Whistler should be sitting. What if she's reported him? What if she was trying to trap him into behaving inappropriately? What if she was chatting to him in front of a whole crowd of students, all piled into her bedroom, gathered round the laptop screen, laughing and telling her what to say? What if she's writing an article about pervy lecturers for the student paper?

What if everyone in class knows?

'Okay, everyone,' Paul says, feeling the words catch in his throat. 'I thought we'd do things a little differently today and just go straight into Craig's story. How does that sound? And then if we have time at the end, maybe do a few writing exercises. Alright?'

The class look up blankly from their horseshoe of desks.

He glances at dowdy, moody Rachel. She knows. Of course she knows. They're friends, they probably tell each other everything.

Just then, the door opens and Alison Whistler strolls into the room.

'Sorry I'm late,' she says. 'I spilled my coffee.'

Paul can't speak.

He feels himself blushing, and his mouth losing all its moisture.

'Right, okay . . .' he mumbles.

Alison takes her seat at the far side of the room like nothing is out of the ordinary. She pulls out her plastic document wallet, her notebook, her biros, her phone.

'Okay,' Paul says again, composing himself as much as he's able. 'Craig's story . . . "Guardian of the Tombs". Did we all print it out and read it through, yeah?'

No one says anything.

Somehow Paul gets through the two-hour workshop. He involves them all in a discussion about Craig's story. He improvises some writing exercises afterwards. And he glances at Alison only occasionally, just once or twice, and she looks back blankly, as if nothing whatsoever has gone on between them. Maybe it hasn't. Maybe Paul's reading way too much into this. Maybe she chats online with all her lecturers. Maybe that's just what people do nowadays.

After class, he feels a tangible wave of relief when she gets up and leaves the room, chatting and laughing with Rachel.

Paul sits with Craig in his office and they go over his story, Paul pointing out how more conflict and tension could be introduced to improve it.

'It starts off strongly,' Paul says, 'but then you never really fulfil that early promise. The guardian figure. He's an interesting character, but couldn't he do something a bit more unexpected? It just all gets a little . . . predictable.'

Craig nods.

Paul can feel him soaking up every word he's saying, taking his advice on board like it's fact. And as Paul speaks he thinks: What the fuck do I know? What right do I have to tell anyone how to write anything?

After the short tutorial, he and Craig walk down the stairwell together and out through the exit, and there, sitting on the bench in a pair of aggressively tight black leggings, is Alison Whistler.

'Can I have a quick word?' she says, standing, taking a drag on her liquorice paper roll-up.

Paul feels himself blush again.

'See you then,' Craig murmurs shyly. 'Cheers.'

As he walks away, Paul wonders whether Craig could possibly have picked up anything weird between him and Alison. He waits for Alison to speak, and realises that she, too, is waiting for Craig to walk out of earshot. Once he turns the corner at the end of the path, she sits back down on the bench. She looks at Paul, her eyes wide and black, her shiny dyed hair blowing around in the wind, visible goose bumps on her thin, pale arms. She's like a cartoon, a sexy cartoon. After a pause, he sits down too, his leg only a few inches from hers.

'You wanted a word?' he says, noticing an embarrassing tightness to his voice which he hopes she doesn't pick up on.

'Hi,' she says.

'Hi,' he says.

part two
first world problems

LAUREN
2014

So? How did it go? Alyssa texted. It wasn't even nine in the morning. It was raining, again, and the bus was cramped and vinegary, and when the man in the seat to my left opened his copy of *Metro*, his suit-jacketed elbow jabbed in my ribs like he was trying to tell me something.

I cancelled, I began to text, then deleted it.

Fine, I wrote instead and pressed send.

Really??? Alyssa texted back, almost instantly.

No. I cancelled at the last minute, I replied.

I felt the man's elbow jabbing at me again, forcing me to scooch even further towards the window. I shifted around and glowered at him but he didn't notice. There were two articles on the page he was looking at: one about gay rights activists in Russia, the other about a boy with sculpted facial hair's '*X Factor* dream' being over. My phone buzzed on my lap again.

WTF, Alyssa's reply said. *He seemed nice!*

'He' was a guy called Carl, who worked in Alyssa's husband's office. She'd shown me his *Guardian* Soulmates profile on her phone one night last week. He was thirty-four and he liked long walks and political theory and the films of Pedro Almodovar. His hair was so dark we both suspected it might have been photoshopped.

I'd only agreed to swap phone numbers to get Alyssa off my back about internet dating for a while. It seemed to be all she talked about recently: 'It's not weird any more,' and, 'I know someone that actually found someone through it,' and 'What if I managed your account for you and just let you know if anyone nice or hot messages?'

Why did we have to be such fucking *girls* all the time, I thought. Why did we always have to be defined by whether we did or didn't have a boyfriend or a fiancé or – in Alyssa's case – a husband of six years who sat around playing Xbox whenever he wasn't working?

I didn't want to get annoyed or fall out with her over this, but at the same time, whenever the subject came up, it felt like she was prodding at a wasp's nest deep inside me.

Please leave me alone, I typed, then slipped my phone into the pocket of my jeans, determined to ignore it from now on. I watched the raindrops slide down the outside of the window.

The man next to me turned the page.

Girl, 13, dies of ruptured stomach from legal high, the paper said, as the bus turned the corner and the sea swung into view. There were tiny coloured specks of fishing boats bobbing on the horizon, and every time I saw the Channel it made me think about how I still wasn't used to living here yet and didn't think I ever would be, which in turn made me wonder what you were doing, right at this exact moment, if you were also on a bus to work somewhere.

The man turned the page.

162 die in factory blaze in Bangladesh.

He turned the page again.

Dog of the Day! Milo (7), Cavalier King Charles Spaniel.

I could see the stack of bin bags from halfway down Bingley Road. There were even more than usual; piled up to shoulder height, glistening with raindrops, they filled almost the whole doorway, completely obscuring the 'Please do not leave donations on the step!' sign I'd made and tacked up on Saturday night. I had to drag the bags into the street to get the shutters open, and one of them caught on a shard of broken pint glass, spilling its contents into the road: Dora the Explorer pyjamas, stained soft toys, and a few cardboard baby books so damp they'd almost turned to mush.

I propped the door open with the fire extinguisher

and began hauling everything through to the back room, two bags at a time, and when I came back on my third trip, there was an old bloke in the shop, shuffling towards the bookshelves in the back corner.

'Excuse me?' I called. 'I'm afraid we're not open for another ten minutes yet.'

But he just nodded and smiled and carried on shuffling towards the books.

Let him browse, I thought. Why not? What does it matter?

I'd begun hoovering when I felt my phone buzz in my pocket again.

I knew it was Alyssa again before I opened the message.

Oh shit HAPPY BIRTHDAY btw! it said.

Date: Mon, 27 Sep 2004 19:33:14 +0000
From: fiveleavesleft@hotmail.com
To: lauren_cross83@hotmail.com
Subject: Re: Re: Hello

hello,
glad you're having fun. knew you would be. you always struck me as a person who knew what they were doing, so, um, congratulations on that.

i realise this makes me sound a bit stupid but what's Canada like exactly? is it like America? whenever i try to picture 'Canada' i just think of a big mountain with a bear standing on the top of it. does that sound about right?

(i've only ever been to places in Europe.)

no Avril yet. if this was a computer game, then we're still stuck on the first level. i don't know. that's not really true. we've got a couple of good support slots booked for next month (have you heard of Nine Black Alps?) and Alex reckons our demo is 'being heard by all the right people' whatever that means. (maybe it means Avril's about to slot it into her tape walkman, any moment.) but yeah, in the meantime I'm still mainly just doing as many hours as they'll give me at the Bull and eating beans on toast and oven chips and those rectangular pizzas that go in the microwave and trying to find another job which is a) more hours, b) daytime if possible and c) not completely soul destroying. (telesales?)

please keep your fingers X-ed for me, and i'll be sure to let you know of any interesting developments in my life if/when they materialise.

oh by the way, in case you were wondering: i bumped into Paul the other day (first time i've seen him since you and he broke up) and he didn't say anything bad about you. so you know, if there *was* any bit of you still wondering whether he's okay or whatever, Paul's fine. he spent most of his time just talking about himself: about this novel idea he had. (no change there then.) i think me and him have drifted apart a bit. can you tell? i don't know. it's just weird i guess, seeing people you used to get on so well with and not having anything much to say to them any more . . .

no, i never met Emily. she sounds like quite the character.

so how's everything going so far? have you found somewhere to live or a job or anything yet?

please send me all your news whenever you get a chance. it's exciting.

okay, really lovely to hear from you, too.

i'm going to go now.

Ian

p.s. we came seventh in the pub quiz.

IAN
2014

'So this is where the magic happens,' Martin says.

He puts his hand on my shoulder and steers me into a large, weird-smelling room at the end of the corridor. There are about fifty to sixty people crammed inside, elbow to elbow at five long rows of desks, talking into headsets and typing on old desktop computers. It's impossible to make out what any one person is saying; their voices all blend together into a swarming, chattering racket.

I want to squirm out from Martin's grip.

I want to run back along the corridor and down the stairs and out through the lobby and away into the city.

I want to buy my guitar back.

I want to drop myself over the stairwell.

I want to travel back in time to 1983 and start all over again.

'This is where you'll be working,' he says, shouting to be heard above the clatter of voices. 'At the moment we're doing a large project on behalf of the government. It's a sort of questionnaire.'

I want to be back in the spare room again, reading *Ways to Happiness*.

I want to work as a large top hat for a city-centre printing firm; at least I'd be outside, walking around in the fresh air.

The room has the sour, chemical smell of fifty to sixty people drinking instant coffee all day without any proper ventilation.

A cheap electric heater buzzes warmth into my trouser leg.

I'm wearing my one pair of smart trousers, my one smart shirt, and my one pair of smart shoes. Everyone else is in jeans and jumpers. Even Martin's wearing a pair of those two-colour jeans with fake worn bits at the knees.

'We'll find you a free terminal in a minute,' he says, 'but first I'd better show you where everything else is.'

So we head back down the corridor and stop outside the door at the farthest end. Its small plastic sign says *Martin Glade*.

Carol Glade, I think.

Martin pushes the door open to reveal a small office with a plush leather swivel chair and a big desk with a new-looking iMac on it.

'Pretty nice, eh?' he says.

'Yep,' I say, looking in at the cool, dark room.

I wait for Martin to tell me to go in and sit down. But he doesn't. We both just stand there in the doorway, looking at his office.

'Top of the range, that,' he says, pointing out the giant, flatscreen monitor.

'Nice,' I say, trying to sound suitably impressed.

'Anyway,' he says after another long pause, letting the door swing closed. 'Back this way . . . follow me.'

He leads me back down the corridor again in the direction of the main room. On the way he points out the toilets and the break area, which is a grim, windowless, L-shaped room with a sink in one corner and a few tables and chairs in the middle.

'How many breaks do we get?' I ask.

'How many do you need?' he says. 'You get one. For lunch. And no more than forty minutes, yeah? Too many breaks end up being a bit, you know, counter-productive.'

We go into the main room again and he directs me towards an empty space, to an old blue swivel chair facing onto a dirty beige computer. There are no windows anywhere, and the overhead striplights turn everything a jittery, grainy, electric yellow, like you're on drugs and it's five in the morning.

'Have a seat,' Martin says.

I sit down.

NO VAPING, says a tatty printout, tacked to the wall above me. BREAK ROOM AND OUTSIDE ONLY.

'Now, for starters, all I want you to do is listen in to Dean here and get a basic feel for what goes on.' He gestures to the man at the next terminal. 'Dean's one of our absolute best, you see. I'll be back in an hour.'

He gives me a wink and pats me hard on the back, then swaggers out of the room.

I wiggle the mouse and my monitor crackles into life. It says 'Quiztime Solutions' on the desktop.

I look over at Dean. He's grey-haired, with sunken cheeks and large bags under his eyes.

'H—' I say, just as Dean's phone makes a shrill chirping noise.

'*Gooood* morning, madam,' Dean says into his headset. His voice is as warm and musical as a radio DJ's. 'And how are *weeee* this morning? . . . Oh, I'm sorry to hear that. Anyway, my name's *Deeeean* and I'm calling from a company called . . . What's that? . . . Oh no, I'm not selling anything, madam. The reason I'm calling is just to let you know that you *maaaay* well be eligible for a . . . Okay then, madam, but if you'll just . . . Well, in that case I'm *truuuuly* sorry to hear that and I hope you have a . . .'

Dean sits back in his chair and sighs and rubs his sagging face hard with both hands. His stubble makes a rasping sound against his palms.

'H—' I say.

Dean's phone chirps again and he leans in. '*Gooood* morning, madam . . .' he says.

As he continues speaking, I feel myself zoning out.

My gaze floats around the room for a while, resting finally on a small black squiggle on the MDF partition that separates Dean's monitor from mine. It's handwriting, I realise. I lean in a little closer to examine it. In tiny, wobbly, childlike biro it says: *I hate it here*.

After a while, I'm given a spare headset and a script so I can follow along. The script is a snaking maze of boxes and arrows that tells you what to say in any possible situation. It seems that the gist of the job is to convince old people to fill out online questionnaires by promising them entry to a (possibly imaginary?) competition. In the three and a half hours that I sit listening in, Dean convinces eleven different old people to fill in the questionnaire.

He really knows what he's doing.

The questionnaire takes about twenty minutes to complete, and all the questions are about how satisfied you are with your current situation in life, what you might possibly do to improve it, how happy you are in general on a scale of one to ten, etc. Dean asks the old people the questions and the old people tell him their answers and he then clicks the corresponding boxes on his on-screen questionnaire.

Occasionally the noise in the room reaches a kind of crescendo; for a few seconds all fifty or sixty voices will be speaking simultaneously, and the sheer volume of it causes my heart to quicken and I have to grit my teeth and grip the arms of my swivel chair and wait for it to stop.

I wonder how I will possibly get through doing this every day, nine till six, five days a week.

It seems impossible.

Each call is almost identical; it's just you saying, 'Hello, sir/madam,' and then someone saying, 'Not interested,' and then that person slamming the phone down on you. If you're lucky, something interesting happens, like they'll tell you to fuck off.

Just before one, Martin reappears. He claps his hands and tells us to break for lunch. On my way out of the room, I try to keep my head down and my body buried amongst the crush of people all heading for the doorway at the same time, but he manages to spot me and taps me on the shoulder.

'So?' he asks, once we're the only ones left. 'Reckon you can handle it?'

Here it is, I realise. My opportunity to just say no. To open my mouth and say, 'I'm really sorry, Martin, but I don't think this is the job for me . . .'

I take a deep breath.

'Sure thing,' I say instead.

What the fuck am I saying?

When Martin grins, I see bits of egg stuck between his teeth. There's a smear of brown sauce at the corner of his mouth, too, and I have the sudden, unshakeable conviction that he's been sat in his comfortable air-conditioned office all morning, eating a Tesco breakfast sandwich and looking at pictures of cars on the internet.

* * *

It's raining outside so I stand beneath the arched entrance to the building. As I smoke my roll-up, I watch a steady stream of businesspeople bobbing along the pavement, all headed in the direction of the Tesco Express.

I will give up smoking on my thirty-first birthday, I tell myself as I grind my fag out with my shoe, then immediately start rolling another one.

There's a miserable-looking woman in a saggy black cardigan stood at the other side of the doorway, smoking a kingsize. I feel ninety per cent sure that she also works in the call centre. We both seem to be pretending that the other person isn't there. I don't blame her. Talking's probably the last thing you'd want to do on your break.

Just as I'm lighting my second fag, Dean steps into the doorway, too. He has a slight stoop when he stands, his head jutting forward as if it's a bit too heavy for his neck.

'Alright, Sue,' he says, shuffling up to the miserable-faced woman and taking a box of Mayfair out of his jeans pocket. 'Got a light, darling?' Dean's normal speaking voice is much sadder and quieter and a lot less musical than his phone voice.

Sue hands him her lighter.

'Cheers, duck,' he says.

'Slow morning,' Sue says, then coughs.

When Sue coughs it sounds like someone shaking a biscuit tin full of gravel.

'How you doing, matey?' Dean says, nodding at me from across the doorway.

'Not bad,' I say, trying my hardest to smile politely and look enthusiastic.

'I'll ask you again in a few days.'

Sue coughs and I drop my roll-up on the ground even though it's only half smoked and the business-people go past the doorway and I look at the time on my phone, and somehow there's only five minutes left until the end of lunch break.

I don't want to go back up the steps.

I don't want to go back up the steps.

I turn and go back up the steps.

In the afternoon, Martin gets Dean to come off his computer and show me how to use mine. So Dean logs off and waddles his swivel chair even closer towards me, extinguishing all remaining inches of personal space between us.

'Bloody computers, eh?' he says.

Up close, Dean's breath is almost unbearable, a sour mixture of coffee and emptiness.

'I remember when this was all paper and pen,' he says.

I nod politely at everything Dean says, taking shallow breaths through my mouth, as he begins to methodically show me what each of the buttons on my screen do, how to log in and out, how to clock all my breaks and toilet trips, how to see a list of how many calls I'd made so far, how to accurately catalogue everything, etc. Then he goes over the script, explaining that it's all in the wording, you see, that you have to say that the person *may* be eligible for our fantastic competition, that that's one of the words that you're absolutely unable to change, no matter what.

I nod my head emphatically in the hope that it might make Dean stop breathing all over me.

'That's about everything,' he says. 'I think you're ready to have a go.'

He plugs an extra headset into my phone so he can listen in while I make my first call. Then points to the button on-screen that I have to click to start the automatic dialler. I move my mouse pointer over it and double-click.

A long, ominous pause, and then my phone chirps, just once, and then I hear ringing in my headset. After a while someone picks up.

'Hello?' an old woman says. 'Who is this?'

When I open my mouth to speak, the voice that comes out of it isn't mine.

'*Gooood* afternoon, madam,' it says. 'And how are we today?'

'Sorry, who is this?' she says.

She sounds like Mum: very old and very far away, as if she's standing at the other end of a dusty brown corridor, past endless shelves of carriage clocks and old photos.

I look down at my script, following the snaking arrows and clipart bubbles to a section that says:

My name's ________ and I'm calling from a company called Quiztime Solutions. The reason for my call is to let you know that you *<u>*may*</u>* well be eligible for the exclusive opportunity to enter our fantastic new competition to win any one of a number of wonderful luxury prizes.

I open my mouth but the pause drags on.

'Hello?' the old woman says.

I'm going to take off my headset and stand up and tell Dean and Martin that I'm really sorry, but this just isn't the job for me, that it makes me feel uncomfortable.

As Dean nudges me on the elbow and taps his biro against the next bubble of script and breathes his horrible breath all over me, I begin to lift myself out of my chair. But as I do so, I think about Carol. I think about Rick from the job centre. I think about a sentence in an email that someone once wrote me. I think about my dad.

I let myself drop back into the chair and begin to speak.

PAUL
2014

The ceiling of Alison Whistler's bedroom has a small hole in it. Alison's downstairs, in the toilet. Her room is small and candle-lit, and right now it smells of incense sticks and sex and unwashed clothes. Paul wonders what the time is, but he doesn't want to check his phone, in case the spell is broken by some sort of message – a query from one of his students, or an email from Julian asking why he's still not received the novel yet, or worse still, an out-of-the-blue nice email or text from Sarah. If I could just stay here, Paul thinks, in this bed with the curtains drawn and whatever music this is that's playing and never have to go back out into the real world again then maybe I could be happy.

Just then his tongue shifts, automatically, to the lump.

Try not to think about it, he tells himself.

You're shagging a nineteen-year-old.

Try to think about that instead.

This is the third time Paul's been up to Alison's room, which is on the top floor of a five-bedroom student house.

She had to sneak him up the stairs.

He'd been taken aback, the first time he saw her room, by just how *bare* it was. He'd wondered where all her books and CDs and DVDs were. Then he'd realised. If you're a young person with an iPhone and a Kindle and a MacBook and a wifi connection, that's all you really need these days. Also: you don't have to pay for anything either.

Like what happened after the second or third time they had sex.

They were lying in bed, smoking, and Paul was secretly enjoying how cinematic and over-the-top it all seemed – the affair between the student and the teacher, with him playing the role of the older man for the first time in his life (Alison considers thirty-one and a half *ancient*) – and Paul found he was viewing himself from above, in widescreen, in grainy black and white, like a scene from a French film.

'Have you ever seen any Godard?' he'd asked.

'No, why?'

'I feel like I'm in a scene from a Godard film,' he explained.

And then Alison had asked which was his favourite, or which he recommended she start with.

'*Breathless*,' he'd said. 'For definite.'

She'd sat up in bed and started typing and clicking on her MacBook, and then less than four minutes later there it was on her hard disk, completely free: a 699MB mp4 of *Breathless*.

'You mean, you don't torrent stuff?' she'd asked when he raised his eyebrows.

'I just sort of *rent* things,' he'd replied. 'So, did you download my book, too?'

He asked it as a joke but Alison didn't smile. She just said, 'Maybe.'

Paul hears the toilet flush one floor below, then her footsteps on the stairs. The door opens and she enters the room in a red towelling dressing gown, carrying a pint of tap water, her hair all messed up and knotted at the back.

'What time is it?' Paul asks.

'Don't know,' she says, putting the pint glass on her dresser, then shrugging off the dressing gown. She's wearing nothing beneath it. She's plump around the stomach and the tops of her thighs, plumper than Paul had imagined when masturbating. There are stretch marks on her belly, and she has lots more weird little tattoos, too. Her mate is learning how to do a kind of home tattooing technique called 'Stick N' Poke' and she'd let him do some on her as practice. So she has an almost-circle on her ankle, a wonky star on her thigh, an Illuminati triangle on her forearm, and what looks like a tiny slice of pizza on her left shoulder.

'There's a hole in your ceiling, you know,' Paul says,

pointing up at it, sure he can hear shuffling sounds above them.

'Oh yeah, that,' Alison says, nodding like a hole in your bedroom ceiling is normal, then getting back into bed and curling up against him.

'What's up there?' Paul says. 'Above your bedroom?'

'Dunno,' Alison says. 'Pigeons?'

'You should probably cover it up, anyway.'

'What for?'

'Well, what if your landlord's put a webcam up there? What if he's up there right now, wanking?'

'He wouldn't do that. He's sweet. And anyway, he's, like, *sixty*.'

'Just cover it up,' Paul says, beginning to play out a nightmare scenario in his head where a video of him and Alison doing it somehow goes viral. Simultaneously, his tongue touches the lump again, causing his brain to send a triangular sliver of worry pinging around his body.

To distract himself, Paul sniffs his fingers.

They smell like a mixture of Alison and smoking.

They're developing a faint orange tinge.

He needs to quit again. He needs to sort himself. He needs to break up with Sarah and book himself a doctor's appointment and very, very quickly write a novel. Jesus. He needs to sort his whole fucking life out.

Last night he spent about half an hour lurking on the NaNoWriMo forum, that thing where people write whole 50,000-word novels during the month of November.

It's already four days in.

Paul's running 6,666 words behind schedule.

'I'd better go,' he says.

'Don't,' Alison says, her hand twisting around his ankle, then rubbing up his calf, his knee, his thigh.

'Sarah . . .' Paul says.

Alison's hand stops moving.

'. . . she'll be back soon.'

This is a lie. Sarah won't be back for another few hours.

'Fine,' Alison says.

'Don't be like that,' he says.

'I'm not being like anything,' she says, sticking her bottom lip out in a sulky pout, pulling the duvet up to cover herself, folding her arms tight across her chest. 'Honestly, I don't give a shit.'

Paul fights back the urge to stay in bed and apologise. He dresses quickly, both of them filling the room with a broody, awkward silence, and then he says, 'Bye,' and hurries off – not even waiting for Alison to check the coast is clear – down two flights of raggedly-carpeted stairs, stepping round the unwashed mugs and plates like a contender in some sort of low-budget TV assault course, then dashes along the hall, his breath clutched painfully in his lungs until he finally hears the slam of the front door behind him.

Outside it's incredibly bright, and weirdly sunny for November, and Alison's musty bedroom already seems like something from a long time ago, maybe even something he's imagined.

At the bus stop, he jams his tongue against the

lump and takes out his phone. It tells him that he has one new Facebook notification and two new Twitter notifications.

On Facebook, David Hastings has tagged him in a set of scanned-in photographs from the early 2000s. Paul thumbs through them. They're all taken in their old student house, in the kitchen and the living room. One of him and Lauren sitting on the sofa, her legs resting over his. One of him and Ian talking at a party. Christ. They all look so young and thin.

He opens Twitter and feels a spear of panic pierce his gut.

From @jfgkdfjdlsjf to @PaulSNovels at 3:42pm:
i know what ur doing

A little later, on the top deck of the bus, Paul tries to find out more about @jfgkdfjdlsjf, but it turns out the account has been protected. All he can tell is that it doesn't follow anyone and that the tweet to him is its only tweet so far.

It's probably some sort of phishing thing, he reassures himself, looking uneasily around the bus to make sure there's no one following him.

That evening, after dinner, halfway through an episode of *Grand Designs*, Sarah picks up the remote and turns off the TV. A flower of silence blooms between them in the small, pale blue living room. Something is wrong. Something has been wrong ever since Paul got home.

He holds his breath and waits for her to speak, to say whatever it is she's been working herself up to say.

'I know what you're doing,' she says in a quiet, steady voice.

Okay, Paul thinks, feeling the floodgates open on a panic so intense it makes his head spin. This is it. Everything's over, she's found me out. *She's* the one who sent me that Twitter message. She's going to break up with me. And – Paul discovers, his hands jammed between his trembling knees – this might not be what he wants after all. Because Paul doesn't know what the fuck he wants any more. He doesn't know anything except: a) he's dying and b) he's making a right dog's dinner of his life.

'I found a lighter in the washing machine,' Sarah says, in the same slow, wounded voice.

Oh! Paul thinks. Oh! Okay!

And sheer relief makes him laugh out loud, just once, a single involuntary, 'Ha!'

'I'm glad you find it funny,' Sarah says, getting up off the sofa.

'Wait. . .' Paul says.

He follows her into the kitchen.

He knows how seriously she takes smoking. How much she hated him doing it. How much she wanted him to stop the first time round, and how much misery he put her through, those endless months he was quitting.

'I've just been stressed,' he says. 'You know, with my writing and everything. I mean, I'm making good progress with the novel now,' (he's written nothing usable in getting on for three months) 'and it's just been putting me in this weird mood. I know I need to give up again, I *know* I do. I'm sorry. I've only been on two or three a day anyway, *if that*,' (he's currently on about ten to twelve), 'but yeah, you're right, you're absolutely right, and I am so, *so* sorry, I really am, look at me,' (Sarah's turned to run water into the sink and Paul suspects she might be crying but when she turns to face him her eyes are cold and dry), 'it's such a fucking stupid thing to do, I was doing so well, and I'll stop again, I promise, I *promise*, starting right now, okay?'

He waits for Sarah to nod.

To look at him warmly.

He wants, more than anything, for Sarah to make him feel like he is not a terrible human being.

'Do what you want,' Sarah says. 'I don't care any more.'

He can't tell if she's talking about the smoking or something else.

'I don't know what I want,' Paul says after a long pause.

He walks slowly back into the living room and turns the TV on. From this moment onwards, he thinks, I'm going to have nothing more to do with Alison. Because the guilt of it sits in his stomach, heavy and undigested, like how it might feel if you ate a shoe.

It's finished, Paul tells himself. It's over. It was a mistake and you've learned from it. Tomorrow you are going to change. You are going to book a doctor's appointment. You are going to start being a good boyfriend. You are going to buy Sarah flowers or chocolates or both. This is a new start, Paul, right here. This is 'the first day of the rest of your life'.

He presses his tongue against the lump.

He changes the channel from *Grand Designs* to *The One Show*.

Date: Mon, 27 Sep 2004 03:13:22 +0000
From: lauren_cross83@hotmail.com
To: fiveleavesleft@hotmail.com
Subject: Re: Re: Re: Hello

Heyyy,
SO I'm staying at a new hostel now that has 24hr computers in the lobby hence why I'm typing this so late . Also hensce why I'm a bit drunk as I'm typing it.

I just wanted to say that I am so sorry and thank you and thank you so much for your sweet email . God I wish we couldve talked more when we were both in Nottingham actually because the trugh of it if I'm completely homnest I don't have any one at all to tlak to. Not here or anywhere. Not Emily. And especially not my mum. And if I'm honest I am not having a greatest time of things either.

Oh god I'm sorry to burden this all on you like this an dyou should just ignore me or tell me to shut the fuck up but I feel so sad and alone sometimes and I don't think coming out here was such a great idea afterall. I know I said I was having a great time and eveyrhthing in my first email but that was just becaue that's what your supposed to write in emails right? Well Im not. I'm having a fucking rubbish time. I AM SUCH A DICK I JUST SEEM TO FUCK EVERYTHNIG UP ALL THE TIMW.

I fucked things up with Paul and now I've only been here less than a week and I feel like Ive fucked things up here too.

I just need someone to talk to an d it seems like youre it maybe because we don't know each other that well wouldn't it be good I fyou could just tell somebody absolutely everything you know? like for once you could not pretend and be completely honest about how awful you were and they wound't judge you? Becuae I wish I could do that and I guess that's what I am doing here now and If you never want to speak to me again after this fi you think I am just some complete drunken crazy random then I will completely understand.

Canada was supposed to be a fresh start and now I have already messed it up. I'm such an idiot. I think I am writing this email to punish myself and you are the unlucky person who is going to receive it as soon as I click send.

Which is now I guess, as I can feel myself about to fall asleep on the keyboard.

I'm sorry and thank you for being such a sweetie. Your lovely emails really made me feel better maybe more than you could realise so thanks. And sorry. I don't expect you to rpe;y, .

All my love
LXXXXXXXXXXXXXXXXXX

Date: Mon, 27 Sep 2004 03:17:01 +0000
From: lauren_cross83@hotmail.com
To: fiveleavesleft@hotmail.com
Subject: DON'T READ THAT LAST EMAIL!!!!

Oh god.

I don't know what time it is there but hopefully you will see both of these emails and just read this one. Just plese delete that other one please. It was a mistake. Theres nothing in it anhyway except complaining. Im an idiot. sorry. Im really sorry. Just please please pelase don't' read it.

thankd in advance

L xxx

LAUREN
2014

Nancy, the first of my volunteers, got in a little before ten. Nancy was small and shy and child-like, even though she was well into her sixties. She'd kept her hair long – it was a very thin, dark grey and kind of damp-looking – and she always wore these floral print blouses and thick brown cords that looked like they came straight from the seventies. I liked her a lot.

'Sorry, I'm late,' she whispered.

I looked at my phone; she was three minutes early.

'You're not late,' I told her and she tugged at her hair and muttered to herself then scurried into the back to hang up her duffel coat. Nancy's first job was to get started sorting through the new bags. It was what she liked doing best. She was scared of the till; the till got her in a flap.

The old man had left without buying anything, and there were no more customers, so I stuck my head through the doorway to the back room and asked Nancy if she wanted to put a CD on. She'd sat down cross-legged on the floor, and she nodded and struggled to her feet, stepping around the piles of toys and books and VHS cases to get to the stereo in the far corner. I went back out into the shop and took my place behind the till. I waited to see what she'd put on. Lately, she'd been getting into Justin Bieber. She'd picked out his first album one afternoon from the music section, and said she liked him because he was 'such a nice little boy'. She thought he was 'polite'. I didn't have the heart to tell her he was growing up to be a dickhead.

If she puts on Justin Bieber, I told myself, then something good will happen today.

The speakers buzzed and I waited for the music to start, but it wasn't Justin Bieber. It was one of my CDs: *XO* by Elliott Smith. I must have left in the machine on Saturday night while closing up. I waited for Nancy to stop and change it, but she didn't.

Jamaal didn't get in for another fifteen minutes.

'What?' he asked, the moment he stepped through the door, his eyes wide and wired. There was a scab at the corner of his mouth that hadn't been there on the Friday afternoon, and he had what looked like a fading black eye, too.

'Good morning to you, too,' I said.

He didn't take his coat off. It was large and black and shiny and he just stood there in it near the door, shifting his weight from one foot to the other. Oh Jamaal, I thought. He looked like a schoolboy still, although according to his caseworker Jeanne, he was almost twenty-one.

'Cup of tea?' I said.

He shook his head.

'Miss? Can I go outside and make a quick phone call please?'

'You've only just got here.'

'It's important, Miss.'

It always made me feel weird when he called me that. It made me feel old and spinsterish. To Jamaal, I was just a grown woman of indeterminate age. An adult. I wasn't *young*, not like him.

'Sure,' I said and watched him go back outside, lighting a cigarette in the strange, cupped-handed way that teenagers often do. He began talking on his phone, but he was doing it in such an over-the-top way, it made me suspect he was just pretending. 'Is it?' he kept saying, too loudly, glancing back through the glass of the door to see if I was still watching, pulling his coat around his chest instead of just doing up the zip.

I'd been told by Jeanne that Jamaal was second-generation Somalian, and sometimes, like this morning, when he came in brimming with anger, I wondered if it was the shitty state of his country that he was angry about: how it'd forced his parents to come and settle here instead. And then I'd feel embarrassed about how little – almost nothing – I knew about Somalia, or anywhere, really, that wasn't England or the United States or Canada, and I would promise myself to go home that evening and look Somalia up on the internet; to do *more* somehow than what I always did when I got home, which was to just turn the TV on or fiddle with my phone, then go to bed.

Or, maybe, Jamaal was just an angry person.

Maybe Jamaal just didn't like me.

Hadn't *I* woken up this morning feeling shitty, too?

Was it too simplistic and presumptuous – a little bit racist, even – to assume that Jamaal's anger had anything to do with his heritage?

I knew nothing about him.

I walked over to the front door, tapped on the glass and waved at him, smiling, trying to coax him in with friendliness, with a sort of gentle feeling of 'You're not in trouble, just please come inside and do something nominal, so I don't have to lie to Jeanne about you on Friday.'

But he turned his back and carried on talking.

I was about to go out and get him when I heard the landline ringing in the back. And a few seconds later, Nancy's sheepish, sing-song voice began calling me: '*Lau*-ren? *Lau*-ren?' Nancy never answered the phone, you see, even though I'd told her numerous times that she could, that she was totally allowed, that nothing bad would happen on the other end of the line. But, like the till, the phone got her in a flap.

I went into the back, stepping over the piles she'd made of books and CDs and cuddly toys and clothes and things we couldn't sell like electrical items and VHS tapes, to get to the little 'office' area in the far corner, where I usually sat tearing my hair out over the accounts. I moved slowly, knowing that if the phone was still ringing by the time I reached it, it would most likely be some sort of PPI scam. I reached the phone. It was still ringing. I picked up.

'Hello?'

'*Gooood* morning, madam,' a man's voice said. He sounded like a radio DJ. 'My name's . . .'

I could hear the chatter of other voices in the call centre around him, and I hung up quickly, dropping the phone back into its cradle a little too dramatically.

'Just another cold call,' I told Nancy, who'd been watching nervously.

She nodded to herself then went back to sorting. She had a Marks & Spencer bag full of paperbacks open in front of her and she was trying to divide them into their various categories. Even from over by the phone, I could see she was messing it up – Alain de Botton and Malcolm Gladwell were mixed in with fiction. And as my eye ran further down the spines, one in particular stood out. It was a lurid yellow. I tilted my head to read the spine: *Human Animus*.

Date: Wed, 29 Sep 2004 13:47:48 +0000
From: fiveleavesleft@hotmail.com
To: lauren_cross83@hotmail.com
Subject: Re: DON'T READ THAT LAST EMAIL!!!!

argh. i read it. i couldn't help myself. i'm sorry!

the only reason i'm telling you i read it is so that i can reply with the following extremely important message:

YOU ARE NOT A DICK, LAUREN CROSS. YOU ARE A NICE, KIND PERSON AND YOU HAVE NOT SCREWED ANYTHING UP AND THERE IS AT LEAST ONE PERSON IN THE WORLD (ME) WHO THINKS YOU ARE PRETTY FUCKING GREAT ACTUALLY AND HOPES THAT YOU ARE OKAY. (OKAY?)

seriously, i hate to think of you over there by yourself, feeling dreadful. you shouldn't be so hard on yourself. what is it you feel you've 'fucked up' exactly?

also, i felt kind of flattered that you chose me to tell that stuff to, so i want to be equally honest in my reply. i still don't feel i've been honest enough yet.

okay, i've had an idea. here's what i'm going to do to balance things out. i'm going to go downstairs and have a fag in the back garden and then i'm going to come back upstairs again and sit down and write you a list of the most painfully honest things i can think of, in an attempt to balance things out and make you feel less embarrassed about your email . . . okay?

off I go . . .

okay, i'm back.
right, here goes:

- i've only ever had one girlfriend (for 3 months, when i was 18)
- apart from 'being in a band' i have absolutely no clue what i'm doing with my life
- sometimes late at night i get scared that 'being in a band' is not a realistic thing to strive towards
- i feel like i will pretty much always just be working in shit bar jobs like the one i'm doing right now
- i got a 2:2 at uni but tell everyone i got a 2:1
- i don't know what to do to make things better for myself and my main technique for ever attempting to get over anything is to usually just not think about it and hope it goes away and hide in my room
- when i was 12 i accidentally wet myself on the Shockwave ride at Drayton Manor
- i think i fancy you a tiny bit.

okay.

i hope that balances things out somewhat. right, i'm going to quickly hit send, before i change my mind, and then I'm going to spend the rest of the evening/ tomorrow/my life walking around cringing.

Ian

p.s. argh

IAN
2014

My left ear's still tingling and sore from the earpiece of my headset as I walk towards the bus stop, the clatter of voices and typing and telephones still rattling round my head. I can hear something else, too – a kind of beeping – and when I turn to see where it's coming from, there's Martin's Audi pulling up to the kerb alongside me. The tinted passenger window rolls down as I approach.

'Want a lift?' he says.

I don't have the energy left to think up an excuse. I just open the door and get in.

Martin's car smells of boiled sweets and aftershave. The upholstery is cream leather and there's some sort of Ibiza chill-out music playing on the stereo, the kind of music that I imagine he puts on whenever he wants to try and get laid. And then, before I can stop myself, I've accidentally imagined him having sex with my sister.

'Good day?' he asks.

'It was alright, yeah,' I say, trying to imagine anything except Martin and Carol doing it.

I imagine myself going back to the call centre tomorrow: sitting in that same seat, making that same phone call, again and again and again. I imagine myself going home. Going to work. Going home. Going to work. Going home. Going to work. One day completely losing it and writing *I hate it here* in wobbly black biro on the desk.

'It's not rocket science,' Martin says.

'Nope,' I say.

He drives like he's trying to impress me, revving the engine at red lights and lurching forward between gaps in the traffic at every opportunity. I want to hold the little handle on the passenger door, but I don't want him to think I'm a coward.

'When do we get paid?' I ask.

'Last Friday of the month.'

The last Friday of the month is still another three weeks away. It's also a week after my and Carol's birthday. Shit. I'd been hoping to buy her a big present to say thank you. I'll have to just make her something instead, or give her an I.O.U.

Just past the university buildings, we stop at a set of traffic lights, and as we wait for a group of pissed students to stumble over the crossing, I realise I've been staring at a man dressed in some sort of puffy, black tube-like outfit, standing on the corner, handing out flyers. He's smoking a fag and bobbing his head along to the music on his headphones, singing cheerfully to himself. For a moment I can't work out what his costume's supposed to be, and then it hits me.

He's dressed as a big top hat.

At the top of the stairs, Martin holds the door for me like I'm the one who's visiting.

'Hell-*o*-o?' he calls down the corridor in a cheesy, Fred Flintstone voice.

'Hi, babe,' Carol calls back in her normal voice.

I don't say anything.

'Look who I found,' he says as we both step into the kitchen.

Carol smiles up at us from the little table in the corner, where she's peeling carrots into a bowl.

'So, how was your first day then?'

The way she says it, she sounds like Mum.

They're both staring at me now, and I feel my neck starting to itch and my left ear throbbing again and I hope it sounds like the truth when I say, 'It was really good, yeah.'

'I've not quite started on dinner yet,' Carol says to Martin, smiling apologetically.

Things have really stepped up a gear in their relationship over the past few weeks. Martin's been round most nights for dinner, which means I've been hiding in my room, either trying to read *Ways to Happiness* or playing

Snake II on my phone. (I'm doing pretty rubbish at both of them.)

'That's alright, babe,' Martin says, shuffling towards her, groin first.

Carol gets up and holds her arms out towards him, and I get the feeling they're about to start openly snogging right in front of me, so I say, 'I'll see you guys later,' and head down the hall to my room.

I close the door and take the laptop down from the cupboard. I have a new plan. I'm going to make Carol a mix CD for her birthday. I'm going to choose a selection of songs that remind her of things from when we were little. Songs we used to listen to on car journeys. Songs Dad played on his guitar. Songs Mum sang along to while she did the ironing. This is exactly the kind of thing Carol would like and, also, it won't cost me any money.

So I start typing up a list of all the songs I'll need: 'Green Door' by Shakin' Stevens, and 'Fire and Rain' by James Taylor, and 'You Can Call Me Al' by Paul Simon. 'Blue Moon' and 'Waterloo Sunset' and 'Do They Know It's Christmas?' Halfway through, I stop, remembering that I don't actually *have* any of these songs on my computer (they were all on an external hard drive which I wiped and sold on eBay for thirty quid) and if I wanted to put them on a CD, I'd have to download them again first.

Easy! a voice whispers inside me. *Just go back online!*

I click on the wifi icon in the bottom corner of my screen, and the pop-up window opens and I scroll down the list of available networks, and there it is, unlocked as always: Rosemary's Wireless.

With great effort, I close the lid of my laptop and put it back up on top of the wardrobe. I take some big, deep breaths and do a few circuits of the room. Over by the window, I look down into the expensive-looking ground-floor flat opposite, at a woman sat at a kitchen table, drinking a cup of tea from a large red mug.

Rosemary?

Could this be you?

I'm half-heartedly imagining a scenario wherein I start a whirlwind romance with the woman in the flat opposite – just by waving at her – when I hear a familiar squeal come from the direction of the kitchen. It's the noise Carol always makes whenever an exciting or unexpected thing happens to her. I can picture her in the kitchen, eyes screwed shut, hands clasped together, and I think: Oh shit. It's happened. Martin's finally proposed.

She runs down the corridor and hammers on my door.

'Coming,' I say.

The door bursts open and there she is, grinning widely, hands clasped in front of her, eyes large and black.

I wait for her to say it.

'Martin's just asked me . . .' she says, out of breath and looking a little bit like she's about to cry, 'to go away for the weekend with him.'

'Oh,' I say. 'Oh wow. That's great. That's really great. When?'

'End of this month. You know, for my birthday.'

Hang on, I think. That's *our* birthday. Our thirty-first.

We'd already arranged to get pissed and order Domino's. She knows I don't know anyone here. And now I'm going to be spending it alone.

Date: Sun, 3 Oct 2004 15:08:08 +0000
From: fiveleavesleft@hotmail.com
To: lauren_cross83@hotmail.com
Subject: Argh

okay, now it's my turn to feel worried that i've said too much.

PAUL
2014

'What's your novel about?' Alison asks. 'Your new one.'

It's early afternoon, a Wednesday, and they're in bed again, in Alison's room. Right now Alison should be in an English lecture and Paul should be writing. He should be at the doctor's. He should be breaking up with Sarah and backpacking around Australia.

As Paul attempts to think of an answer, he reaches across Alison's body for the fags and lighter on the bedside table and his forearm casually brushes against her boob. Two months ago, if someone had told Paul that his forearm would be brushing against Alison Whistler's bare left breast, he'd have done a backflip in excitement. But now it makes him feel nothing. Nothing at all. Like my novel, he thinks, which he'd spent about half his life wanting and wishing and yearning for, and then, when it finally *happened* and he actually got published . . . nothing.

Paul spends as long as he possibly can lighting his cigarette, trying to think of something impressive to say.

'It's about . . .' he says.

But he has no idea.

The other day, after class, he'd glanced over the first chapter and realised just how slight and unexciting his prospective story was – how *unimaginative* it was. Because all he was doing was writing about the first serious relationship he'd ever had at uni with a girl called Lauren Cross and then changing the names round a bit.

Jesus.

Is that what Dostoevsky did?

Change the names round a bit?

I'm a fucking fraud, Paul thinks.

And to make matters worse, he's been keeping Julian at bay with a string of bullshit emails about how it's 'coming along really well' and 'just another week now!'

He should just quit.

No one's forcing him to do it.

He should just give up writing completely and go round the bars again, handing out his CV.

What will happen when I die? Paul wonders. Will I make it into that obituaries page at the back of the *Guardian*? Will anyone set up a tribute page on Facebook for me? Will Alison covertly attend my funeral?

'It's about the dislocation between who we are and who we think we are,' he says finally.

'Right,' Alison says, nodding seriously.

That actually sounded pretty good, he thinks. I should write a novel about that.

'But I don't want to say too much more,' he says, 'because I often find that when I'm right in the middle of working on a draft, there's always the danger I might damage it by talking about it too early. I hope you can understand.'

'Sure thing,' Alison says, nodding.

'That hole's still there,' Paul says, pointing at the ceiling with his cigarette.

'Yep,' Alison says. 'Hi, Mr Singh,' and she waves up at the hole and grins and pulls the duvet a little further down to flash the hole her tits.

'Hold this,' Paul says, handing her his cigarette.

He stands up in bed.

'What're you doing?' she says.

He grabs the spermy wad of toilet roll and condom from her bedside table, stands on his tiptoes, and plugs the hole with it.

'There,' he says proudly.

'Great,' Alison says. 'Thanks. That's fucking disgusting.'

She makes no effort to remove it.

Paul climbs back into bed. Her laptop is playing very aggressive-sounding hip hop. When Paul first asked Alison whether she was a goth or not, she'd laughed and then replied, 'I'm not really an anything,' and this had made Paul feel extremely old-fashioned and uncool.

Alison hands Paul his cigarette back, then picks up her phone.

Paul smokes it right down to the cardboard as Alison's chipped black fingernails tick against the glass of the touchscreen like miniature raindrops.

'What're you doing?' he asks, when the ticking shows no sign of stopping. 'Playing Snake?'

'What's Snake?' she asks, distracted.

Like almost everything Alison says, Paul is unable to tell whether she's joking or not.

'What *are* you doing?'

'Writing.'

'Writing what?'

'My story. Jesus.'

'Please put your phone away,' Paul says, as she continues pecking away at the screen with her fingernails and he suddenly feels extremely old and fucked and sorry for himself.

'I think I'm dying,' he says.

'Lol.'

'I'm being serious.' Paul feels his heart quicken as he speaks. He's finally talking about it. It's becoming real. 'I've got this lump in my mouth, on my gum.'

'Show me,' Alison says, dropping her iPhone on the duvet.

'Really?' Paul says, surprised at her reaction.

'Sure.'

She climbs onto Paul so that she's straddling him, and he opens his mouth and she peers in.

'Where is it? I can't see anything.'

'There,' Paul says, as much as he can with his mouth open, sort of pointing the lump out with his tongue.

'Move your tongue out of the way then.'

He moves his tongue out of the way, and as she's examining him he fixes his gaze on the wonky little pizza-slice tattoo on her shoulder.

Why would anyone get a pizza tattoo?

Last week she shaved off a huge patch of hair on the left side of her head, to reveal a professional tattoo she had done last year, the thing he thought was a snake or a rose, which turned out to be a massive curling lizard. She's fearless, in a way that Paul has never been. She does not give one single, solitary fuck about the future.

When Paul was twenty, all he ever *did* was worry about the future.

He'd tie himself in knots, wishing he was not in the current moment, whatever it happened to be, yearning instead for some indistinct, far-off point when he could say with confidence, 'I, Paul Saunders, am a published novelist.'

And look where that's got him.

His gaze drifts down to Alison's left nipple, which is an extremely pale pink, almost the same colour as the rest of her skin. There are two small oval scars either side of the teat, from where it used to be pierced. She has these little scars, from previous piercings, almost everywhere.

She takes her hands away from his face and gets back into bed. He waits for her to speak. She picks up her phone and looks at the screen then drops it on the duvet and kicks her feet impatiently.

'Well?' Paul says.

'It's probably nothing.'

'But you saw something?'

'There's a very small sort of skin-coloured lump there, yes. But I'm not a doctor.'

'So you *saw* something then is what you're saying?'

'Yes, I saw something.'

Okay, it's real, Paul thinks. I'm actually dying.

Oh fuck.

I need to write my novel.

I need to write my novel really, really quickly.

'You should just get it checked out at the doctor's,' Alison says. 'It's probably nothing.'

'You're right,' Paul says. 'I'll get it checked out.'

I need to go to the veggie café and write my novel.

Whenever Paul gets home from Alison's, he sprays the clothes he's taken off with Febreze before stuffing them deep in the washing basket. In the shower, he scrubs his body so hard it turns a blotchy, sore-looking pink. He cleans his teeth twice and washes his hands three times and sniffs his fingers repeatedly, trying to convince himself that they just smell of soap. Finally, he makes sure to delete all new text messages to and from Alison (who, as an extra precautionary measure, has been saved as 'Craig' on his contacts list).

I'm not actually doing this, Paul thinks, whenever he does it, because I am not the kind of person who would have an affair.

There have been two more tweets from @jfgkdfjdlsjf:

eat shit and #die

and

you are a massive #pedo wanker and soon everyone will find out what youve been doing #dickhead

Paul is starting to suspect that it's Alison sending them.

He's looked back through her @AliWhistle account and it uses the same kinds of grammar and is also all written lowercase.

Or is that just how everyone under twenty writes things these days?

Who is this? he tweeted back, once.

No reply.

He's spent hours searching through Alison's whole life online, dredging up accounts for Tumblr, Flickr, Pinterest, YouTube, Blogger, Vine, Instagram, Ask.fm, Last.fm, looking for clues, but all he ever finds are reblogged gifs of rotating neon-pink sunglasses and screencaps of foreign films with non sequitur subtitles and purposefully kitsch vector animations and strings of puzzling acronyms and cutesy misspellings and lowercase poems which aren't really poems and ironic comments about wanting to become the wife of Kanye West.

LAUREN
2014

I finally managed to get Jamaal to come inside and stand behind the till, which he was more than capable of operating, and I persuaded Nancy to take a break from her sorting and hang out some clothes, so that I could price up the books in the back room. At least that was what I said I was doing. What I actually did was just sit on the carpet and – after checking over my shoulder (in case what? he came in and saw me?) – look at Paul's book. PAUL SAUNDERS it said in bold black capitals on the neon-yellow spine.

I'd sort of forgotten he'd published a book; I'd sort of forgotten Paul completely, to be honest.

I leafed through to the back page where, on the inside cover, there was a large black-and-white photo of him, his mouth fixed in a serious expression and his nose longer and more crooked than I ever remembered it being. I'd seen this picture once before, on the back flap of the hardback edition, in a Waterstone's when it first came out. When was that? Four years ago? I'd taken Alyssa in with me, for moral support. I'd only known her a few months at that point, but we were close, right from the start. We stood there in the entrance and flicked through it, trying to get a sense of the story – to make sure it wasn't, you know, about anything to do with *me* – and when it wasn't (I'm embarrassed to tell you this), I actually felt disappointed.

Ha.

How does that even make sense?

And then, when we finally turned to the back inside flap, and Alyssa saw that photo of Paul for the first time, his weird overly long nose and sombre pout, all in over-saturated black and white, the picture cropped so you could only see his face, intensely staring out of the frame like he thought he was Ernest Hemingway, well, when Alyssa saw it, she burst out laughing, spitting the last bite of her Boots Meal Deal all over the pyramid of new release hardbacks.

'Bloody hell,' she'd said. 'He's not much of a looker, is he?'

I flipped to the dedication at the front.

To nobody, it read.

Nice one, Paul, I thought. Just as bitter as always then.

'Lau-*ren*?'

Nancy again. I got up and stuck my head into the shop.

'What's up?' I asked.

'I'm going,' Jamaal said. He was right by the door, one foot already through it, rain and wind whistling in, and Nancy had stationed herself behind the till. Apart from the two of them, the shop was deserted.

'Come on,' I said. 'Please don't do that. What am I going to tell Jeanne on Friday?'

'Tell her whatever you want, Miss. This is bullshit. I'm off.'

I glanced across at Nancy, who couldn't handle even the mildest of swearwords, and sure enough she'd begun worriedly rubbing the corner of the counter with her thumb, blushing and looking as if she might burst into tears.

'Just stay till one at least?' I pleaded. 'Please?'

'No,' he said. 'Fuck this. It's not like you even care about this charity anyway, Miss.'

'What's that supposed to mean?' I said, genuinely confused.

'Well, you get *paid* to work here, don't you?'

He waited for me to answer, his eyes burning.

'That's not the point,' I said quietly.

'No, it isn't. The point is that this is a waste of fucking time and I'm off. So, bye.'

He slammed the door so hard it rattled and bounced open again, and Nancy and I stood in the shop for a long moment without speaking, collecting ourselves.

'Shall I put some Justin Bieber on?' I said eventually.

Nancy shook her head.

IAN
2014

As the days roll on, it takes all my willpower not to just click the Internet Explorer icon on my desktop. I'm being a hardliner: no internet. Not until I feel better. Between each routed call, there's a thirty-second gap to fill, which most other Quiztime Solutions employees seem to be using to look at Facebook. I'm taking a leaf out of Dean's book: in between calls, I'll play a hand or two of Solitaire or do a few clicks on Minesweeper. And tomorrow, I tell myself, I'll bring in a book or a crossword. Anything to distract me from the urge to go back online, which is low-level but continuous, like toothache.

Go ahead, a voice whispers between calls.

Reactivate your Facebook account.

What's the harm?

How much damage can it do?

I don't listen, though.

I know exactly what will happen.

If I go back online, I'll just make myself even more miserable than I am at the moment. I'll look up certain people I used to know, and stare for whole evenings at a time at certain old Facebook photos and I will wander around certain streets in Nottingham again via Google Street View, and most of all, I will tie myself up in knots again over a certain person whose name I don't want to say, even in my own head, wondering what would've happened if only I'd handled things differently.

There's a list of names in the bottom right-hand corner of my monitor at all times. My name is about halfway down it. There's a clock, too, which is constantly timing exactly how long it takes me to do various things throughout the day. If my name turns blue, for instance, this means that I'm on an active call. If it turns green, it means I'm available to receive calls. And if it turns red, it means I am on a 'personal comfort break'.

Sometimes, I'll read down the list of names – Dean Fossgill, Esther Wu, Hayleigh Forrester, Jade Goodwin, Dalisay Rivera, Lewis McAndrews, etc. – and find it so strange that here we all are, sitting in this same cramped, weird-smelling room together, talking all day, just not to each other.

At lunch we slope off in different directions in silence.

So far, my lunch routine is: go for a piss, smoke a

roll-up in the entrance, then do a circuit of the Tesco Express. By the chillers, I'll stare in at the various Meal Deal items and promise myself that I'll come back and fill my basket with them the very moment I get paid. Then, back upstairs, I'll take my homemade sandwich out of my rucksack and carry it into the break room and sit down at the long table and eat it in silence.

No one ever really talks in the break room.

Most people just silently do things on their phones.

Today, for instance, there are three of us: me, The Lad With The Pearl Earring, and The Girl Who Always Wears The Same Pink Top.

The Lad With The Pearl Earring is eating a Tesco Meal Deal and silently doing something on his phone. He's in his early twenties and could easily beat me in a fight. The earring isn't actually pearl; it's one of those David Beckham sparkly ones.

The Girl Who Always Wears The Same Pink Top is eating noodles from a small Tupperware box. She's a bit younger than me, and is from an Asian country, I'm just not sure which one. She has long black hair and her skin is a pale brown colour. As she eats, she leafs through a crinkly, tea-stained copy of yesterday's *Metro*. It's only when she looks up from the paper and catches my eye and smiles a small, pained smile at me, that I realise I've just been flat out *staring* at her for the last few minutes. I quickly look down at the empty bread bag that I carry my sandwiches around in and feel my cheeks flush with heat and my ears begin to tingle.

When lunch break finishes, I go and sit down at my computer, put on my headset, and change my name from red to green. Then I lift myself back out of my chair a little in order to subtly look around the room and find out which way The Girl Who Always Wears The Same Pink Top has gone.

Turns out she's sitting almost directly across from me, just behind the *I hate it here* scribble.

At exactly one forty we click ourselves back off break, and the room once more fills with the sound of chattering and typing and chirping phones and people apologising and people hanging up. In the gaps between my own calls, I strain to catch The Girl Who Always Wears The Same Pink Top's voice, and when I finally make it out, it's very soft and musical and accented in a way I can't quite place.

'My name's Dalisay,' she says, 'and I'm calling from a company called Quiztime Solutions . . .'

I scan down the list of names on my screen, and when I read hers – Dalisay Rivera – something tinkles inside me like a bell.

In the early hours of the morning, I crouch down by my bed and unpeel the Sellotape around the top of my bedside table box. I lift the lid and peer inside at my collection of sentimental objects. I stick my hand in and rummage around amongst the cinema stubs and Fuji Film packets and pin badges and gig flyers and home-made greetings cards until I find the thing I'm looking for: a bulging brown envelope containing six long and as yet unanswered letters from my friend Andrew in Japan.

Andrew is my best friend.

He's very thoughtful and serious.

He's Canadian, although I met him back in Nottingham, when I was working in HMV and he was a customer.

Andrew always seems to know the right thing to do with himself.

For example: after Nottingham he moved to Japan forever.

I get back into bed and prop myself up with pillows.

As I read back through Andrew's letters in chronological order, I feel a ball of guilt slowly grow inside me.

At the start of Andrew's first letter, it's around the size of a marble, but by the 'hope you're okay' at the end of letter six, it's as big as a bowling ball.

I'm sorry, Andrew, I think, folding the letters and slipping them back into their envelopes. Just hang on, please. I will reply as soon as something good happens.

I close the lid of the cardboard box and shuffle down in bed and close my eyes.

I think about Dalisay.

I imagine us walking along a garden path past swirling, photoshopped fairies. We're holding hands, and the sun is shining, and she's wearing her best pink top and smiling at me with her calm brown eyes, and the bell is ringing again in my stomach, loud as a fire alarm.

Then the daydream begins to shift around on itself,

slowly transforming into something else, a feeling I've not experienced in a long time, the feeling of wanting to write a song.

First I hear a soft, ascending melody, which I'd most likely play finger-picked.

Then I hear a second counter-melody which would probably become the vocal part.

I even hear a few of the lyrics.

I lie there, very still, the duvet tight across my chest, and wait – as if standing on the front porch of myself, holding the door open – for the feeling to leave my body.

PAUL
2014

Paul looks at the knobbles of Sarah's spine beneath her pale pink nightie as she curls away from him, over on the other side of the mattress. The top of her head is outlined by the bluey-white glow of light emitted from her iPhone as she reads an article on Jezebel or The Huffington Post or one of the many other American websites she always seems to be looking at.

Lately, Sarah's not been sleeping.

Lately, all Sarah ever seems to do in bed is lie on her side and read articles, sideways, on her phone, facing away from him, the nightie stretched tight across her back.

When they're in bed together like that, Paul tries not to think about Alison – to keep his mind as empty as he can, like a meditation technique – because he worries that his brain might give him away otherwise, that it might make a small, whirring, Alison-Whistler-pitched motor noise that Sarah will pick up on and challenge him about.

He shifts onto his back and his eyes drift up to the shadowy, hole-less ceiling of their bedroom.

'I'm not smoking any more,' he says into the darkness.

A pause, just long enough for Paul to wonder if Sarah's drifted off to sleep.

'Good for you,' she says.

'You don't believe me.'

'It's not that, exactly.' Her voice is cold and very far-away sounding, as if it's coming from somewhere deep inside her. 'It's more that I don't give a shit any more.'

She presses a button on her phone and then they're both in the dark.

'I want a baby,' she whispers.

This was not what Paul was expecting at all. He shuffles himself up to her and slides one arm around her, resting his hand very gently on her hip. Sarah doesn't move.

'I'm thirty five,' she says, still facing away from him.

'We could have a baby,' Paul says, inching even closer towards her and brushing a wisp of hair from her neck in order to gently kiss it.

Doctor's appointment, Paul thinks. Doctor's appointment, Jonathan Franzen, mouth cancer, Australia, Rachel, Alison, baby.

'We could have a baby,' he says again.

Sarah doesn't reply.

She just shifts a little away from him and curls herself into a ball.

Sarah takes the second half of the week off work and goes to her parents' house in Surrey, again, leaving Paul to wander aimlessly round their flat wondering if she's ever going to come back. She seems sad, almost constantly now. She knows, Paul thinks. It's obvious. She knows what I'm doing and it's breaking her heart. I should just finish with her. Tell her the truth. Oh god, what the fuck am I doing with my life.

Right now he's standing in their bedroom, rooting through Sarah's knicker drawer.

What exactly is he expecting to find in there?

Sarah's knickers are different to Alison's. Sarah's knickers come in five-packs from Marks & Spencer and are bigger and more sensible and don't have any bows or see-through bits on them.

Paul's hand touches an object that definitely isn't knickers.

He pulls it out.

It's a Polaroid of Sarah.

She looks much younger, about twenty, Paul guesses, and her hair is longer and darker and shinier. She's posing in a pastiche of one of those Bettie Page 50s pin-up girls, and she's wearing stockings and suspenders and high heels and nothing else.

He tries to work out who might have taken this picture,

tries to remember the various bits and pieces she's told him about previous boyfriends, his brain buzzing around uselessly within the choppy, fragmentary chronology of it all.

The Sarah in the picture looks so much happier than Sarah now, and Paul knows that it's *him* that's making her feel this way; him who's sucked all the life out of her.

For a moment, he remembers a thing in perfect clarity: a thing she told him on one of their first dates, in the Cornerhouse bar. She was drinking a gin and tonic and she leaned in across the table towards him, wearing a black dress and gold hoop earrings, and said that she'd always wanted to be a dancer when she was younger, that she took classes as a teenager and was planning to get back into it, actually, that she was going to join the gym again and get into shape, and then pick up from where she left off, because when she was dancing it felt like 'nothing else mattered'. And then she'd laughed, saying she realised how corny that sounded, and he'd said, 'No, no, that's good. You should do that.'

Paul slips the photograph back beneath the knickers and shuts the drawer.

Date: Wed, 13 Oct 2004 16:04:59 +0000
From: lauren_cross83@hotmail.com
To: fiveleavesleft@hotmail.com
Subject: Re: Argh

Ian,

Please don't be worried! Your email was lovely. Really, *really* lovely actually. Thank you so much. I don't think anyone's ever been that honest with me. I feel flattered too.

It's only taken me a while to reply because all my time's been taken up with Emily – traipsing round, hunting for a flat, handing out our CVs, etc.

No luck on that front as yet, I'm afraid to report. We're still living out of suitcases in a double room at this cheap hostel place which I'm 99% sure is flea-infested. I keep finding these itchy red dots on my legs in the mornings. Gross. Anyway, if we don't find somewhere soon, I'm going to have to just stump up and pay for a better hostel for us both (Emily's refusing to chip in; she wants to spend all her money on booze and joss sticks and things with mirrors sewn into them.)

If I'm completely honest, so far she's annoying the fuck out of me. I guess when I agreed to come here with her, I didn't actually know her that well; she was just someone on my course who always seemed to be having a good time and knew what they were doing. It was funny when you said you thought of me as that kind of person: well, that's exactly how I've always thought of Emily. Things always seem to just work out for her somehow, and I think maybe I decided to come away with her to watch up close how that worked, maybe even take away a few tips. Well, so far what I've learnt is: to get what you want, you just have to complain really loudly about [anything] and eventually someone else will come along and sort it out for you.

Oh dear, I don't know. I realise that *I'm* complaining too, by writing about it, and if I'm not careful, I'll accidentally create an infinite loop of complaining that will swallow us both completely.

Canada is amazing. I wish you could see it too. Everything's so BIG and CLEAN and BRIGHT here. And the people are so nice. I couldn't get my head around it at first. I was still in England mode. We were waiting at this bus stop the other day, on our way out to look at a (way too expensive) apartment, and this lady started talking to us, just chatting to us about the weather out of the blue, and my first instinct was to think 'Okay, what's she after?' You know, as in: is she going to ask for change or try and steal our bags or something dodgy like that, but it turned out she JUST WANTED TO TALK. Weird, right?! People here are actually friendly for no reason! It doesn't make sense! We English are so repressed! I'm going to stop using exclamation marks now!

You were right to picture mountains by the way: from most places in Vancouver, almost everywhere really, you can look up and see the Rocky Mountains in the distance, which I still haven't quite got over. (I've not seen a bear standing on any of them yet, though.)

Ooh, before I forget, I've got to tell you about this thing they do in the local paper here. It's a bit at the back, called 'I SAW U', and it's for people who are too shy to speak to each other! I've become a bit addicted to reading it. Here's an example:

Purple Pants and Leather Man
There were a lot of people on that westbound 14, and you stayed at the front of the bus. You caught my attention. I saw you look in my direction several times. I tried to catch your eye and smile as I moved towards the back, but I couldn't see you over everyone between us. I was the girl in the blue hoodie. You were dressed in bright purple pants and leather jacket. Having chatted would've made my day. Perhaps some other time?

How did your gigs go, by the way? Any word from Avril yet? I see exciting things for you on the horizon.

Thanks for your list! I think we're about even now.

Your friend,

L x

p.s. Please stop smoking.
p.p.s. I think I fancy you a tiny bit too. (Always have.)

LAUREN
2014

After Jamaal left, I expected a sudden rush of customers, but it stayed dead quiet all morning, just a student couple who didn't buy anything and, a little before midday, The Man Who Always Buys One CD, whose choice for today was *Permission To Land* by The Darkness (a steal at £1.25). I was standing behind the till with Nancy, trying – *again!* – to show her how the receipt roll worked, when Peter, the new boy, came in.

I'd forgotten about him starting.

He'd dropped his form in towards the end of last week and I'd told him to come in for a half shift today, just a few hours over lunchtime, to see how he got on. I'd had a good feeling about him straight away. He seemed nice. He said he was taking a year out, before he went off to uni the following September, and he reminded me of someone but I couldn't think who.

'Hey,' he said from the doorway, waving awkwardly, the sleeve of his hoodie pulled down over his knuckles so just the tips of his fingers poked out.

'Hi, Peter,' I said. 'Come in. This is Nancy. Nancy, Peter.'

He had one of those haircuts where the fringe is all long and swoopy across his forehead, and there were a few bright red patches of acne on his cheeks and chin.

'Hi, *Pe*-ter,' Nancy said, rubbing the spot by the till again. 'I might . . .' she said to me, quietly, gesturing behind her.

'Sure,' I said, and she almost ran out from behind the till and off into the back room.

'Is she alright?' Peter asked.

'She's just a bit shy,' I explained. 'She probably thinks you look like Justin Bieber,' I whispered (immediately feeling bad afterwards for making a joke at Nancy's expense).

'Right,' Peter said, a little embarrassed. 'So, shall I, um . . .' He motioned towards the till.

'Yep, come round,' I said.

Just then the speakers crackled and the music started up.

Sure enough, it was 'Baby' by Justin Bieber.

'See?' I said, and Peter grinned.

Isn't it weird how some people can immediately put you at ease like that? It was as if there was this warmth coming from him and I felt like I could just say whatever I wanted, that I didn't have to hold back or tone myself down or whatever.

I wondered again; who *was* it he reminded me of?

And then I realised: it was you.

Date: Fri, 15 Oct 2004 11:46:08 +0000
From: fiveleavesleft@hotmail.com
To: lauren_cross83@hotmail.com
Subject: Re: Re: Argh

okay, glad my email wasn't too weird. i can breathe out now. phew.

thanks for the I Saw U ad! i imagine i'd get addicted to those too if they printed them over here. please send more if you get the chance. i wish they'd had them in the Nottingham Evening Post. i'm always so crap at ever making the first move. (or the second or third, come to think of it.)

anyway.

Canadians sound nice. weird and nice. i think i want to live in Canada now. anywhere but Nottingham actually. i'm getting so sick of it. every time i go out, i seem to bump into another person i know that i don't really have the energy to talk to. i keep catching myself daydreaming about moving to a new city. starting again and all that. i don't know. (is that my complaint quota used up for the day?)

Here's my one bit of exciting news: we played a support slot and got a (very small) mention in this week's NME. if you like, i could type it up for you?

i'm trying not to get too carried away about it. i realise it's only a couple of lines, but, you know, it's another small thing that suggests this band might not actually be a complete waste of time.

oh god, i hope so. i've been doing a bit of CV-handing-out myself. just shops and pubs and things. but i just keep daydreaming about a version of things where i would actually get to play music as my job. does that just sound impossible to you?

i hope you have some luck with flat hunting soon. how's Emily? still winding you up?

today i went downstairs to get a bite to eat and Alex had left his dressing gown in the kitchen sink. i guess he must have got something gross on it. i don't know why i just told you that. maybe because it's about the most exciting/only thing that's happened to me so far today.

anyway, i'm going to go now. got a lunchtime shift at the Bull in fifteen minutes.

yours sincerely,

Ian 'probably going to be late for work' Wilson

xx

p.s. I'll give up smoking on my next birthday (Nov, 20th). how does that sound?

p.p.s. what are you doing when your year in Canada runs out?

IAN
2014

'Hi, my name's Dalisay and I'm calling from a company called Quiztime Solutions.'

Whenever I hear her voice from behind the partition wall, the bell inside me tinkles madly, and sometimes I even find myself getting jealous of whoever she's talking to on the other end of the line. Why can't it be me she's phoning with the chance to win an exclusive, five-star luxury break for two?

I wonder where in China or Korea or Malaysia she's from.

I wonder why she's working here.

I wonder whether she has a boyfriend.

My phone chirps and I lean forward and click onto the first page of the questionnaire, ready to start filling it in if the person agrees to go ahead with the survey. (The person almost never agrees to go ahead with the survey.) The phone rings in my headset, then a gruff male voice barks, 'Hello?'

'Hi there, sir, I'm calling from . . .'

'Fuck off, mate,' he says and slams down the phone.

This is quite common.

I'll get sworn at, on average, around ten times an hour.

I wonder how many times an hour Dalisay gets sworn at.

I don't like the idea of someone telling her to fuck off.

At about eleven this morning, as I was returning from a 'personal comfort break', I purposefully took the long way round the room and as I passed her monitor I saw the familiar, dark blue stripe of Facebook on her screen.

It would be so easy to just double click the Internet Explorer icon on my desktop. Reactivate my account. Send Dalisay Rivera a friend request.

But instead I continue my game of Solitaire, dragging a three of clubs across the pixellated green card table and dropping it onto a four of diamonds.

My dialler chirps and the phone rings in my headset and then a woman's voice says, 'Hello?'

'Hi there, madam, I'm calling from . . .'

'Fuck off,' she says, before slamming down the phone.

In my second week, two new people start: a boy and a girl, both in their early twenties. Martin leads them around the room, giving them the full tour. When they reach my terminal, Martin puts his hand on my shoulder. I take off my headset and swivel round in my chair.

'Alright, Ian, mate,' he says. 'Think you could show Chloe the ropes?'

Chloe is pale and nervous-looking. She smiles meekly at the floor. The boy is tall and handsome and confident.

'Sure,' I say.

'Grab a seat then, Chloe,' Martin says, winking at me, 'And our Ian here will show you *just* what to do.'

As Chloe goes to fetch a spare chair over, Martin purses his lips and grabs hold of an invisible arse and pumps his hips at me.

I try to ignore him.

I plug an extra headset into the dialler for Chloe, and while she's putting it on I watch Martin lead the tall boy off round to the other side of the partition.

'Have you done anything like this before?' I ask.

Chloe shakes her head and stares into her lap.

I show her what to do, what all the buttons mean, etc., and I can hear Dalisay doing the same thing from behind the partition wall. Martin must have assigned Tall Boy to her and I feel a sharp, sour pang in my gut.

I try to focus on Chloe.

Once we've covered the basics, I make a few example calls while she listens in. After a few minutes of no answers, I actually get through to someone willing to fill in the questionnaire. The dialler window tells me that the person I'm speaking to is called Mrs Wilson, and that she lives at 24a Heathcote Avenue in Stockport. After I've told her about the fantastic holiday competition and asked her all the generic personal info questions – height, age, ethnicity, religious beliefs, gender, sexuality, etc. – we get onto the main body of the survey, which is designed to assess her happiness levels on a scale of one to ten.

As I ask Mrs Wilson the questions, with Chloe listening in on the second line, I become doubly aware of just how uncomfortable and intrusive they are.

'On a scale of one to ten, Mrs Wilson,' I say, 'with one being not at all happy, five being neither happy nor unhappy and ten being extremely happy, how happy would you say you are *over all*, Mrs Wilson?'

A long pause.

I can hear *Deal or No Deal* playing in her living room.

'I don't know . . . three?' Mrs Wilson says.

'And can I ask why that is, please?' I say, tapping the corresponding bubble on the script with the end of my biro so Chloe can see exactly where I'm up to.

'Well, last year my son committed suicide.'

Chloe shifts a little in her chair.

I type *son killed hmslf* into the available text box, click save, and then move briskly along to the next question.

'I'm very sorry to hear that, Mrs Wilson,' I say. 'Anyway, moving briskly along . . . when you picture yourself in one year's time, Mrs Wilson, do you ultimately see yourself as: a) less happy than you are today,

b) roughly the same level of happiness, or c) happier than you are in your present situation?'

'I don't know . . . B?'

'That's great,' I say automatically, only catching myself once I've said it.

After the call's been wrapped and logged, I pause the dialler and turn in my swivel chair and Chloe looks *even paler*, if that's possible.

'Think you're ready to have a go?' I say.

'Mind if I just nip to the loo for a moment first?'

This is the first full sentence Chloe's said since she sat down.

'Down the end of the hall on the left,' I say, and Chloe quickly trots off, out of the room.

I listen for a while to Dalisay laughing and joking with Tall Boy, over on the other side of the partition.

On a scale of one to ten, with one being not at all happy, five being neither happy nor unhappy and ten being extremely happy, I am hovering at about one and a half.

I find Chloe's name on the list.

It's been 'personal comfort break' red for just over three minutes now.

It gets to ten before I realise that Chloe's done a runner.

As I walk down Oxford Road, the sun clips the tops of the buildings and makes the puddles sparkle, and I accidentally think about that song again, the one that appeared uninvited in my head.

If someone were to hand me a guitar, I reckon I could play it.

'Spare change, mate?' a homeless man calls from a newsagent's doorway. I shake my head.

I reach the music shop just as they're getting ready to close. The man with the beard is already lowering the first of the shutters.

As I get closer, I can see an item in the left-hand bay that makes my stomach flip: standing between a shiny snare drum and a bright blue ukulele is my guitar. I get right up to the window and tilt my head in order to make out the spidery writing on the price tag dangling from its headstock.

£999, it says.

Fucking hell.

'You alright there, mate?' the man asks when he notices me. 'We're closing up, but if you know what you want, I could go in and grab it?'

'Just browsing,' I say, stepping out of the way to let him get at the second shutter.

PAUL
2014

'I'd like to make an appointment,' Paul says in a low and trembling voice to the receptionist at the doctor's surgery.

I am going to die, he thinks.

'What day, please?' the receptionist says.

'As soon as possible,' Paul says.

While she scrolls through the calendar on her computer, Paul turns and looks around the empty waiting room. The walls are painted a bile green and the frenzied, multi-coloured swirls of the lino flooring look a bit like a Jackson Pollock nervous breakdown. On the coffee table are copies of *Marie Claire*, *What Hi-Fi?* and *GQ*.

'Nothing till next week,' she says.

What about right now? Paul wants to say. There's nobody here. I don't understand. Just let me go in. I'm going to die.

'That's fine,' Paul says.

'Next Wednesday at four?'

'Great.'

If I die before next Wednesday it will be your fault, Paul thinks, stumbling onto the street, fumbling a cigarette into his mouth.

Maybe I should get one of those e-cigs, he thinks as he lights it and takes a couple of deep, dizzying blasts.

During the short walk back to the flat, Paul doesn't really look where he's going. Since the lump's appearance, he's stopped worrying about all other possible ways of dying. Because, if you're going to die from *this*, he reasons as he steps into the road without really checking his left and right, then at least you know you aren't going to die from anything else like being hit by a car.

In the entrance hall, he checks the post box (nothing). On the way up the stairs, he checks his emails on his phone (nothing). Back inside the flat, he sits down on the sofa, lifts his laptop onto his knees and checks his emails again (still nothing).

On the NaNoWriMo forum, people are reaching the halfway point. They're posting messages of encouragement and motivational quotes.

On the penis extension forum, someone has posted an advanced, five-minute stretching technique called 'The Helicopter'.

On Facebook, David Hastings has invited Paul to the event 'Dave-O's Wicked Stag Do!!!'

Oh god, Paul thinks.

When Paul lived with David, in his second and third years at university, David always seemed to be head-butting things and watching *Jackass* and walking around with his top off and doing chin-ups on the metal bar he'd bolted to his doorway. Once he smashed a full pint of orange squash against the living room wall because someone beat him at *Tony Hawkes Pro Skater*.

Paul looks at the date of the stag do: December 12, which is just under a month away.

He reads the description:

'Now then lads,' it says, 'as u know I am getting married on the 15th of jan and so I need one final blowout and you as my best lads past and present are hearby cordially invited to get fuckfaced with me in the manner of your choosing. Fun will include but is not to be limited to: drinking, smoking, drugs (bring your own!), go karts (if we can be arsed??) and other festiveties (I.e. Strip club? Curry? Other suggestions more than welcome!!). COME ON LADS DON'T LET ME DOWN NOWWWW!!!!!!!!!!!!!!!'

To accompany the event, he's posted a picture of one of the men from *Jackass* (Steve-O?) doing the 'metal' sign with both hands, his tongue extended, next to the tanned buttocks of a stripper.

I'll probably be dead by then, Paul thinks.

He feels a strange twinge of nostalgia, thinking about all those evenings when he and Dave and Ian used to sit in their living room, just smoking joints and watching late-night telly and talking shit.

He surprises himself a little by clicking the 'Join' button.

Date: Mon, 18 Oct 2004 16:04:59 +0000
From: lauren_cross83@hotmail.com
To: fiveleavesleft@hotmail.com
Subject: Re: Re: Re: Argh

Ian,

YES PLEASE SEND THE REVIEW PLEASE YES.

That's so ace! I can't wait to read it!! Congratulations!!!

To reciprocate, here are my two top bits of news:

1) We have somewhere to live that doesn't have fleas!
2) We both have jobs!

I guess it's been a rather productive week . . .

So yeah, we have a flat – it's called a 'duplex'. It's bright pink if you can believe that. Imagine a really big fondant fancy with a door and windows in the front. We live in the rooms at the back, above two Chinese nurses, and to get to our section you have to climb up these rickety wooden stairs. And at night you can stand outside on the balcony and look out at the lights of the city (Richmond, which borders Vancouver) and watch the planes coming into land at the airport.

My job's in a trendy cafe called Cake Hole in Gastown (which is like the swanky-but-cool area maybe and also happens to be the most touristy bit of the city). I've only done one trial shift so far and it's only part time but after I finished the manager let me take some cakes home afterwards and said I could come back again. That's a good sign, right? And Emily's working flat out at Chapters now too (which is like the Canadian version of Waterstones) and loving it and in answer to your question: I'm actually getting on with her a lot better now that I don't have to see her ALL THE BLOODY TIME.

I'm glad you liked the I Saw U's as much as me.

Here's a couple more for you then:

Dancing with myself
U were sat across from me in Relish with ur friends and I found u very attractive. U have an eyebrow piercing. I was the one dancing like an idiot till my friends got there. I danced all night but never worked up the courage to speak to u! I am an idiot!

Commercial
I was walking towards Nanaimo on Commercial, and you away. I was wearing an open black hoodie with a white shirt and jeans, you had a long white jacket and black slightly wedged shoes. We both did a double take and I should have run back and said hi, so this is me doing that now just a few moments too late.

With Your Mom

You were the Korean (?) girl with your mom at Tim Horton's on Robson, Saturday morning. We exchanged smiles but I didn't want to embarrass you. I was the cute half-Asian guy in the purple sweater. Next time I promise I wont be so shy.

What are you doing for Christmas by the way? Do you go home and see your family? I think I'll be spending mine out here . . .

L xx

p.s. I'm not really sure what I'm doing once my working visa here runs out. But I don't think I'll go back to Nottingham. I feel pretty much the same as you about it. I'll probably end up staying with my mum for a little while but no doubt she'll drive me mad after a couple of weeks. So, I guess my answer is just: Not sure.

p.p.s. I hope there have been no more dressing gowns in your sink recently.

p.p.p.s I've been sort of talking to you in my head a bit, sometimes, as I'm walking around. That doesn't make me sound like a nutjob, right?!

(Actually, don't answer that.)

LAUREN
2014

I'd just finished showing Peter how to use the till – he picked it up straight away, he'd done shop work before – and I was about to sort through the remaining tower of donations with Nancy, when Alyssa appeared in the doorway.

'Surprise,' she said, stepping into the shop, shaking a Sainsbury's bag at me.

'What's that supposed to be?' I said.

'Lunch.'

'I don't think I can leave the shop today.'

'Come on. It's your *birth*day.'

I looked back at Peter, who grinned and raised his eyebrows. I went back over.

'Right,' I said, keeping my voice down so Nancy didn't

hear, 'now I know this is throwing you in at the deep end, but think you could handle things here for a bit on your own, just for half an hour?'

'Well, there's Nancy too,' he said. 'She can help me out if I get stuck, right?'

'Yep,' I whispered. 'But if she asks where I've gone, just say I've popped next door.'

'I'll be fine,' he said.

'Thanks,' I said, touching him on the arm, which struck me as weird, even as I did it. (I've never been much of a 'physical contact' person.)

'Happy birthday!' he called as we left.

It'd stopped raining, just about, so we sat on a bench in the square, a little way down the road from the shop. Alyssa took her jacket off and laid it over the damp slats of the bench, hamming it up, playing the role of a Disney prince.

'Why, thank you, kind sir,' I said, trying to join in, but my heart wasn't really in it.

Once we'd sat down, she talked me through the contents of the Sainsbury's bag: 'just cheese' sandwiches, BBQ Transformer Snacks, Mr Men cupcakes, and a large bottle of Appletiser, which she cracked the top off and swigged from before handing to me.

'Aren't I a bit old for this now?' I said gently.

'That's the point,' she said, blowing a stray bit of hair from her forehead. 'That's the joke.'

'Right.'

I tried my best to smile.

'So? Go on, Birthday Girl. What happened?'

'What happened when?'

'What happened last night?'

'Oh shit. I don't know. Nothing happened. I cancelled on him. Said I wasn't feeling well.'

'He sounded nice.'

'I'm fine on my own,' I said. 'You really need to stop thinking that being single is some kind of problem or disability. Because it isn't. *Okay*?'

I could feel that wasp's nest buzzing inside me again and I had to stop and take a deep breath. I didn't even really know what I was getting so angry about, really. Alyssa was just trying to help.

'Right,' she said, only half listening, peeling the pink circle of icing off the top of her cupcake with her teeth, half a cheese sandwich still in her other hand. 'Well, there's this bloke at work called Gary who I think *might* be single, if you wanted me to find out and put a word in with him?'

'Fucking hell!' I said, standing, my sandwich falling off my lap. The pigeons went for it immediately, swooping down, making the whole scene about ten times more dramatic than it should've been.

'What?' Alyssa cried. '*What?!*'

I took another deep breath and sat back down.

'I'm fine,' I said.

'You're thirty-one.'

'So?'

Alyssa was four years younger than me. She'd been married since her early twenties, to Dave, a boy she'd known since A-Level college. She'd never been outside this town, except on holidays and training courses. Which was *absolutely fine*, I reminded myself. But it also seemed to lead her to different conclusions about things.

Be nice, a voice said inside me. *She's your only friend here and she's just trying to cheer you up, because, admit it, you've been acting pretty down lately.*

'Thirty-one's fine,' I said, in a purposefully lighter tone, trying to snap myself out of it. 'Thirty-one's the new, um, twenty-eight. Please stop trying to make it into something it's not.'

'That spotty lad at the till looked alright,' she said, grinning.

'He's eighteen,' I said, unable to stop myself from smiling too.

'Hot MILF action.'

'Right, now can we please stop being such fucking clichés,' I said, forcing the grin off my face, 'and just talk about anything other than *men* for once?'

'Like what?'

'I don't know. Like how the planet is probably going to become uninhabitable in our lifetime and there's probably no point in procreating anyway.'

'Cheerful.'

'It's true.'

I wasn't sure if it *was* true or not; it was just a thing I'd skim read on my phone the other evening between TV programmes, some elderly academic likening our attempts at recycling and emissions management to 'rearranging deckchairs on the *Titanic*'.

As the pigeons pecked away at the rest of my sandwich, I imagined an end-of-the-world scenario: global warming had caused the earth to reach unbearable levels of heat and everyone knew that soon they'd all be cinders.

I imagined myself going to the phone, trying desperately to call you, and realising I didn't know your number.

'Give me that Appletiser,' I said.

Alyssa passed me the bottle and I took a big swig.

Date: Mon, 25 Oct 2004 15:08:08 +0000
From: fiveleavesleft@hotmail.com
To: lauren_cross83@hotmail.com
Subject: Re: Re: Re: Re: Argh

thank you for being interested in reading the review. (i'll type it up at the bottom.)

we've had someone from a label get in touch off the back of it, too – they're only a tiny vinyl-only thing in Leeds, but still. fingers crossed. Alex has sent them over a CD and he's also been spending an inordinate amount of time making us a Myspace page, which he insists is extremely important.

have a look: myspace.com/thepostcardsUK

it's got the three songs off our demo and an acoustic one I recorded last week, here in my room. hope you like it. (if you don't like it, please lie and tell me you liked it.) also, if you look in the 'top friends' bit, i've got my own personal account on there, too, so if you wanted to join, we could be 'friends' on it or something, maybe?

congrats on your job/flat/fondant fancy/etc!

i've got an interview for Christmas temp work at the HMV tomorrow. kind of dreading it. i don't know. feels like i'm selling out – cheating on Selectadisc. is that pathetic??

yeah, probably going home to see my parents at Christmas. we usually just sit in the living room and eat chocolate oranges and watch TV for three days straight. last year my sister brought her new boyfriend down on boxing day, too, and he turned out to be a prize dickhead, so i'm kind of hoping they'll have broken up by now. (is that mean?)

(i've been talking to you in my head a bit too. that's kind of what the song, the acoustic one, is about actually, if you must know. i feel like i have all sorts of questions to ask you. would it be okay if i just asked you some questions? i don't want to bombard you with them though, without your prior consent, you see, but i just want to know lots more about you . . .)

i can hear Alex shouting at the TV downstairs which means the football must be on. sometimes, when the football's on, it's kind of terrifying: i went out for a walk the other night and the streets were completely deserted and then someone must have scored a goal because suddenly i heard this massive roar coming from every house and it sounded a bit like what i imagine the end of the world might sound like.

okay, here's my first question (i couldn't wait till next email, sorry): do you like football?

also: do you have any brothers and sisters? (i have one sister.)

and finally: what's your favourite band or singer? (i think mine is Elliott Smith.)

i guess i'd better try and get some sleep. Just looked at the time on my computer and realised that my interview's in less than eight hours.

shit.

wish me luck,
Ian x

p.s. NME review:

Opening up for the Alps were Postcards, a local band who seem to have already developed a small but rabid following. From their short, nervy set it was easy to see why. This three-piece buzzsawed their way through a blink-or-you'll-miss-it performance full of howling, wiry guitars, clattering drums, and occasional moments of soaring, angelically melodic brilliance. Beneath the fuzz there's some real talent at work.

IAN
2014

Martin appears in the doorway and claps his hands. 'Great job this morning everyone. Only a few hundred surveys left before we've hit our target. So let's really smash it the rest of this week, yeah, and as soon as we get it finished, I'll order us in some pizzas. How does that sound?'

Everyone makes an *ooh* noise.

On my way out the door, he puts a hand on my shoulder.

'Quick word, mate?'

I follow him down the corridor and into his office, which smells suspiciously like McDonald's.

'Have a seat,' he says, sliding himself into his big leather chair. 'I've been having a listen through to a few of your calls from the other day. And I don't think you're performing at your maximum potential to be honest, mate.'

'Oh,' I say.

'Now don't be alarmed. I'm not going to fire you. But I just feel like you're just not really putting your heart and soul into this. You sound like you're just reading out the words from the script if I'm honest. And we both know you can do better than that, yeah?'

'Yep.'

'It's not rocket science.'

'No, it's not.'

'Look at Danny.'

'Which one's Danny?'

'Danny,' Martin says, touching the place on his earlobe where a sparkly earring would go. 'Danny.'

'Right,' I say. 'Danny.'

'He only started a couple of weeks before you did and he's consistently coming up in the top three in the weekly chart.'

I didn't know there was a weekly chart.

'Whereas you . . .' Martin says, opening a spread sheet on his computer, then swivelling the monitor to face me, 'you're right down here near the bottom.'

He points to my name on the screen. It's second from the bottom. Below me is someone called Andrew Smith.

'Which one's Andrew?' I say.

'Andrew's been off since before you started with spinal problems. Anyways, all I'm saying, mate, is that this afternoon I really want you to step it up a gear, yeah?'

'Alright,' I say, lifting myself out of my chair. 'Cheers.'

I wonder what he'll do exactly if I don't step it up a gear.

I wander back down the corridor.

I stick my head in the break room.

Today there are eight or nine people in there, including Sue and Danny and Tall Boy and Dean. They're all eating Tesco sandwiches and silently doing things on their phones. I carry on down the steps towards the exit, rolling a roll-up as I go.

Four days left until I give up.

Four days until my thirty-first birthday.

For once it's not raining, so I decide to go for a walk.

I head down Deansgate in the opposite direction to the Tesco Express, and on a whim I turn into a side road near the fancy, white-brick solicitor's offices. At the end of the street there's a small park that I've never seen before: a rectangular patch of bright green, just-mowed grass with a few metal benches dotted round the edges. It's the kind of place you might take someone for a picnic. It's almost empty, just one woman sitting on her own, eating her lunch.

I can't remember the last time I went for a picnic with anyone.

I'm reaching for the gate, my hand's just about to touch it, when I see a dash of pink beneath the woman's coat and realise that of course it's Dalisay, sat there eating her sandwiches. My hand falters and stops in mid air then slips back into my jacket pocket.

I never know what to do in situations like this.

Do I sit on a different bench?

Or do I go over and say hello?

Or do I perhaps turn round and head back to work as quickly as I can, hoping she didn't see me?

I feel extremely pathetic, the whole rest of the afternoon. Each time I hear her voice from behind the partition wall, I cringe. I bet Danny wouldn't have run away from a girl on a bench. According to *Ways to Happiness*, 'to fully achieve happiness you must first be prepared to grab it by both horns'.

I'm such a coward.

I should've gone up and said hello.

In between calls, I lose six games of solitaire in a row.

Before you leave each day, you have to fill in a sheet, saying exactly how many minutes you've worked and exactly how much in pounds and pence you believe you've earned, then add that figure to your running total for the week. It's beginning to look like a massive amount (even though I know in reality it's only slightly above minimum wage).

Only a few days left until payday.

I've had to borrow twenty quid off Carol, to see me through the week.

I sign my name in the correct box and file my sheet in the box file by the door, and as I'm heading down the main set of stairs, I realise that I'm right behind Dalisay. She's only two or three metres in front of me.

She pushes open the main door at the bottom, then stops and holds it open for me, too.

'Thanks,' I mumble.

I stick my hands deep in my coat pockets and fumble around amongst the bits of fluff and the stray filter tips for my almost-empty pouch of tobacco and papers. We step out onto the street. It's already gone dark and the wind is making a whistling, howling sound, like a dog trying to join in when someone plays the piano.

I turn right and start walking in the direction of Piccadilly, extremely, painfully aware that Dalisay's turned the same way too.

Shit.

She's walking just a few steps behind me.

I try to focus on rolling my cigarette, but my fingers feel numb and wonky like they're made out of sausages.

I slow myself down, so we're almost level.

The wind keeps blowing my tobacco away.

I'm trying desperately to think of something interesting to say.

When I finally finish rolling my cigarette, I look up and there she is in the left-hand corner of my eye, just a quarter step behind me.

I stick the roll-up in my mouth and light it.

'You shouldn't smoke,' she says. 'It's a bad habit.'

I turn to look at her and she's smiling.

'Sorry,' I say.

I slow myself down a little more and now we're walking side by side. I attempt to blow my smoke away from her face but the wind catches it and blows most of it straight back at us.

'Sorry,' I say again.

'Why are you apologising?'

'I don't know.'

She's still smiling.

I try to smile back and my face feels like a Microsoft Paint drawing of a smiling face. We walk along Deansgate, past Richer Sounds and the Church of Scientology and a large shop that just sells bathtubs. I allow myself to stop smiling.

'I'm giving up soon anyway,' I say. 'For my birthday.'

'When's your birthday?'

'This coming Friday.'

'Cool.'

'I don't suppose . . .' I say.

'What?'

This is it.

I am *grabbing happiness by both horns.*

'Well, I was just wondering . . .'

'Yes?'

I'm about to just blurt it out when a beeping sound makes us both jump. I spin round and there's Martin's Audi, pulling up to the kerb. Fuck's sake. Not now. The tinted window slides down as we both approach.

'Alright, mate?' Martin says. 'Want a lift?'

Dalisay hangs back, confused.

'I'm fine thanks,' I say.

'Fair play,' he says. And then, really, really obviously, he winks at me.

He pulls away from the kerb so fast his back tyres squeal, lurching off into the Deansgate traffic.

'Martin goes out with my sister,' I say.

'Oh, okay, right,' says Dalisay.

A long pause.

'He's awful, isn't he?'

'Yeah.' Dalisay smiles with relief. 'He is.'

'Anyway . . .'

We've stopped walking now. We're just standing by the kerb, looking at our trainers. They're both Converse, I realise, except mine are black low tops while Dalisay's are red high tops. Fuck it. I'm just going to say it.

'I was just wondering if you fancied having a drink with me on my birthday, maybe? I've only just moved here, you see. To this city. And I don't have that many friends yet, and I was going to hang out with my sister but now she's going away. For the weekend. With Martin. So, um, yeah.'

Did I really just say that?

'Oh shit, I can't,' she says. 'I'm helping my aunt all weekend. I've already booked the Friday off.'

'Right.'

I drop my fag on the pavement and grind it out, feeling a little kite of hope come crashing down inside me.

'But what are you doing right now?' she says.

PAUL

2014

'What did you think?' Alison asks.

She's done her room up like a French restaurant, covering a borrowed collapsible card table with a chequered red-and-white table cloth and sticking a candle in an empty wine bottle and streaming a compilation album called *Café Parisien* on her free Spotify account. Every fifteen minutes or so, the jaunty accordion music gets interrupted by adverts for car insurance and macho outdoor assault course training.

Paul takes a big swig of red wine, swivels a little in the office chair she's borrowed from one of her housemates, and looks down at his empty plate. She made them pasta. Just penne pasta, with what Paul suspects was a jar of Dolmio stirred in.

'It was nice, yeah,' he says, unable to summon any kind of enthusiasm.

He feels deeply embarrassed by this whole evening.

I'm thirty-one and a half, he thinks. What the fuck am I doing here?

He watches her face fall.

'No, really,' he says. 'It was nice.'

Alison stands and starts collecting up their plates.

'You can say it was shit if it was shit,' she says.

'It was nice,' Paul says.

'It was shit,' Alison says.

'I think I'd better go.'

'But what about the film?'

The film is *Breathless*. That was the whole point of French Restaurant Night. Also, earlier on, Alison said, 'Wouldn't it be great if we were in, you know, *actual* Paris?' and fluttered her eyelashes at him cartoonishly, her face flickering in the candlelight, and Paul knew just what she was hinting at.

'Yep,' he'd said noncommittally.

'We should go, lol,' she'd said, trying to pitch it as a joke, a throwaway comment. But Paul could tell how much she really wanted it. She'd been moaning recently about the frustration of only ever being able to see him in her room.

'No, I think I'd better go,' Paul says firmly.

Without warning, Alison drops their empty plates on the floor. One of them smashes and both sets of cutlery go pinging off into the bedroom.

'Just fucking go then,' she snaps.

Paul stays in the swivel chair, paralysed with shock. He reaches for his wine glass and gulps down the rest, his hand trembling.

'GO,' she screams, and he jumps in his seat, then stands.

She pads over to her bed and sits on the edge of it, her head in her hands.

'I was going to say this later on, anyway,' he says quietly. 'I don't think we should see each other any more.'

'No shit,' she mumbles.

Paul quickly gathers his coat and his phone and leaves the bedroom. As he's going down the stairs, he doesn't notice the scuffed bedroom door on the floor below, standing open. It's only as he's almost past it that he realises. There in the doorway is Rachel Steed, staring at him, eyes burning.

'Hello Rachel,' Paul says, not quite able to meet her gaze.

She doesn't speak.

Just stares at him, her mouth pursed, her eyes narrowed, her hair all ratty and unwashed. She's wearing her Rip Curl hoodie and a pair of faded pink pyjama trousers, and she's holding an empty white bowl with a fork in it.

Paul feels her eyes boring into his back as he races down the second set of stairs, along the hallway, then slams the front door behind him.

Date: Sat, 20 Nov 2004 14:34:12 +0000
From: lauren_cross83@hotmail.com
To: fiveleavesleft@hotmail.com
Subject: Re: Re: Re: Re: Re: Argh
Attachment: HBDI.jpg

Hi there, New Myspace Friend,

How strange. It feels like some sort of secret society. Is that the idea? When I first joined, I agreed to let it do that thing where it checks through all your email contacts, and it turned out loads of people from uni are on there too, all being really pretentious and 'cool' – posing in black and white, taking their photos from funny angles, etc.

Everyone's very serious, aren't they? It seems like the only music and films and books anyone wants to list are ones they hope no one else has heard of. I don't know, it just makes me wonder how much about a person can you really find out from an arbitrary list of things they (pretend to) like?

Maybe I'm being overly harsh, but I think it's all just touched a nerve; it all reminds me a bit too much of Paul, of how he was when we were together. I don't know what he was like with you lot when you lived with him, but he'd always be making me these tapes and CDs in a very serious and joyless way and then about a week after he'd given one to me, he'd quiz me about it. I used to dread it, by the end. It was like getting homework.

I'm getting side-tracked, though. What I was supposed to be saying was: I'm keeping my fingers crossed for you about the record label and the job interview and I think you are very clever and talented. I felt very proud to know you when I read that review and also, also, also: I absolutely **<u>LOVE</u>** your new song, the quiet one of you on your own. I listened to it on headphones on my break in the cafe on Jenn (the manager)'s computer (seems I'm definitely staying on by the way!), and it made me cry a little, it's so pretty. I had to take a couple of deep breaths afterwards. So, um, good work!

I wish I could work out how to put it onto my iPod. All I've got on here are a bunch of songs that Paul loaded on, which I'm completely sick of.

Speaking of which, I don't want the memory of Paul to completely put me off music any more and I know I need to broaden my horizons a bit. I've not heard Elliott Smith before. Which one of his albums should I start with?

I think my favourite band or person is . . . Cat Stevens. Which probably isn't a particularly cool thing to put on your Myspace page. Have you seen the film Harold & Maude? If not, WATCH IT NOW, IT'S BEAUTIFUL.

My other answers are: No, I don't like football, and no, I don't have any brothers or sisters.

Here are some more for you:

Is your sister an older sister or a younger sister?
How did your interview go?
And . . .
If you could only eat one thing for the rest of your life, what would it be?

L xxx

p.s. HAPPY BIRTHDAY FOR TOMORROW!!! Please find attached a photo which Jenn took of me holding a cake from the cafe. I took it home with me and at some point tomorrow I'm going to eat it in your honour.

LAUREN
2014

'How was that?' I asked when I got back.

'Pretty good,' said Peter, but he sounded unconvinced. 'We almost sold a pair of jeans, actually. This lady came in and tried them on in the changing room but then she decided she didn't want them in the end.'

'She wasn't wearing a red baseball cap, was she?' I asked, thinking: please, not Piss Lady.

'She was actually, yeah. How come?'

I went over to the cubicle in the corner, pulled back the curtain and the sharp, sour smell hit me in a wave. Sure enough, there was a pile of soiled clothes – knickers and jeans – tangled on the floor, kicked beneath a chair.

'Did I do something wrong?' Peter asked as I hurried off to the back room for a plastic bag.

Nancy was in there, eating her sandwiches and sipping her Cup a Soup, playing some sort of colourful, Tetris-like jewel game on the computer.

'*Lau*-ren?' she asked. 'Can I—'

'Not now,' I snapped.

I could feel it again: that buzzing, waspy frustration rising up inside me.

I went back through to the changing cubicle with an inside-out carrier bag and picked up the jeans and knickers using the bag as a glove. I felt warmth through the thin plastic and gagged a little.

'Oh,' Peter said, when he saw me come out and the smell finally hit him. 'Oh god, I'm really sorry. I didn't realise. Or I would've . . .'

'It's fine,' I said, hearing myself snap at him, too.

'Are you sure? Cause you look a bit . . .'

'What?' I shouted. 'I look a bit *what*?'

Nancy had come out from the back room and they both watched me as I burst into tears.

'Right,' said Peter, taking charge. 'Right, come with me.' And he guided me, gently, one hand on my shoulder, into the back room where he cleared a space among the piles of donations and dragged up a chair. I'd stopped crying by then, and I felt embarrassed and sheepish as I sat down, letting him rush round, asking Nancy where the kettle and the teabags were, then coming back and asking if I'd like a hot drink.

'Cheers, yeah,' I said. 'One of my teas, please. The herbal ones near the kettle.'

But Peter remained where he was, awkwardly shifting his weight from one foot to the other.

'Is there anything, um, you want to talk about?' he asked shyly.

'Not really,' I said. 'Thanks though.'

The kettle had begun boiling; it rattled and whistled like a tiny, nightmare steam train.

You get paid to work here, don't you? Jamaal's voice echoed in my head.

Just after three, Nancy's husband, Bob, came to collect her. He was like a male version of Nancy – shy, small, childlike, early sixties – and he always wore the same pair of gigantic white trainers and the same light grey, perma-creased trousers. If I understood it correctly, they'd met online, through some kind of dating service for people with special needs, and they seemed really, really happy together. He was the one who made Nancy's sandwiches and filled her thermos with Cup a Soup in the mornings.

'Alright Bob,' I said.

'Afternoon, Lozza,' he said, leaning against the counter while Nancy fetched her coat. 'Busy day?'

'As always.'

According to the journal roll, we'd made a grand

total of £16.47 so far. (According to the last managers' meeting, we should be bringing in at least ten times that.)

'All ready for Christmas?' he said, looking around the undecorated shop and then winking at me.

I smiled and nodded.

'You can go, too, if you like?' I said to Peter once Bob and Nancy had left.

'Think I'll stick around to the end,' he said. 'If that's alright?'

'Thanks,' I said. 'Weird first day, I imagine. Hope it hasn't put you off.'

'Nope,' he smiled.

I could tell that he still felt a bit awkward about before, about me crying. I was embarrassed, too. I wanted to change the subject.

'So, uni next year then?' I said.

'Yep.'

'Where are you going?'

'Nottingham,' he said. 'Nottingham *Trent*.'

'I did English at Nottingham,' I said.

'Really?' he said excitedly. 'Did you like it?'

'What, the course or the whole thing?'

'Whole thing.'

I thought about this for a long time. Did I like it? Did I have a good time? It all seemed so unreal now; it was like remembering scenes from a corny TV drama. Mainly, I just felt embarrassed by how young and spoilt and full of self-pity I was.

'It had its ups and down,' I said. 'I'm sure you'll have a great time though.'

'Right,' he said, nodding solemnly and stretching the cuffs of his hoodie over his fingers just like you used to do.

Date: Sat, 4 Dec 2004 15:08:08 +0000
From: fiveleavesleft@hotmail.com
To: lauren_cross83@hotmail.com
Subject: Re: Re: Re: Re: Re: Re: Argh

hello,

thank you for the cake. it looked like it tasted very nice. you have a tan. you look happy. it's a nice photo.

(full disclosure: i've printed it out and stuck it near my desk. i hope this is okay.)

i had a nice birthday by the way: Alex took me out and got me drunk and when i told him i was giving up smoking the day after my birthday, he said you were a bad influence on me.

anyway, you'll be pleased to know that you are now corresponding with an official HMV Seasonal Temp, which is most of the reason it's taken me so long to reply to your email. that and about a million band practices (we have another gig coming up – this time we're headlining and Alex is convinced some A&R people are coming up from London). Still no word back from Leeds label yet.

HMV is okay so far. the people are nice. i feel like a traitor to Selectadisc though. i keep telling myself it's alright because i'll probably just end up spending most of my wages back in there anyway, so actually it's like some kind of small-scale Robin Hood manoeuvre.

thank you for saying the nice things about my song, too. i'm not good at taking compliments, i never know what to say. but thanks. it means a lot.

my sister is older by five minutes than me (but acts like she's five years older). she's called Carol and she's weird and a bit boring. i don't know. that came out sounding meaner than i meant it to. she's not weird. i think we're just drifting in different directions. she did something to do with accounting at uni and whenever i get into the same old arguments with my parents about 'getting a real job' or whatever, she's always the example they dredge up. i feel guilty now. i should probably ring her up or go and visit.

yeah, myspace is weird isn't it. i don't know, mostly just hoping it will be good for the band. speaking of pretentious: have you seen Paul's profile?? he's in my friends' list if you want to have a look. (be prepared to cringe massively though.)

how are things with you? do you feel weird about spending Christmas away from home? are you still enjoying work? please send me more news and details about Canada even if it's just boring stuff. i like getting emails from you.

oh, yes, almost forgot: yesterday a Canadian man came in and bought the new album by a Canadian band called Stars on import (in case you're interested, the album's called Set Yourself On Fire, I like it a lot – highly recommended) and we got chatting about it and him and Canada and i told him about how i knew someone who was living there, etc. he comes from Toronto but he has been to Vancouver lots. he was very nice. that's it really, that's the story. sorry it's not more exciting. i think i just wanted to tell you that i had met a Canadian person and sold him a Canadian CD.

Elliott Smith albums: maybe start with either XO or Figure 8. or maybe the self-titled one. fuck it, they're all really good.

Ian

p.s. i think i would only eat crisps.

p.p.s. isn't it your birthday sometime soon too or have i remembered that wrong??

p.p.p.s. i've kind of accidentally started smoking again.

p.p.p.p.s. I GOT ALEX TO ORDER HAROLD AND MAUDE INTO THE LIBRARY. THANK YOU SO MUCH. YOU'RE RIGHT. I THINK IT'S THE SADDEST, MOST BEAUTIFUL THING I'VE EVER SEEN.

IAN
2014

The bar in Wetherspoon's is three-deep with noisy, red-faced old men. I leave Dalisay standing at the edge of the crush and push my way towards the front. When I finally get there, I ask the barmaid how much a pint of Coke and a pint of Fosters might cost.

'Four twenty-eight,' she says. 'And it's Pepsi, not Coke.'

'Make it a half of Fosters and a small Pepsi then,' I say.

'The small is only ten p cheaper,' she says.

'Great,' I say. 'One of those then, please.'

We carry our drinks to a booth in the corner near the back and sit down facing each other. Dalisay tries to pay me back for her drink, sliding a pound coin across the table.

'Thanks,' she says, when I refuse. 'Things are so expensive here.'

'In Wetherspoon's?'

'In England.'

I want to ask which country she comes from but I can't quite work out a way to say it without sounding rude.

'How long have you been working at the call centre?' I say instead.

'Almost a year.'

'Wow.'

'How long has your sister been going out with Martin?'

'God, about *nine* years, I think.'

Just then an old man with a blotchy red face stumbles up to our booth and leans in over us, his mouth hanging open, his chin all wet and shiny.

'Are youse two related?' he asks in an almost impenetrable Mancunian accent, pointing a swollen pink finger first at me, then at Dalisay, then back at me again. 'Are youse two brother and sister, yeah?'

Dalisay raises her eyebrows at me, honestly puzzled.

(I am ninety-nine per cent sure he's making some kind of racist comment.)

'Come on, mate,' I say, but my voice gets swallowed by the roar of the bar before it can make its way into his ear.

'Where are you from, love?' he asks, grabbing onto the edge of our table and swaying dangerously backwards and forwards as Dalisay squints up at him, trying her hardest to decipher his accent.

'I beg your pardon?' she says, incredibly politely.

'*Where . . . are . . . you . . . from*?' he barks, so loud it makes an older couple at the next table look over.

'Oh,' Dalisay says, finally twigging. 'I'm from the Philippines.'

'And what made you want to come over here, then?' he says. He's teetering on his heels now and narrowing his eyes, and there's a string of spit dangling from his chin.

'Alright, come on, mate,' I say, a little louder, lifting myself out of my seat.

Oh god.

What am I doing?

I'm not a big guy.

I've never been in a fight before.

'What's it gorra do wiv you, mate?' he slurs, and he moves towards me lifting his fists up limply.

I raise my hands and press my fingers gently against his ribcage, to stop him from coming at me, and even just that mild bit of pressure sends him stumbling backwards, away from our table. He trips over a flap of folded carpet, lurches out towards our table for balance but misses completely and sits down hard on his arse. A few more people look over and someone at the bar cheers.

He starts swearing to himself, shaking his head. As he pulls himself back to his feet and swerves off in the direction of the gents, I see a doorman come running for him.

'Really sorry about that,' I say.

(The Philippines, I think.)

'Wow,' Dalisay says. 'You saved us.'

I know she's only joking, but I still feel kind of proud of myself.

'People here drink a lot,' she says.

Again, I'm not sure if she means in Wetherspoon's or England.

'Yeah, they do.'

I take a sip of my half.

A long pause.

'What's it like,' I ask, 'in the Philippines?'

'You heard about the . . . the typhoon? Last year?'

'Shit, yeah,' I say.

(I think I saw something online.)

A long pause.

I try to think of something else to say, something positive.

'What's it like, apart from that?'

(I really don't know what I'm saying.)

'You know it's a third world country, right?'

I nod.

(I didn't know that.)

'Things cost so much here, by comparison. Back home, for instance, you could buy a whole meal with how much it cost us for just these two drinks.'

'No way.'

'It's pretty screwed.'

'I should move there,' I say, before I've even thought about what I'm saying. 'I'm completely broke.'

'Okay,' Dalisay says quietly.

I know I should just shut up, but for some reason I don't.

'I mean it,' I hear myself say. 'Recently I've just been eating things out of tins. And I had to sell my guitar, and the bloke in the guitar shop ripped me off, I know he did. He only gave me four hundred quid for it. Fuck's sake. I'm sick of having no money.'

I look down at our almost empty glasses.

I've said the wrong thing, haven't I?

Dalisay's gone quiet.

She's not smiling any more.

'Do you have any family over there?' I say.

'All my family are back there except my tita . . . Sorry, my *aunt*. I'm staying with her at the moment and just sending most of the money I make back home to my family. I have two brothers in college.'

'How old are you?'

'I'm thirty-six.'

She looks mid twenties at the most. Her skin is very smooth and there are no wrinkles round her eyes or mouth. She's wearing her pink top again. She's not smiling at me. Something's changed between us. I'm suddenly extremely aware that I've fucked this up and I wish I knew what the right thing to do or say was: the magic combination of words that would make Dalisay Rivera instantly like me again.

'I'd better go,' she says, standing up and pulling on her coat.

'I can walk you out, if you like,' I say, downing my last inch of Fosters.

'It's fine. Really,' she says. 'Thanks for the drink. See you in work.'

Before I can get up, she's gone.

PAUL
2014

On the way to his seminar, Paul sits on the top deck of the 42, fiddling nervously with his phone, refreshing his emails every few seconds. Australia, he thinks. Jonathan Franzen. Doctor's appointment. NaNoWriMo.

Almost at the Precinct Centre, a new email arrives.

It's from Julian:

Why haven't you been replying to my emails?

I could just tell him, Paul thinks. Tell him that I've written nothing at all. That I think I'm going to just give up writing completely, actually.

Meanwhile, the NaNoWriMo people have broken the 41,000-word barrier on their novels.

Or maybe do a Jack Kerouac, Paul tells himself,

dinging the bell. Just clear your head of all this extraneous shit and write it all in one go, over the course of a weekend.

In the silent, airless corridor of the first floor of the New Writing Centre, Paul walks past a framed picture of Martin Amis, past an office room where the admin people sit, past a large stationery cupboard, and pauses outside his seminar room. It's gone five-past. He peers in through the thin rectangular window in the door and they're all in there, everyone except Alison. Rachel Steed sits on her side of the desk, next to Alison's empty place, fiddling with a pale blue iPhone.

Before anyone spots him, Paul dashes on down the corridor, past the staff room, past his office, past Greg's office, and out through the double doors at the far end.

In the toilets, he locks himself in the corner cubicle, drops his trousers, lowers himself onto the ice-cold seat and takes a few deep breaths. As he shits, he slips his phone out of his pocket and starts composing a group email.

Dear all, he types. *Sorry for any confusion re today's class. Due to unexpected circumstances I am no longer able to attend our seminar group. A reminder: everyone who's had their stories critiqued already should now be working on their second drafts. For reference and guidance, perhaps look back over the Lish/Carver example we covered in Wk 4 (photocopies can be found in your course handbook).*

We will critique two stories next week instead.

Sorry again and see you all next week,

Paul

What a mess, he thinks, tearing off a wad of toilet paper with one hand, hitting send with the thumb of his other.

Just then, his phone buzzes and chirps in his hand.

One new Twitter notification, from @jfgkdfjdlsjf at 1:11 p.m.:

i can see what youre doing

Paul hears a shuffling sound above him, looks up, and from a circular hole in the ceiling directly above his cubicle, a bloodshot eye winks down at him.

'Fuck!' Paul cries, dropping his phone on the tiles as he stands and gathers his trousers, fumbling his way out of the cubicle. He buckles his belt, retrieves his phone – the glass has shattered, the cracks flowering up the touchscreen like tiny petals from the bottom left corner – and looks up at the ceiling, which is now just a normal square of ceiling again.

Date: Sat, 18 Dec 2004 01:34:12 +0000
From: lauren_cross83@hotmail.com
To: fiveleavesleft@hotmail.com
Subject: Re: Re: Re: Re: Re: Re: Re: Argh

Ian,

Sorry i've taken a while to get back to you too. A girl at the cafe left and I've gone up to almost-full-time which, weirdly, I'm enjoying more than I thought I would. (If I'm honest, I've still been feeling a bit wobbly occasionally, just panicking, generally, about almost everything – What am I going to do when I get home? What am I going to do with my life in general? Etc. Etc. – and working a lot is taking my mind off it.)

In answer to your question: yep, my birthday was a few days ago (the 15th) but I purposefully didn't tell anyone (including you). For some reason I've never really had that great a time on my birthday, it always makes me feel a bit superstitious and precarious and so I decided this year not to tell anyone until it was over. (Every year I tell my mum not to get me anything, but every year she does anyway.)

Thank you for the recommendations by the way. I found a 'hip' record shop and went in and bought XO and that Stars album as a birthday treat. I love them both. New music! Hooray!

I'm going to have to keep this short as I'm really, really tired, but I just wanted to say a massive thank you for how much you've been here for me recently even though, you know, you're on the other side of the world, and to let you know how much it's meant and kind of kept me sane.

It's especially nice and comforting for me sometimes just to think that you are a person, moving around, somewhere in the world, doing whatever it is you're doing.

I hope you're feeling happy and that things work out for you with the band soon. I really think they will. You're very talented.

Your friend,

L

LAUREN
2014

'Sorry, *how* much is this?' a girl asked, holding up a small, pale blue typewriter, her top lip curled. The way she was dressed, she looked like she probably ran her own style blog, and each day she'd take a new photo of herself and upload it with a name for the style she'd created: Nautical Biker Gypsy from the Future or whatever. Today her look seemed to be Ungrateful Typewriter Wanker.

'Twenty pounds,' I said, pointing out the stuck-on, handwritten price label.

'Oh, right, so is that the actual price then?'

I nodded, and she huffed and put the typewriter back on the shelf. As I carried on hanging out an armful of shirts and blouses, I watched from the corner of my eye as she took out her phone and typed something into it.

'They've got them on eBay for a tenner,' she called across the shop a moment later, approaching me with her held-out iPhone. 'And that includes postage.'

'Right,' I said. 'Well, that one's twenty, I'm afraid.'

'Think I'll leave it then.'

She left the shop and I finished hanging out the blouses and walked back to the counter.

'Your phone made a noise,' Peter said, nodding at my phone, which I'd left, face down, by the till.

I turned it over. It was a text from Dad: *Happy Birthday sweetheart. Let me know if there's anything you'd like this year x*, which was, I suspected, almost word for word the message I got last year. I wondered what the time was, wherever he was in the world currently, and whether he'd just woken up when he sent it, or whether he'd been awake for hours already and only just remembered, and whether there really *was* 'anything I'd like' from him.

I put my phone back by the till, face down.

'Are you on the internet?' Peter said, out of nowhere.

'What, like Twitter and Facebook and things?'

'Yeah.'

'Me personally or the shop?'

'The shop.'

It was a thing that Jenny, the area manager, had been hammering recently at all our regional meetings: about making sure we used social networks to promote our branches as much as possible. But I'd just never quite got round to it.

'Not really,' I said.

'Do you ever put things on eBay?'

'No. We use it sometimes to price things, but I don't know. I'm not much of an internet person.'

'I could do it, if you like? You know, set it up and things?'

'Really? You wouldn't mind?'

'I'd like to help,' he said, smiling.

'That'd be great,' I said, feeling a hot sharpness at the corner of my eyes. His kindness had caught me off guard. Why wasn't he more self-absorbed? Why wasn't he busy taking selfies or downing goldfish or whatever it was the kids were doing these days?

'How about you?' he said. 'Are you on Facebook?'

'No.'

'Twitter?'

'Nope.'

'Instagram?'

I laughed.

'Why not?'

I thought about it. It wasn't anything I'd ever had to explain to anyone before, but I knew it had to do with my mum. With how – even at the toughest, most horrible moments – she'd been so quiet and dignified about everything. She hadn't complained, *at all*, while all that was going on inside her. And yet every time I used the internet, there seemed to be this chorus of voices, this sort of deafening waterfall of misery, everyone complaining about *everything*, all the time: about the weather being a bit shit, or their coffee not being quite what they'd ordered, or their job being ever so slightly annoying, or not having enough money to buy new earrings, or whatever, and it seemed like that was just what you *did* now, you complained about everything, and that that was what social networks were for, and I'd decided I didn't want to take part.

And then I thought about how worthy and over the top all that sounded, itself like some sort of *complaint*, and I gave up on explaining it, before I'd even tried to formulate it into a sentence.

'I don't know,' I said instead.

Date: Mon, 3 Jan 2005 01:34:12 +0000
From: fiveleavesleft@hotmail.com
To: lauren_cross83@hotmail.com
Subject: Re: Re: Re: Re: Re: Re: Re: Re: Argh

merry christmas (AND HAPPY BIRTHDAY!!! did you get my silly e-card thing?) to you too. hope you had a nice Christmas day.

mine was kind of awful: got in a big argument with my dad about how i should be putting my energies into something 'more realistic' than music (i.e. accountancy like Carol). also, Martin, her boyfriend, was there again, and he tried joining in and i had to go and pace around the garden for a bit to stop myself from shouting at him.

i like thinking about you out there, moving around in the world, too. i kind of wish you lived a bit nearer though. we should definitely hang out when you get back, if you want . . .

the gig went well i think, but no industry people turned up in the end. and still no news about the single yet. feels like band things are drifting slightly. if i'm 100% honest, i'm panicking and your email has helped, so thank you.

Andrew (nice Canadian man who has come in a few times now) said i should tell you to check out a bar called The Railway Club (if you haven't been already?). apparently there's this little toy train that runs round the ceiling.

i wish i had more good news. i don't know. guess i feel a bit flat today. i wish we were hanging out somewhere.

IAN
2014

On Thursday afternoon, about half an hour before home time, Martin tells us to finish off whatever call we're on, then come through to the break room. We've hit the basic target a day early, and, true to his word, he's sent out for pizzas.

'One slice each, yeah.'

I log out of the dialler and take off my headset and shut down my computer. Then I stand and stretch, trying to make the deep ache in my spine go away. Dalisay's head pops up from behind the partition wall.

'Hey,' she says, taking off her headset, shaking out her hair.

'Pizza,' I say.

'Pizza,' she says.

'Sorry about the other night. If it sounded like I was just complaining.'

'Don't worry about it,' she says, gathering her bits and pieces.

To my right, Dean's finishing up the end of his call. He removes his headset, rubs his face and groans loudly into his palms.

'Are you having pizza?' he asks.

'I guess so,' I say.

I want to follow Dalisay, but Dean grabs my elbow.

'Here you go, lad,' he whispers, slipping a small shiny object from his rucksack and fumbling it into my hand. 'This might help wash it down.'

It's a hip flask.

'Cheers, Dean,' I say, unscrewing the lid. I take a swig, much bigger than I'd planned. I was expecting whisky, but it's vodka. It makes me shudder. I pass it back and Dean glances around the room, then takes a big swig, too, his Adam's apple bobbing up and down in his thin grey throat.

'Ah,' he says, smacking his lips.

Down the corridor, Martin's laid out three large margaritas on the break room tables and he's getting everyone to walk past him, one by one, with paper plates.

'One slice only,' he shouts across the chatter.

Dean and I join the back of the queue. I swear I can feel the vodka working inside me already. My cheeks are tingling and my ears are buzzing. Dalisay's only a few people ahead of us in the queue. She's talking to Tall Boy again. He's moving his hands around and leaning into her and she's gazing up at him and moving the hair from her ear and smiling.

'Want a bit more?' Dean whispers, nudging me in the ribs.

I look around. We're right at the back. Everyone's focusing on the pizza.

'Cheers, yeah,' I say, ducking my head a little as I take another, even bigger swig from the flask. I pass it back to Dean and he does the same. By the time we reach the front of the queue, we've emptied it.

'One slice each, yeah,' Martin says to us.

'Cheers, Martin,' I say.

Then everyone stands around in twos or threes, nibbling their pizza, not really saying very much. Some people are doing things on their phones. Dalisay is *still* talking and laughing with Tall Boy. Meanwhile Dean is leaning into me, going on about how rubbish the internet is. Something has shifted inside him now. He's become sweary and narrow-eyed. I feel worried. I look around the room for a way out.

'All this fucking Facetube business,' he hisses. 'What's it all *for*?'

'I don't really go online that much, to be honest,' I say.

'I mean, look at that muppet over there,' he continues, nodding towards Danny, who's leaning against the wall, tapping at his phone. 'Fuckin' bragging in here the other day, he was, about how he'd got *over a thousand* friends online, right? *Right?* And then he just stands over there on his own, stroking his electronic penis. I mean, how does that even work?'

'I really don't know what to say,' I say.

'Fuckin' idiots, the lot of you.'

'Are you drunk?' Carol asks when I get in.

I'm trying to stand normally but my knees keep buckling. She's over by the oven, stirring a big pan of pasta sauce.

'Can I have some of your dinner?' I say.

'You are,' she says. 'You're rat-arsed.'

'It's Friday night.'

'It's *Thursday evening*.'

'I'm going to my room.'

I close my door and sit on the end of my bed and pick *Ways of Happiness* up off the floor. I throw it hard at the wall. Then I go and get my laptop down from the top of the wardrobe and sit with it on the edge of the bed. Once it's booted up, I click the wifi pop-up and, before I can change my mind, I quickly select Rosemary's Wireless.

Back online, the first thing I do is log into Facebook. The little red dots at the top of the screen tell me I have forty-six unread messages and six hundred and twenty-three other notifications.

I type 'Dalisay Rivera' into the search bar and hit return.

Four different Dalisay Riveras appear on my screen.

The one I'm searching for is right at the top of the list. I click on her thumbnail and it leads me to her profile page, which is almost blank unless we become friends.

I move my cursor over '+1 Add Friend' and click.

Chapter One

After university, Pete Simpson took a job serving drinks at a music venue in the city centre. The shifts were long and miserable and most nights he would find himself stumbling home at three or four in the morning, his clothes stinking sweetly of spirits and mixer, and his legs wobbling like jelly from standing up for twelve hours or more, often with only a fifteen minute break (during which he would perch on a step outside and stuff as many curly fries into his mouth as was humanly possible).

This was not the job Pete had hoped for when he graduated – he'd pictured himself, sitting at spacious desk, writing copy for adverts, perhaps – but then nothing seemed to be turning out quite the way Pete had imagined. He was living with his first real girlfriend, Laura, in a two-bedroomed terrace that they had begun renting over the summer.

But things had seemed to sour in their relationship over the last year or so. The move had been an attempt to try to live like adults and really start a life together, ~~but~~ neither of them were ~~even slightly~~ happy.

~~Their relationship was like a sinking ship.~~

~~And~~ as Pete Sanderson stumbled along the streets of Sherwood, he knew deep down that he was going to have to finish things ~~with Laura~~. *This will break her heart, he thought, ~~sadly~~. But it's for the best. Neither of us is happy, ~~but~~ I'm the only one who's able to see it. I must let her down gently, ~~too,~~ for she is as fragile as an ornamental teapot that used to belong to her Grandma.*

~~That night,~~ as he arrived home, he found her in the bedroom, still awake, scribbling ~~once again~~ in the hard-bound notebook she carried almost everywhere with her.

Deep in Pete's bones he knew it was time to deliver this death-blow to their relationship, before it was too late, before they both grew into one of those bitter and loveless couples that you see so often, who are only staying together out of the terror of being alone.

'What's the matter?' ~~Lauren~~ asked ~~innocently,~~ looking up from her notebook.

Poor thing, Pete thought.

She really doesn't know what's coming, does she?

'We need to talk,' he said.

PAUL
2014

Oh dear, Paul thinks as he puts his pen down and swigs his last half inch of Kronenbourg. He's sitting at one of the back tables in the Wetherspoon's opposite Whitworth Park.

He'd printed off his 'novel' – all forty-seven pages – and bought a brand new red Uniball gel ink pen for two pounds sixty-five from the student shop, but there's no way to make this any good, he realises, just halfway through the first chapter, no matter *what* he scribbles all over his manuscript.

He stands and buttons his coat.

Then he opens his laptop case, puts the pages of his novel inside, zips it up, and walks out through the pub, past a few florid old men drinking pints of real ale, past a wild-haired mad woman whispering into the ear of a plastic baby, and back onto Oxford Road, where it's already gone dark. Great. Another day wasted.

Lately, Paul's been having these fantasies about stealing a car and driving it off a bridge. In the fantasies he's always pursued by a cop, played by Michael Douglas, and the whole thing takes place in America and, right at the end, Paul screams, 'See you later, fuck-face!' and then floors the accelerator and his car swerves off a bridge and crashes into the sea.

On his way to the bus stop, he wonders how long he's got left.

How many days or weeks or months.

On the NaNoWriMo forum, people are writing their final chapters.

They're excited.

They're beginning to talk about redrafting and agent letters and Christmas.

Just then Paul hears footsteps echoing off the wet brickwork of the Manchester Museum archway and immediately convinces himself it's a mugger, coming for him. Paul is always imagining things like this. For instance: each night, last thing before bed, he'll need to go and double-check the front door to the flat is locked, otherwise he'll lie there waiting for masked men to burst in and hold Sarah and him hostage, forcing them to do lewd sexual acts, just for the fun of it.

As a precautionary measure, Paul takes out his phone and pretends to receive a phone call, hearing the footsteps – they are definitely real footsteps – quicken behind him. He feels his heart quicken, too.

'Hello,' Paul murmurs into his cracked, silent phone.

He's not very good at acting.

He doesn't know what to say next.

He pretends it's the doctor's surgery on the other end of the line, calling him back after a scan.

'What a relief,' he says. 'That's great news. Thanks so much for letting me know.'

But maybe talking on your iPhone isn't the best way to scare off a mugger.

It seems, suddenly, like the worst thing you could do.

'Right, bye,' Paul says, picking up his pace, hearing the footsteps behind him getting louder and quicker, too.

Fuck, he thinks, unable to just turn round and look.

Fuck fuck fuck fuck fuck.

He jams his tongue against the lump.

The lump is his talisman.

It's supposed to stop other bad things from happening to him.

So why isn't it helping now?

'Scuse me, mate?' a hoarse voice behind him says. 'Scuse me?'

Paul stops and turns round.

Why am I stopping? he thinks, tonguing the lump. Why am I turning round?

The man is wearing a dark blue coat with the hood pulled up, his face in shadow. 'Let's have a quick look at that phone, mate,' he rasps.

This can't be happening.

'Sorry,' Paul says, rooted to the spot.

'Give us your fucking phone, mate, yeah?'

'It's got a crack on it,' Paul says as he obediently hands the man his phone.

'What's in there?' the man says, nodding at the laptop bag in Paul's left hand.

'Oh, it's just . . .' Paul says. 'It's just a really old, shit laptop.'

It's a top-of-the-range MacBook Pro.

It still has over a year left on its extended warranty.

'Well, fucking give it us or I'll stab you up, yeah?'

Paul knows right then – for certain – that they are the only two human beings on this dark, whistling stretch of Oxford Road. The man isn't tall or particularly well built. He's about the same size as Paul. He has narrow eyes and a scab on the left side of his mouth. He isn't holding a knife. He's just holding Paul's phone.

'I . . .' Paul says.

'Fucking *give it us*,' the man hisses, shifting his weight from one foot to the other, his eyes darting up and down the empty street then back to Paul. 'Give it us or I'll stab you up, you fucking bellend.'

So Paul hands the man his laptop, too, his beautiful, shiny MacBook Pro 13" with retina display and additional RAM.

The man turns and runs away with it.

Paul breathes out, dizzied from a sudden rush of adrenaline.

He might be sick.

He staggers across the pavement and rests himself against the cold, damp wall of the Manchester Museum, feeling pinpricks of rain on his neck and cheeks and forehead.

My novel, Paul thinks, as a strange, manic delight begins to bubble in his stomach.

My novel!

Immediately, he begins drafting a new email in his head:

Dear Julian, I'm sorry but my laptop's been stolen. It had absolutely everything on it. I'm so stupid. I'm such a fucking idiot. I should have backed things up externally. I know. But I didn't. And the one hard copy I had was in the bag too. Can you believe it? Which ultimately means, Julian, that my novel – which I'm afraid to say was actually becoming kind of amazing – I hate to tell you is now lost, completely, forever.

Date: Wed, 12 Jan 2005 01:34:12 +0000
From: lauren_cross83@hotmail.com
To: fiveleavesleft@hotmail.com
Subject: Re: Sorry

Sorry, again again again, for my late reply.

I've mostly just been super busy at the cafe. Also, a weird thing happened which I feel strangely nervous about telling you for some stupid reason.

I'm being silly. I'll just say it.

Okay, well, *first* of all I went to that bar your friend suggested, The Railway Club, with Emily and Jenn from work last week and we all got really smashed, but in a fun, silly way. It was probably one of my best nights out here so far actually. And afterwards, Jenn took us to this nightclub with Japanese-style karaoke booths at the back and Jenn sang Britney Spears and I sang Cat Stevens and Simon & Garfunkel songs and Emily sang New York, New York three times in a row.

And anyway, so that's that, and I'm at work a few days later and then something happens that's just so ridiculous I still kind of can't quite believe it . . . are you ready for this?

I GOT AN I SAW U OF MY OWN.

What are the chances, right?!

Here it is in all its ridiculous glory:

BRITS ABROAD
Railway Club, Saturday night. You were out with your friends and I was the 'boring' British bloke at the bar who recognised your accent and made you laugh about what might be happening on EastEnders. You said I looked Scottish (whatever that means). As you were leaving you told me where you worked but like an idiot I've forgotten. Please get in touch. I'd love to make you laugh again.

So . . . yeah. That's Part One of the story.

Let's have a quick interlude now, where I go and make myself a cup of Emily's weird herbal tea and gather my thoughts . . .

Okay, I'm back. So here's Part Two:

Well, I went on a date with him (Emily and Jenn both badgered me, relentlessly, I had no real choice) and I *really* thought it was going to be awful, so we arranged for him to just pop in and have a coffee on my lunchbreak, but guess what: it was actually okay.

He's nice.

He's called Michael, and he's a little bit older (31) and there's just something extremely calm and quiet and reassuring about him. This sounds so stupid but as I was talking to him I felt the frantic, chattering thing inside me – which if I'm honest has been going pretty much non-stop since god-knows-when – actually fall silent for a while.

I felt like a better version of myself. If that makes any kind of sense?

So I've decided that I think I'm going to meet him again.

I don't know, it might be nothing, it probably *is* nothing, but he's really nice and I like him and I'm just surprised at how easy it was to talk to him.

Please, please, please say you're happy for me, Ian. I need you to be a friend about this.

L

x

LAUREN
2014

On the bus home I got a text from Carl, the guy I'd cancelled on: *How about tonight instead?* The bus stopped and more passengers got on. A woman asked if I was reading the paper on the seat next to me. I shook my head and she picked it up and sat down and opened it and started leafing through, her elbow digging softly in my ribs.

Dog of the Day!
162 die in factory blaze in Bangladesh!
Girl, 13, dies of ruptured stomach!

I could hear Ginny meowing behind the front door, before I'd even got it open. She wound around my legs, almost tripping me up as I went through to the kitchen and opened the cupboard and found there were no packets of food left, just a box of those dry things she always turned her nose up at. So I took the rest of the lasagne out of the fridge, spooned some into her dish and then slid the rest onto a microwavable plate.

'There you go, Garfield,' I said, putting her portion down on the floor.

She sniffed it, looked at me confused, sniffed it again, then began to lick the top of it.

I set ten minutes on the microwave, then went through to the living room and sat down on the sofa, turned on the TV, flicked through the channels, and fiddled with my phone.

I typed 'Somalia' into Wikipedia.

Somalia, I read, *(Somali: Soomaaliya; Arabic: الصومال aṣ-Ṣūmāl /soˈmaːliə/ so-**mah-lee-ə**), officially the* ***Federal Republic of Somalia***[1] *(Somali: Jamhuuriyadda Federaalka Soomaaliya, Arabic: جمهورية الصومال الفدرالية Jumhūriyyat aṣ-Ṣūmāl al-Fiderāliyya), is a country located in the Horn of Afr . . .*

I let my eyes stray a little down the screen.

. . . has a population of around 10 million. About 85% of residents are ethnic Somalis,[3] *who have historically inhabited the northern part of the country. Ethnic minorities make up the remainder and are largely concentrated in the . . .*

I skipped on further.

. . . succession of treaties with these kingdoms, the British and Italians gained control of parts of the coast

and established the colonies of British Somaliland and Italian Somaliland.[17][18] *In the interior, Muhammad Abdullah Hassan's Dervish State successfully repelled the British Empire four times and forced it to retreat to the coastal region,*[19] *The Dervishes were finally defeated in 1920 by British airpower.*[20] *Italy acquired full control of the northeastern and southern parts of the area after successfully waging the so-called Campaign of the Sultanates against the ruling Majeerteen Sultanate and Sultanate of Hobyo.*[18] *Italian occupation lasted until 1941, yielding to British military administration. Northern Somalia would remain a protectorate, while southern Somalia became a United Nations Trusteeship in 1949. In 1960, the two regions united to form the independent Somali Republic under a civilian government.*[21] *Mohamed Siad Barre seized power in 1969 and established the Somali Democratic Republic. In 1991, Barre's government collapsed as the Somali Civil War broke out . . .*

What's wrong with me? I thought.

It felt worse, somehow, to read the article without really processing it correctly than to not read it at all, so I closed it and put my phone as far away from me as I could without standing, right on the other arm of the sofa, face down.

I closed my eyes and focused on the movement of breath in and out of my lungs and the sofa beneath me and my hands in my lap and my whirring brain and my slightly full bladder and a pin-prick itch on my left shoulderblade and the aching arches of my feet and something that felt like a spot about to happen on my chin if I chewed my lip a certain way.

I opened my eyes, picked up my phone, and replied to Carl's text.

Date: Wed, 12 Jan 2005 01:34:12 +0000
From: lauren_cross83@hotmail.com
To: fiveleavesleft@hotmail.com
Subject: ?

Please reply.

IAN
2014

'Be good,' Carol says on Friday morning, squeezing me tight. 'Don't do anything I wouldn't do.' We're standing in the car park. It's so early it's still dark.

'Can I use your car while you're gone?' I say.

This is a joke.

I've never learned to drive.

'Don't you dare,' she says, smiling.

I wheel her suitcase over to Martin's Audi and he pops the boot from inside and I lift it in.

'I've left your present in the kitchen,' she says.

'I'll give you yours when you get back,' I say. 'It's still, um, on order.'

'Please don't accidentally burn everything down while I'm away.'

We hug again, and then she gets into the car and I turn and walk back towards the front door. Behind me I hear the squeal of Martin's tyres as he races out of the drive.

There's a parcel and a card on the table by the kitchen window.

I open the card first. *Ian, Happy Birthday!* it reads. She's taped a tenner inside, with a big curly arrow pointing at it and the message, *Have a drink on me!*

I unpeel it and put it in my pocket.

The present is a long, green Marks & Spencer's scarf.

I've never once in my life mentioned anything to Carol about needing a scarf and I look at it for a long time, wondering what could possibly have made her choose it, what exactly it was about a long green Marks & Spencer's scarf that she thought I might like.

I try my very hardest to like it.

But at the same time, I can't help but take it as an indicator of how little we really know each other any more.

On the bus into work I look around at all the other passengers on the lower deck and think: I am now a thirty-one-year-old man sat here on this bus. I smoked a roll-up at the bus stop, before I remembered I was supposed to be quitting. The tobacco was there in my coat pocket and I was still on autopilot. It's okay, I tell myself. Today is a write-off. But you will definitely quit tomorrow. I catch a quick glimpse of my face reflected in the window of the bus and wonder if it looks however a thirty-one-year-old man's face is supposed to look.

I fiddle with the end of my green scarf and look out of the window and hope that Carol is having a nice weekend away with Martin.

Just before my stop, my phone beeps.

I open the message, hoping it might somehow be from Dalisay even though she doesn't have my number.

It's from Mum:

Happy birthday love hop you ar having a lovely day love nun, it says.

While Martin's away, Dean stands in as manager. He's wearing an old grey suit instead of his usual jeans and jumper, and he stoops in the doorway and claps his hands in a pale imitation of Martin and tells us all to get cracking and that he'll be back in a bit to check up on us.

Dalisay's terminal remains empty. I keep my eye fixed on the doorway all morning, willing her to walk through it, before finally remembering that she said she was helping her aunt.

There's a tangible lack of enthusiasm in the room.

It's still somehow a week till payday.

We're all at our lowest ebb.

I log into Facebook but she's still not accepted my friend request.

I click in the search bar, type 'Lauren Cross,' and hit return, knowing there'll be nothing there, there never is, but checking anyway.

I scroll through the results and, as usual, none of them are her.

The dialler chirps.

The phone rings in my ear.

I don't know how much more of this I can take.

PAUL
2014

Paul sits in the doctor's waiting room, attempting to read a list of the *Fifteen Guaranteed Ways to Give Your Girl a Screaming Orgasm* but he can't really concentrate. He keeps reading number six ('The Bowling Ball Technique') over and over, his stomach churning and fluttering.

'Mr Saunders?' the receptionist says eventually.

'That's me,' Paul says, raising a trembling hand.

'Doctor O'Brien will see you now. Room three.'

Paul stands. He puts *GQ* back on the coffee table. He leaves the waiting room.

This is it, he thinks, as he walks along the corridor. This is the moment my life changes forever. It will just be doctors and hospitals from this moment onwards.

Everything will smell of disinfectant. I will never go to Australia or give my girl a screaming orgasm or publish another novel ever again.

He pushes open the door to room three and the doctor, a doughy, grey-haired man in his late forties, smiles at him warmly.

'Paul,' he says, like they've met before. 'What can we do for you, then?'

Paul lowers himself shakily into the chair.

He's not eaten anything except a Mars bar in the last forty-eight hours.

'It's . . . It's . . . Well, I've got this . . . lump . . . on my gum.'

'Right, okay,' Doctor O'Brien says, nodding, like a lump on the gum is a perfectly normal thing for a thirty-one-year-old male to have. 'And how long have we had this lump, do you think?'

'Maybe two months?' Paul says. 'I'm not too sure.'

'Right, let's have a look then,' Doctor O'Brien says.

He stands up and comes out from behind his desk. He puts on an eyepiece and a pair of rubber gloves and picks up a little mirror on a stick. 'Can you show me which gum it's on, please?' he says. 'Just tip your head back a little further for me, would you?'

So Paul tilts his head and closes his eyes and opens his mouth and points at his inside-right lower gum with a trembly finger.

'Oh, *yeeesss*,' Doctor O'Brien says quietly, to himself.

Yes? Paul thinks.

Paul feels the doctor's finger go inside his mouth and

press hard on the lump, then prod at the skin surrounding it. He opens his mouth as far as it'll go to accommodate all the doctor's fingers and that little mirror on the stick, which clicks, occasionally, against Paul's back teeth.

'Right,' the doctor says. 'You can put your head back up now.'

Paul opens his eyes and lifts his head. Doctor O'Brien is pulling off his gloves and dropping them into a bin. Paul scans his face, trying to work out the verdict.

Doctor O'Brien sits back down.

'Do you chew gum?' he asks.

'Sometimes,' Paul says. 'I mean yeah, I used to chew it quite a lot, yeah.'

'I thought so,' Doctor O'Brien says. 'What you have there Paul is a buccal exostosis. In other words a bony outgrowth on the gum. These are most usually caused by excessive chewing, or sometimes from stressful situations, if you grind your teeth in your mouth, perhaps. Essentially it's your mouth's reaction to a sudden increase in stress on the teeth and gums. You've actually got a second one coming, too, on the other side, but it's not quite as developed.'

Paul shifts his tongue over to the other gum and prods it gingerly and sure enough, there's another, smaller lump there, too.

'Oh,' Paul says. 'So it's not . . . um . . . it's not . . . you know? Bad?'

'Not at this stage, no. If they *keep growing* then yes, maybe you'll need some minor surgery, but we're talking about if it suddenly starts making eating a problem for you. Have they been growing very rapidly, would you say?'

'No, I don't think so . . .'

Paul's hardly listening now. He's too busy feeling the ice-cold waves of relief flood through him.

You have been given another chance, a benevolent, godlike voice says inside him. *Do not fuck any more things up. Untangle yourself like a big black ball of tights. Start again, from this point here.*

'There is something else actually,' Paul says. 'I'd like to give up smoking.'

Date: Sun, 30 Jan 2005 01:34:12 +0000
From: lauren_cross83@hotmail.com
To: fiveleavesleft@hotmail.com
Subject: Worried

Ian,

I'm worried i've upset you.

I keep telling myself that you're just busy, working a lot, or maybe things have happened with the single, or maybe Avril has finally got in touch, but whatever I decide to tell myself, none of it's really doing the job of shifting this ball of worry that I've been carrying around in my stomach ever since I sent you that last email.

We are still friends, aren't we? I want to hear back from you. I want you to email and tell me everything's fine between us, that you've been doing [something or other] and I'm just being a nob, and you were about to email me anyway, because it would really upset me if things *weren't* okay.

I *know* I/we said that thing early on about fancying each other (and then never really mentioned it again). I've not forgotten it. And I keep thinking about that and then worrying that the stuff with Michael has upset you. Please tell me I'm overreacting. Tell me to get over myself. Anything.

Also, I suppose I should tell you the full truth here, even though I'm so scared it will screw things up even further between us: I've started seeing Michael properly. It just feels like the right thing to do. I hope you can understand that.

Oh god, this all feels like such a mess now between us, and I'm so scared I'm just digging myself a deeper hole. I just want you to know that, no matter what, I think you are absolutely fantastic and I will always be here for you and you have been so sweet and kind and helped me so much and I'll always remember that.

But even more importantly: please get in touch and tell me that I'm just being stupid and that nothing's changed between us and that we're still friends like before.

love,

L xxx

LAUREN
2014

'I've taken the liberty of getting you a drink,' Carl said, easing himself awkwardly out of his seat in order to lean across the pub table and kiss me. He smelled of the kind of aftershave my dad sometimes wore, and he was wearing a shiny burgundy shirt, tucked into a pair of dark blue jeans, and his hands touched my waist a little too familiarly as he pecked my cheek. His profile had said thirty-four, but he looked much closer to forty-four. 'I hope that's okay?' he said, nodding down at the wine glass.

I looked at it, standing there opposite his pint of lager.

Was it okay?

Was this what people did on blind dates?

'Thanks,' I said, feeling a cold, prickling embarrassment sweep across my skin.

I sat down and Carl slid himself back behind his side of the table, then leaned across it as if it was a job interview. It was quiet in the pub – why the fuck had we chosen my local? – just a few people perched on stools at the other side of the room, and I was thankful for that at least.

An hour, I told myself. You need to stay here for at least an hour.

'This is a nice place,' Carl said, looking around. 'I've not been here before.'

'Right,' I said, feeling a gloomy hourglass up-end itself inside me.

What was I doing?

Wasn't this my birthday?

Why was I spending it here with Carl?

'I've just come back, you see,' he continued, 'from South America.'

He sat back and took a big, proud swig of his pint. His skin was smooth and tanned and slightly oily, and his eyes wouldn't quite meet mine. Instead they flitted from his drink to the jukebox to a woman who was laughing loudly, over by the bar.

Maybe I'm just as much of a disappointment, I thought.

'Have you ever been travelling?' Carl said.

And just then, as if on cue, 'Californication' came on the jukebox.

I thought about my year in Canada: about Emily and Michael and you.

'Not really,' I said, trying to smile, feeling the bones creaking in my face, the grey sand collecting in a heap on the floor of my stomach.

Only fifty-nine more minutes to go . . .

Date: Fri, 8 Apr 2005 01:34:12 +0000
From: lauren_cross83@hotmail.com
To: fiveleavesleft@hotmail.com, jude_is_drunk@hotmail.com, ottomail@yahoo.co.uk, simon_johnson256@hotmail.com, stonersmoker84@hotmail.com, fizzypixiepeach@yahoo.com, sanguine_sarah_s@hotmail.com, craigyboy_mc@hotmail.com
Subject: I'm (almost) Back

Hi everyone,

Just to let you all know, I'm going to be coming back early from Canada and if anyone wants to meet up that would be really good. It feels so long since I've seen you all and so much has happened and I'd really like to see you guys. I'll be staying at my mum's for a week or two, then the plan is LONDON.

I know how dull group emails can be, so I'll spare you all and keep this one brief.

I've got a new phone now – the number's 07896 187879 – and like I said, would be great to see you.

love,

Lauren

IAN
2014

I'm woken by the front door slamming, then someone stomping down the hall. The light goes on in the living room. I look up at Carol from my place on the sofa and try to remember what I was doing. The last thing I remember clearly is going to Morrisons and blowing my birthday tenner on an oven pizza and a bottle of White Label rum.

'What time is it?' I ask.

Carol doesn't answer, just walks over to the sofa, then flops down on it next to me. I look at my laptop. The browser's still open on Dalisay's Facebook wall. I remember what happened now: Dalisay accepted my friend request and it turns out she has a boyfriend. A man with thick muscly arms and spiky black hair called Marcos.

'What's the matter?' I say.

'Can I have some of that rum?' Carol says.

Before I can answer, she picks up the bottle and pours a big slug into a mug that still has an inch of cold tea in the bottom, then knocks the rum/tea mixture back in one.

'You alright?' I say, knowing what a stupid question this is.

Her eyes are red and puffy.

'I broke up with Martin,' she says.

'Fuck,' I say.

'This morning. We've spent the whole rest of the day talking about it and then he drove me home just now.'

The display on the DVD player says it's just gone five in the morning.

Carol has the voice of someone who's about to start crying at any moment. I'm already pre-empting it, moving my hand to stroke her back, just as she begins to curl forward and put her face in her hands. And then she's sobbing loudly into her palms as I stroke the bony knobbles of her spine, feeling each sob juddering up through her skin and muscle and bone.

'Shhh, shhh,' I whisper, pretending to be Mum, or Dad, or someone.

A little later, I go out to the kitchen and make us instant coffees. I pour rum in them, too, and we sit on the sofa, our feet resting against the coffee table, and I let her talk more about what happened. I don't really say anything though because there's nothing much to say except, 'I'm sorry.'

She tells me how in the morning she opened Martin's present – a shiny purple Agent Provocateur bra and knicker set that she just didn't like – and looked at it and realised that Martin didn't really know anything at all about her and never truly would and that the only reason she was even with him, if she was completely honest with herself, was out of an overwhelming terror of being left on her own.

'I'm sorry,' I say, once she's finished.

'I'm thirty-one years old,' she says.

Me, too, I think.

'What the fuck am I doing with my life?' she says.

I don't know, I think.

'You'll be fine,' I say, and pour us out the rest of the rum.

I get off the bus and walk the short walk to work. It's a dull, grey, spidery Monday morning and I'm hungover and wishing I'd not chosen today to finally, finally, *actually* give up smoking. As I go in through the front door and up the main stairs, I grit my teeth and stick my hands deep in my trouser pockets.

I wonder if Martin will say anything.

My plan is just to keep my head down and hit my target number of surveys and in between calls I'm going to start searching for another job.

I sit down. Turn on my computer. Plug in my headset. Log into the automatic dialler. Slowly the room fills up. Just before nine, Dalisay comes in. I pretend to be reading an article about global warming that someone shared on Facebook and wait for her to say hi, but she doesn't. She just walks past me and takes her seat behind the partition.

At nine, Martin appears in the doorway. He's dressed as smartly as usual but there's a small razor nick on his cheek, and his eyes seem smaller and darker, and just for a moment I actually feel sorry for him.

He doesn't know what he's doing, either, I think.

'Alright, everyone,' he says in a slightly quieter voice than normal, clapping his hands limply. 'Let's get started, yeah?'

He catches my eye and I wince on his behalf as he turns and heads off down the corridor.

I complete the happiness survey with two old women and one old man, and no one seems particularly happy today.

The highest score anyone gives me is an overall five out of ten.

I never normally pay that much attention to the caller information on the dialler, but about halfway through the morning I notice I'm dialling the flat directly below Carol's: Ms R. Langley, it says, Flat 7, Bridport House. No way, I think. I pass the door to Flat 7 twice a day at least, on my way up and down the communal staircase.

The phone to Flat 7 rings for a long time and then finally someone picks up.

'Hello?' a woman's voice says.

I go through the usual spiel; I tell her my name and why I'm calling and promise her the possibility of entry to a competition where she *may* be in with a chance of winning a luxury holiday if only she has the time to take part in a short questionnaire.

'Oh, go on then,' she says.

So I start the questionnaire.

I ask her all the usual questions.

Towards the end, in the 'general overall happiness' section, I ask how happy she'd consider herself overall, on a scale of one to ten.

'I don't know . . . four?'

I ask her why that is.

'Well, it's not been the same since my husband passed away.'

'I'm very sorry to hear that,' I say, and type *husbnd dead* in the little box on my screen. 'Anyway, moving briskly along,' I say, 'when you picture yourself in one year's time, do you see yourself as: a) less happy than you are today, b) the same level of happiness, or c) happier?'

'Well, c, I hope,' she says with a small, sad laugh.

At the end of the call, I thank her for her time and wish her all the best and tell her that we'll be in touch if she wins the holiday.

What I really want to say, though, is, 'I live directly above you!'

I want to ask if there's anything I can do.

I want to tell her that I'm sorry her husband died and

that the world has become such a miserable place for her that she would rate it an overall four out of ten with one being not at all happy and ten being very happy indeed.

'Just one final question,' I say, making sure to speak in the same measured tone as before, as if this is a thing that we ask everyone who takes part. 'Can you confirm your first name for me, please?'

'Rosemary,' she says.

At the start of lunch break, Martin walks up to my desk. 'Can I have a quick word, mate?'

I follow him down the corridor. Today there's none of the usual swagger in his step. Today he's just sort of hobbling.

The light isn't on in his office and the room smells damp and old, like he's possibly slept in it.

He's going to ask me about Carol and I'm going to have to tell him a lie.

'Have a seat,' he says, sliding himself into his big leather swivel chair.

I take the seat opposite, and when we do finally look each other in the eye, Martin's are sore and bloodshot.

'I think we both know what this is about,' he says quietly.

I nod.

'I've had another listen to your calls,' he says, 'and I can't see any improvement whatsoever. In fact, if anything, *mate*, they've gotten a bit worse actually.'

'Oh,' I say.

'Yeah. Seems like you've got a completely different set of priorities to the rest of us here.'

I don't speak.

I can't think of anything to say.

'*Non job* priorities,' he says.

'Like what?'

'Like trying it on with that Chinese bird.'

'Come on,' I say. 'That's not fair.'

He folds his arms and leans back in his swivel chair and looks at me for a long, tense moment. He doesn't look like a person who is making a decision about my future at Quiztime Solutions, though. He looks like a person who's already made one.

'Is this it, then?' I ask. 'Have you just fired me?'

'Work it out,' he says. 'It's not rocket science.'

As I leave the building I automatically reach into the pockets of my coat for my tobacco and papers before remembering that I threw them away, first thing this morning. I can feel the dry dust of old tobacco in the corners of my coat pockets, but it's not quite enough to make a roll-up out of. That sweet, stinging, need-a-cigarette feeling grows in my stomach as I start to walk down Deansgate, my head spinning.

I turn the corner.

At the gate to the park, I stop. There's Dalisay again, sat on one of the benches, eating her sandwich.

Deep down, I knew she'd be here.

She pretends not to notice me until I'm right up close.

'You okay?' she says, once I've sat down next to her. 'You look . . . funny.'

'I'm fine,' I say. And then, after a pause: 'I think Martin just fired me.'

'*What?*' she says, genuinely surprised. 'What for?'

'Don't worry about it.'

I feel dizzy and out-of-synch, like the sound of me is running about a half-second behind the picture.

I reach out and try to hold her hand.

My fingers grope for – and briefly manage to touch – her red woollen mitten before she yanks it away.

'What're you doing?' she snaps.

'I don't know,' I say.

'I have a boyfriend, you know. Back home.'

'I know,' I say. 'Marcos.'

'Yeah,' she says. 'Marcos.'

'I saw him on Facebook,' I say.

I watch the pigeons pecking around in the grass for a while.

'I'm sorry,' I say. 'I don't know what I'm doing.'

'As in right now?' she says. 'Or generally?'

'Both,' I say. Then, 'I think I might leave Manchester.'

I'm not sure if I mean it, though.

'Me, too,' she says. 'My mom's been sick, and I'd been saving some money to fly home for Christmas anyway. But I feel like I might end up going early.'

'How early?'

'Couple of weeks?'

Just then her red plastic wristwatch begins beeping and she fumbles in her mittens to stop it, in the end offering her wrist to me to do it for her.

I press the little button.

'Thanks,' she says. 'Well, end of lunch.'

She stands up and I stay sitting on the bench.

'You staying here?' she says.

I shrug.

LAUREN
2014

'Have you seen *The Motorcycle Diaries*?'

Carl's speech was slurry even though he'd only had two pints. I suspected that he'd been drinking somewhere else, too, since much earlier in the evening.

I shook my head, my eyes drifting once more to my phone, which I surreptitiously slid off the table, letting it drop into my lap then touching its button and glancing at it, wondering why I was even being covert; it wasn't as if Carl was paying attention. He was just enjoying talking now, slurring wetly in my direction. I'd heard about his camera collection, his gym membership, his current job, the job he was retraining for, and his year-and-a-half motorcycle odyssey across South America.

21:37, my phone's display said, which meant I'd been

here for thirty-six minutes. It felt like much longer. Days, perhaps. I'd had one and a half small white wines, and spoken somewhere in the region of fourteen sentences.

'Oh shit,' I said, looking up from the blank screen of my phone, forcing my eyes to widen as far as they'd go. 'I just got a message from my flatmate. I think I need to go, actually.'

'Everything okay?' Carl slurred, confused.

'My cat's fallen ill,' I said, grimacing apologetically, standing, pulling on my coat, all in one quick motion.

I don't know what Carl thought when I just left like that, really quickly, without even kissing him on the cheek or giving him a hug or saying any of the things you're probably supposed to say, even if you don't really mean them: 'We should do this again,' 'It was great to meet you,' etc.

It felt good to be back outside and I began the walk home slowly, enjoying the cold air on my face. I only lived six streets away and I tried my hardest to maintain a steady, even pace. I'd been reading about various mindfulness and meditation techniques recently, and one of them was a walking meditation, where you just focused on your steps, letting your head clear, thinking only of your feet, rhythmically touching against the ground, plodding along at a simple pace, one-two, one-two, one-two . . .

But as I walked, I found myself thinking again about my lie to Carl, about Ginny being unwell, and instead of keeping my footsteps steady I picked up pace, with each new step convincing myself that perhaps something *was* wrong with her, that by talking about it, by saying it out loud, I'd kind of willed it into existence and that I'd get home and find her dead.

I sat down on the edge of my bed, still breathless from my almost-run. Ginny was asleep, curled tightly, nothing at all the matter with her. I stroked her the wrong way on purpose, uncovering a newish patch of grey-white hairs amongst the black. She opened one eye a little, then closed it, curling herself even tighter.

When I turned on my laptop, its fan whirred and buzzed and rattled. Something was going wrong with it. It was on its last legs.

It took an age to log into Hotmail. I sat on the bed and stroked Ginny the wrong way and watched the little circle on the screen revolve, chasing its own tail, as I waited for my inbox to load.

Finally I typed 'voicemail' into the search bit at the top, opening the email from Michael that simply said 'Here you go', and then clicked on the link to the almost completely blank page that, he'd assured me, would always be there, no matter what.

I pressed the play button, and there was another long pause while the file buffered. Then a crackle, then a whistling tone, and then, 'Welcome to answerphone. You currently have no new messages and three saved messages. To hear your messages press . . .

'First saved message: Hello, love, it's me. Just phoning to say happy birthday. What time is it there? Give me a ring when you get this.

'Second saved message: Hello, love, only me again. Thought it might be a bit later by now. Or is it still early? I can never work it out. Anyway, whatever time it is, I just wanted to say that I love you very much and hope you're having a nice day, and I've posted a little thing, even though you said you didn't want anything, but I don't hold out much hope of it getting there in time anyway. Okay, I'll call again in a little while. Bye!

'Third saved message: We're not having much luck at this, are we? Oh sod it . . . Happy birthday to you, happy birthday to you, happy birthday to *you-hoo*, happy birthday to you.'

part three
be right back

LAUREN
2005

On the flight home, Lauren waited for Michael to offer her the window seat. He shuffled his way towards it, then, once he'd sat in it, looked over his shoulder and grinned at her. There were slivers of airport bagel caught between his teeth. You didn't actually tell him you wanted the window seat, Lauren reminded herself. He isn't psychic.

This was a thing she'd been working hard on recently: coming to terms with the fact that people weren't psychic. Also: lowering her expectations. It was like limbo. Last week she discovered a clump of grey hairs at Michael's temples and forced herself to get excited about them.

Look, she forced herself to think, real life!

As the plane began to taxi, she slipped her hand into both of his and felt the grainy, calloused texture of his palms with her fingertips. He was like someone, a celebrity she couldn't quite think of right this second. The plane picked up speed, rumbling, the engines beginning to howl, and Lauren marvelled at just how unfazed Michael was: by planes, by take-offs, by anything.

This was why she'd chosen him.

Because it was a choice, wasn't it?

There was Michael and there was Ian and you chose Michael and now you need to stop thinking about this and questioning it or else you will never be happy.

Ian was like an Elliott Smith song: pretty and delicate, but always on the brink of falling apart.

Michael was like a desk: solid and useful and around for a long time, which you could lean on if you had to, or eat your dinner off. Whatever that meant.

'Michael,' she said, but he didn't hear her over the engine sounds.

So she wiggled her fingers, not to free her hand, just to communicate her excitement at the idea of going home.

Michael was from Winchester.

Look, she thought, looking at him. Look at how happy this fully grown man from Winchester is just to sit there and look out of the window!

The plane was calmer now.

The seatbelt lights blinked out.

The grey hairs at Michael's temples were multiplying. Each day there seemed to be more of them. Lauren suspected that if she kept her eyes fixed on the spot next to his ear for the whole nine and a half hours of the flight, she might even see a few new ones appear.

Michael turned his big, square-jawed face towards her.

'Alright?' he said.

At night, in bed, he always spent a long time doing the things she asked him to. He knelt between her legs and worked hard on her, like she was one of his websites.

'Yep,' Lauren nodded, forcing her mouth into a smiling shape.

You have made the right choice.

She watched him remove the in-flight shopping magazine from the netting by his knees and begin to leaf through it. He flipped straight to the back, past all the kids' toys and novelty items, to the practical things like alarm clocks and cufflinks and watches with rotating faces that glow in the dark and still function underwater.

She would probably buy him a rotating, glowing underwater watch for his birthday, whenever it was. His *thirty-second* birthday. Lauren did not know how old this was, not really. All she knew was that it was somewhere past that invisible line into 'adult'. A place that, from where she was sitting, seemed impossible to get to.

She unwrapped her headphones and touched the buttons on the seat-mounted display in front of her, scrolled through, selected an episode of *Friends*, and as it began, allowed herself to entertain the daydream that this was how their new life would unfold, a couple of weeks from now, once they'd both moved into Michael's uncle's spare room in Stoke Newington. Lauren and Michael (Joey! *That's* who he reminded her of! He was like an unfunny Joey!) would become the centre of a new circle of friends, a circle of friends that they would both make together, in this new city, the nation's capital, which they were both going to find jobs and start again in!

Because Michael is The One.

He has to be.

He saw you.

He would really like to make you laugh again.

(He's not done it so far.)

Stop it.

You're just winding yourself up again. You're looking for cracks, like you always do. You're always finding faults and picking at them until they get bigger and you're not going to make that mistake again this time. You are not going to fuck this relationship up, Lauren, no matter what, and if there are *any faults then they're due to you being too unrealistic, demanding too much, and you need to learn to modify the way you think about things, the way you approach the world. You need to calm down and realise that things are a bit duller, a bit more realistic, a bit more shitty in real life.*

Michael is solid and realistic and dependable.

He makes websites for a living.

You have made the right choice.

* * *

At the baggage claim, Lauren insisted she was just tired, that *that* was the reason for her moody, pouty silence. Really though, she wasn't sure. All she knew was that from the moment she set foot back in England she'd felt a kind of cement-coloured malaise expand inside her like a miserable balloon. And all those things she'd developed in Canada, all the things she'd been convinced were solid, permanent improvements – her posture, her confidence, her general outlook – began undoing themselves, like some snag of her was caught in Vancouver, and the further she got from it, the more the jumper of her unravelled.

She sat on a bench, wondering why she always seemed to be waiting for boys to fetch her luggage.

There was Michael, lumbering towards the belt of the carousel, snatching his own suitcase off it. Lauren's popped out through the flaps soon afterwards.

She didn't tell him, though.

She didn't make any indication that she'd seen it.

If Michael picks up my suitcase, she said to herself, then this is a sign that everything will work out okay.

She began gripping the edges of the bench and gritting her teeth as it sailed towards him.

If Michael recognises my suitcase then we are going to be happy.

The suitcase was about to slip past him and still he made no move to grab it.

If Michael recognises my suitcase then I have made the right decision.

'There! THERE!' she shouted manically, when it was

almost at the other end of the belt, causing a few people to turn and look at her, puzzled. 'That one there! The big green one with brown bits!'

He made a dash for it, almost knocking over a toddler in his attempt to reach it, but it was too late. It disappeared through the flapping mouth at the other end, and Michael turned and smiled and shrugged as if nothing whatsoever was wrong.

IAN
2014

I press the touchscreen on the Jobmatchmachine and scroll through the listings. Nothing. Not even a top hat. So I walk back to the soft red seating area and take my seat and wait for my name to be called and when it is, finally, it's Rick again of course. He waves at me and lifts himself out of his seat as I walk towards him. At first I think he's grown a goatee, but as I get closer I realise it's actually a dark brown scab that's crusted all the way round his lips. In between little cracks in the scab I can see bright red dots of blood. I wonder if it's okay for him to be working here like this. Shouldn't he be at the doctor's? Shouldn't he be at home?

'Back again,' he says cheerily, dabbing the corner of his mouth against the back of his hand then examining it.

'Yep,' I say.

'What happened?' he says, looking over some printouts, which, I assume, have all the details about my Quiztime Solutions experience on them.

'I wasn't quite meeting my targets,' I say. 'So they let me go.'

'And when was that?'

'Six days ago.'

'So what have you been doing since then?'

I've been lying on my bed a lot in a foetal position, feeling miserable.

I've been sitting in the living room, drinking rum with Carol.

I've been ignoring all sorts of messages and notifications on Facebook.

'Looking for work,' I say.

'Right,' says Rick, dabbing his mouth again.

He clicks his mouse and leans in towards his monitor.

'Do you have anything where I could just walk around outside?' I say, but Rick isn't listening.

He leans in towards the screen and clacks his tongue loudly against the roof of his mouth. 'Alright,' he says. 'Alright. I've got a warehouse here. Think you could handle working in a warehouse?'

'Maybe.'

'A small team of motivated individuals are needed for work in this busy warehouse environment to boost our staff during the seasonal period,' Rick reads from the screen. 'You will be expected to unpack and repack various consumer goods in this exciting temporary goods-handling position. Well? Any good?'

'I don't know,' I say.

'I'll print it out,' he says.

As he gets up to go and collect the printout, I take one of the *Depression Counselling* leaflets from the desk, fold it in half, and stuff it in my jacket pocket.

Today, at four fifty-five p.m., Dalisay flies home to Manila. I know this because she sent me a Facebook message last night, telling me so. She said it was nice to meet me and wishes me all the best for the future and told me that she would say a prayer for me. I've not replied.

I look at the clock in the corner of the screen.

It's four fifty-six p.m.

I go over to the window.

The not-Rosemary person in the expensive ground-floor flat opposite is hanging tea towels on a clothes-horse. It must be very warm in her flat because she's only wearing a T-shirt. I wave at her, just a little wave, but she doesn't notice.

I leave the room and walk down the corridor, doing my coat up on the way.

When I reach the kitchen doorway, I stop.

Carol's at the kitchen table, still in her pyjamas.

She's been off work pretend-sick for just over a week now. I know this because I'm the one who has to keep calling in and lying for her. She just mopes around the house in her pyjamas and dressing gown all day, letting mugs of tea go cold everywhere. Last night I went round collecting things for the washing up and I found one on the edge of the bath and another right in the corner of the living room, behind the TV.

I don't mind though. Not really.

(If I'm completely honest, I'm enjoying the company.)

'Want anything from the shop?' I ask.

'More rum,' she says.

It's become a sort of in-joke between us, all this rum drinking we've been doing, except I wonder sometimes whether there's actually anything funny about it.

On the way down the stairs, I pass Flat 7.

Once I'm outside, I take out my e-cig and take a long, hard drag. Even though it's vapour instead of smoke, Carol still won't let me do it indoors.

I'll give up nicotine on my thirty-second birthday, I promise myself as I exhale.

Halfway towards Morrisons, an aeroplane goes by overhead.

When I get back, Carol's still sat exactly where I left her. I suspect that if I dipped my finger in the two thirds of tea in her mug, it would be stone cold. I sit down opposite and take the bottle of White Label rum from its bag and stand it between us, next to the salt-shaker person, who seems to be hugging onto the thing of pepper for dear life.

'How're you feeling?' I ask.

Carol's eyes are bloodshot and her hair looks unwashed, and I'm worried that if she carries on much longer with this fake illness, it might turn into a real one.

'I feel great,' she says. 'Really fucking fantastic.'

'Want to watch some telly?'

'Not particularly.'

I move my finger around in a little pile of salt, sweeping it into a line.

'Do you want to go home?' she says.

'*Home* home?' I say.

'I've spoken to Mum and told her I'm coming back early for Christmas this year. Thought you might like to come too. Or you could just stay here.'

'How early?'

'First thing tomorrow morning.'

'Count me in,' I say.

A pause.

'Um.'

'What?'

I move the salt around with my finger.

'Can I borrow five hundred quid?'

PAUL
2014

In the hushed corridor of the New Writing Centre, Paul knocks gently on Greg's door, which is propped open. Greg looks up briefly from his computer, then fixes his attention back on whatever it is he's typing. An email, probably. Some sort of admin nightmare. Greg is director of the Writing and American Studies programme at the university. He's also a widely published, critically respected poet, who nearly always seems to be swamped beneath the twin demands of academia and family life, leaving him little time to ever get anything of his own written. The few times Greg has talked to Paul about his life, he's made it sound like he gets about one half-minute per day to fumble a pen and a scrap of paper from his pocket and scribble down a beautiful crystalline line of poetry, before his admin work or his wife or his two-year-old daughter comes to drag him away again. Yet he publishes a new book every other year. Greg is kind, too. He exudes a soothing, calming warmth. He will understand, Paul thinks. This is going to turn out okay.

'Hi, Greg,' Paul says. 'Can I have a quick word?'

'Sure, sure,' Greg says in his soft, deep voice, still focused mostly on his typing. 'Come in. Have a seat. I'm just trying to get these emails finished.'

Paul steps gingerly into the room, then just stands there.

'Have a seat,' Greg says again, still without looking up.

'Do you mind if I, um, close the door?' Paul says, trying to make his voice sound measured but worried.

Greg stops typing and turns in his swivel chair, folding his hands in his lap.

'Absolutely, yeah,' he says, a new concern in his voice. 'What's on your mind?'

What a nice guy, Paul thinks.

'Not more bad news, I hope?'

'Kind of, actually.'

Since the mugging, Paul's been pitied by almost everyone he knows at the uni. Poor bastard, they probably think whenever they pass him in the hallway or see him sat alone in the veggie café, not even attempting to write any more, just dabbing the crumbs of cake off his plate and staring into space. *See that guy there?* they probably whisper amongst themselves, *well, he lost his whole novel. Just like that. Some mugger nicked his laptop and the only hard copy along with it. I heard it was amazing, too.*

Paul can't look Greg in the eye.

So he looks instead at the bookcase on the opposite wall, at the rows of paperbacks and hardbacks crammed onto the shelves in no particular order, searching out the luminous yellow spine of his own first novel.

'It's quite, erm, *sensitive*,' he says, 'the thing that I need to talk to you about.'

'Right,' Greg says, leaning forward in his chair.

Paul leaves a suitably dramatic pause. He attempts to subtly frame his features to make himself look exhausted.

'I've had some pretty bad news about my health,' he says quietly, his eyes fixed on the dusty front wheel of Greg's swivel chair.

'Oh no,' Greg says. 'Oh, bloody hell, mate.'

'Yeah,' Paul nods, trying to summon tears into the corners of his eyes. 'It's . . . um . . . It's quite serious, actually. And as you can imagine it's been quite a shock for me and for Sarah and everything and it's, you know, it's knocked me for six . . .'

'I can imagine,' Greg says. 'Is there anything . . . I mean . . . How can I put this? Is there a definite diagnosis yet?'

'They don't know, you know, the *extent* of things yet. But yeah . . . it's . . .'

Paul wonders if he's actually going to say the word.

'It's cancer,' he says, feeling the two syllables deliver their one-two gut punch, just the way he'd hoped.

'Oh Paul,' Greg says, lifting himself involuntarily out of his seat.

Paul keeps his eyes fixed on the wheel of Greg's chair. He clears his throat. He says, 'I know I've only got a few weeks left until the end of the semester, but the truth is, I'm finding it really hard to give it my all. And I was wondering if . . .'

'Don't worry about *us*,' Greg says, softly, soothingly; saying exactly what Paul had hoped he would.

'I can get one of the PhDs to cover your remaining classes, mate, if *that's* what you're worried about.'

'Thanks so much, Greg,' Paul says sombrely, trying to contain the happiness and relief deep within him; sealing it off as a tingling feeling somewhere around his stomach. 'Right, I'll be off then.'

'I'm so sorry, Paul,' Greg says, offering his big, warm, soothing hand to shake, and Paul hopes that if Greg senses the clamminess of his own palm, he'll put it down to the illness rather than nerves. 'Do keep us all posted, mate. I'll sort everything here for you and speak to HR, and then I'll send you an email to wrap things up sometime next week then?'

'Great,' Paul says. 'That sounds great.'

Thank fuck for that, Paul thinks as he walks out of the New Writing building, past the library and the veggie café in the direction of the city centre. It's almost five o' clock on Friday. Damon will be finishing work soon.

Paul will send him a text. See if he fancies meeting in town for a pint, maybe. Somewhere noisy. Somewhere full of people and life.

Sarah's staying at her parents' again this weekend.

It's the third weekend in a row.

Paul suspects that there will be a Monday when she just doesn't come back.

It's okay, he tells himself.

Things will work themselves out.

She'll see that I've changed.

I'm different.

I am a new Paul now.

All my updates are being installed.

I'm not dying.

I'm not teaching any more.

The nicotine patch on my arm is tingling, which means it's doing its job.

I'm not a writer.

I'm not an anything.

I'm just a human being, walking down a street in Manchester.

Also: he has a brand new phone. Okay, it's not *quite* as good as an official iPhone, but he can still look at the internet if he wants to, which is the main thing anyone really needs a phone for these days. And if he's lucky, he won't have to see or be reminded of Alison Whistler ever again.

Since the eyeball incident, he's not logged back into Twitter.

And, anyway, he tells himself – ignoring the gaze of a

tramp in a newsagent doorway and resisting the urge to go inside and buy a packet of fags – what can anyone actually do now? I don't even work there any more.

I'm a free man.

Paul only has one more payment due from the university.

Don't worry about it, he tells himself.

You'll look for a job, first thing tomorrow morning.

Tonight, let's get drunk and celebrate.

LAUREN
2005

Lauren tried again. She walked through the door marked 'nothing to declare' and squeezed Michael's hand defiantly. *This is the rest of your life starting, right here! Two Brits Abroad, now home again.* She wondered what Michael would make of her mum, and realised with a mixture of embarrassment and guilt that so far she'd only told him negative things: that she nagged and meddled and never really understood her.

The plan was to spend a couple of weeks at Anne's house, before they moved to London, where they would use Michael's uncle's flat as a base from which to find jobs and a home of their own. This was Michael's plan. He'd made all the decisions. Lauren was just following along. So far, she'd not really mentioned that her mum was loaded.

They walked through the exit and scanned the small crowd, and Lauren automatically looked for her name amongst the taxi drivers' hand-written signs, simply because she was the kind of person who'd always wanted to see her name written on one. She thought briefly of a nice memory of Paul; one summer evening in Nottingham train station, she'd surprised him on the platform after he'd been home for the weekend. That was not so long after they'd started going out, in that first flush of excitement, before things turned sour.

So if Ian was a song and Michael was a desk, then what was Paul?

Paul was a really pretentious, plotless novel.

Things will be different this time round, Lauren.

You will learn how to grow up.

You will learn how to have grey hair and one day be thirty-two years old.

You will get a job doing something important and you will make a new group of friends who will be [something] and you will [something something something].

She spotted her mum and waved. As she walked self-consciously towards her, Lauren noticed that she looked different somehow; a little thinner, a little older, and she was wearing a baggy blue jumper and some kind of silly hat, a purple one with a floppy brim, the kind of thing they might have joked about a year ago if they'd seen someone else wearing it.

As they hugged, Anne said, 'Hello, sweetie,' into Lauren's neck and kissed her, and Lauren wondered if her mum was anything at all like she'd described to Michael. She felt another twinge of embarrassment, remembering how much time she'd spent painting her as this tyrant, and made a promise to herself to tell him more nice things about her, the very next time they were on their own.

Lauren stood back to get a good look at her.

She never normally wore a hat.

Lauren touched the brim of it.

'Come on,' Anne said, swatting Lauren's hand away, 'let's get out of here.'

'What's this for?' said Lauren. 'I thought you always said you didn't suit hats.'

IAN
2014

I'm walking so fast down Oxford Road, I don't really look where I'm going. I dodge round a group of students, step slightly into a doorway, then feel my foot knock something over. There's a jingle of change and I see pennies and ten p's rolling off all over the pavement and out into the road. Shit. I've kicked the homeless man's rain-sodden Costa cup over.

'Shit, I'm so *so* sorry,' I say, trying to gather up as many of the coins as I can from around the students' feet, who don't seem to notice or care.

The man sits in the doorway, cross-legged, his stained coat draped over his knees, watching me.

I can just make out the music shop from here. They've not started pulling the shutters down yet, which means it's not quite gone six. I've still got time.

I hand the man all the remaining change I can find on the street.

'Cheers, mate,' he says, grinning hopefully.

'Oh,' I say. 'I don't think I've got any spare change I'm afraid.'

I reach deep into my jeans pocket, trying to feel around amongst the old filter tips and bits of tissue for any loose coins and without thinking I pull out the massive wad of twenties that Carol let me get out on her card. The homeless man looks at them. I look at the homeless man looking at them. I put them back in my pocket.

'Sorry,' I say.

As I turn to go, I spot a face I wasn't expecting.

It's *Paul.*

Paul Saunders: my old flatmate, Lauren's ex-boyfriend, strolling down the road towards me.

I turn back, stepping over the homeless man's cup again, and ducking into the newsagent. I hang around by the photocopier, peering out of the window through a gap in the index-card adverts, waiting for him to go past.

He looks exactly the same, facially. His hair's mostly gone though. And he's wearing the kind of clothes – brown cord blazer, fitted shirt, smart jeans, expensive shoes – that let you know immediately that he's got some kind of swanky lecturing job at the university.

The more I think about it, I knew he was here all along.

His first novel had come into HMV. We'd put it in the discount paperback bin. One afternoon I'd turned to the back flap and looked at his author photo (cropped so you couldn't see he was balding) and it'd said:

> Paul Saunders was born in 1982. *Human Animus* is his first novel. Saunders has been widely published in journals and anthologies, both print and online. He lives, and drinks, in Manchester.

Come on, come on, I think, shifting from foot to foot, desperate to get to the music shop before they pull the shutters.

I check the time on my phone: two minutes to six.

Once Paul's finally gone past the window, I duck back out of the shop, stepping carefully over the cup of coins, and walk along the road behind him, praying he doesn't turn round.

He doesn't, and I make it to the doorway just as the man with the beard steps outside.

'Can I help you, mate?'

'Yeah, I've come for . . .' and I turn to point my guitar out in the window but it's gone.

The man waits for me to speak.

'. . . the Tele Custom,' I say, pointing to the space in the window where it used to be. 'The cream and black one?'

'Oooh, sorry, mate,' he says. 'Sold that the other day.'

As I wait for the mp3s to finish downloading, I take a big swig of rum straight from the bottle. I open a new tab and type 'postcards band uk' into Google. No surprises. There are, in total, the same four mentions of us as always on the internet: our Myspace page, two small posts on the Drowned in Sound forum, and the Discogs listing for our only seven-inch. That's it. You can't actually buy it anywhere. (Not even on eBay.) You can't download it. You can't read the lukewarm, 3/5 review the NME gave it.

Next I log into my emails.

Not my Gmail though, my old Hotmail account, which I only ever use these days for offers and mailing lists and petitions.

It says I have 999(+) new emails. I scroll through the first few pages and all of them are spam.

I compose a new email, to lauren_cross83@hotmail.com:

hi,
how are you?
sorry it took me a while to reply.
hope you're okay,
Ian x

I click send, then close the browser.

Once all the songs have finished downloading, I log off Rosemary's Wireless.

On my way towards the front door, I look in at Carol. She's in her room, packing. I carry on down the hall, out of the door and down one flight of stairs, until I'm stood outside Flat 7.

I knock on the door and wait.

The door is answered by a small, stout woman with short black hair and flushed red cheeks.

'Can I help you?' she says.

Behind her I can see into the flat. It has different carpets to Carol's – they're brown and orange; a queasy, swirling 70s design – and the flat in general looks much more old-fashioned and cluttered than Carol's. A hot, foggy smell, like boiling potatoes, drifts into the hall.

'Are you Rosemary?' I say.

'Yes,' she says, confused. 'Sorry, *who are you*?'

'I'm from flat eleven,' I say, pointing at the ceiling. 'I've just come to let you know that you should really encrypt your wireless connection.'

PAUL
2014

In the kitchen, at three a.m., attempting to make toast, Paul knocks a teapot off the counter – not just any teapot: a delicate, mostly ornamental teapot that Sarah's had since childhood, that was handed down to her from her now-deceased grandma, and that Paul has always been scared of touching – and it smashes into tiny, irreparable pieces on the tiles.

'Fucking shitting fuck,' he says.

This evening he ended up going out drinking by himself because Damon was busy.

He sat in the corner of Kro Piccadilly, miserably eyeing up women in tight shiny dresses and drank seven pints of strong continental lager. From the all-night Spar, he bought a ten-pack of Marlboro Lights and then just wandered around the city centre weaving in and out of the groups of pissed-up men and women, feeling vaguely like if someone started a fight with him he wouldn't actually mind – that, for maybe the first time in his life, he understood that urge to punch someone's fucking teeth in that sometimes came with drinking.

'Not tonight, mate,' the massive bouncer told him outside Lovely Legs in Chinatown. 'Come back when you're able to stand up straight, yeah?'

Wandering along Oxford Road, past the groups of students, wondering where Alison was and three times almost calling her from his almost-iPhone, Paul stopped to pick up a flyer off the pavement. He squinted at the blurry, neon-purple text and was only able to read the name of the club (*VODKA L@GOON*). Then he noticed there was something smeared on the flyer, and sniffed his fingers, and realised it was dog shit.

Then he was sick down the side of the precinct centre.

Then he fell asleep on the bus home.

(He's still not washed his hands.)

After chugging down a pint and a half of tap water, Paul steps over the smashed teapot and carries a plate of toast through to the living room.

He sits down on the sofa, turns on the telly, flicks through the channels, and stops on *Babestation*, where an almost naked, baby-oiled woman squirms and gyrates on a silky purple bedspread, her lips moving but no sound coming from them as she gives a tit-wank to a cordless phone.

Paul leans forward and squints at the small print

crawling across the bottom of the screen: *£2.20 per minute from a landline, prices from mobile networks may vary.*

He takes his phone out of his pocket, wipes his shitty thumb across the screen, and taps the Facebook app.

He and Alison are still friends.

He's waiting for her to delete him. On her wall, she's uploaded a new set of photos, titled 'Peaks and Trofs', which turns out to be twenty-three photos of Alison outdoors, somewhere in the Peak District, hiking with a group of grinning, fresh-faced, racially diverse kids about the same age as her, and then later, the whole bunch of them larking around in a bar, playing a game with the beer mats, mugging for the camera, then starting a Scrabble tournament. It looks so wholesome and fun and youthful, Paul has to quickly exit out of the photos, feeling for the first time like he shouldn't be looking at them, like he's intruded on a private, intimate moment, a day which Alison and this group of goons will recall with real fondness, maybe, when they're all thirty-one and a half years old, eating toast on a sofa.

He lifts the last bite to his mouth, licks the crumbs off his fingers, then looks at the time.

The babe on *Babestation* flutters her eyelashes at him, flicking her tongue up and down the oily plastic shaft of the phone.

He types in the number on the screen and presses call.

* * *

'The absolute main thing,' Terry says, a week and a half later, 'is that you don't go wandering off too far from your designated area. I know it's cold, but just stay roughly where I drop you, okay?'

Paul nods as much as he's able, stuffed into the passenger seat of the grubby, dog-smelling Ford Focus.

'And make sure you look like you're enjoying yourself, yeah?'

'Yep,' Paul says.

'I'll be back about lunchtime, to top your flyers up and let you grab a bit of grub.'

Terry pulls up to the kerb outside the Subway in Fallowfield.

Oh god, Paul thinks, as he wrestles himself out of the car. Why does it have to be here? As he reaches back into the footwell for his sack of flyers, the top part of his costume gets caught in the doorframe and he has to shimmy his body to get it free. He hears it tear a little.

'Careful,' Terry hisses.

'I'm fine,' Paul says, standing up and brushing himself down.

Underneath the main tube part, he's wearing a black Lycra onesie. The flyers in his sack are for *Supraprint Commercial Printing and Dissertation Binding Services!*

Terry beeps his horn, revs the engine, then pulls away into the busy morning traffic.

Only eight hours to go.

This is the Tesco Express nearest to Alison's house,

the same one Paul bought that box of twelve Durex Fetherlite from. She could walk past at any moment. And if she did, would she recognise him? Paul reminds himself that he is mostly just a foam tube: that, apart from his blacked-up face sticking out from a hole three quarters of the way up, he's disguised.

A group of student lads walk past. Paul offers them flyers. Two of the three lads accept them, and Paul turns to watch them walk off in the direction of the uni. A few paces away, about equidistant from Paul and the nearest bin, they all drop their flyers on the ground. Terry has already gone over this a number of times: every few minutes, Paul must retrieve any large quantities of discarded flyers and throw them away himself, otherwise Terry will get into trouble and, as a consequence, Paul won't get paid. For his shift today, Paul stands to make forty-five quid before tax (it's up to him if he wants to declare it).

He's stopped carrying the leather document wallet around with him.

He's just a top hat now. An anonymous, blacked-up top hat.

He offers a flyer to a student girl and she shakes her head and doesn't look him in the eye.

Paul hears his phone whistle – a cheeky, suggestive noise, which means 'text message' – somewhere deep in the sack of flyers that's dangling from his shoulder. He gets the flap open and tries to find it, knowing his actions are useless: the stretchy synthetic fabric of the bodysuit would stop his fingers from being recognised on the phone's touchscreen, anyway. He'll have to wait until Terry comes back at lunchtime.

The other option, Paul thinks, is to stuff the flyers in that bin over there and do a runner. In costume. To Didsbury.

Pacing up and down the small strip of shops, he mostly hangs around outside the tanning salon because their wall clock is visible from the street. He still has seven hours and ten minutes to go. Is this really his job now? He wonders if he'll even be able to last a *day*, let alone the three-to-four-days-a-week that Terry's looking for.

Paul steps out into the path of a thin, hunched-over student boy and thrusts a flyer into his bespectacled face.

'No thanks,' the boy says in a soft Birmingham accent, swatting it away.

Oh shit.

Paul turns quickly, but it's too late.

Craig's face crumples in a mixture of embarrassment and dismay.

On Sarah's tiny, metallic turquoise netbook, there's a full list of her search history. Paul discovers it accidentally one afternoon, after a furtive wank in the living room with the curtains drawn. He opens the Chrome history, about to get rid of the entry for 'xvideos.com – tattooed emo teen brunette' when he sees the list. It probably goes all the way back to when she first bought the computer, two and a bit years ago.

'Home fertility test,' it says, between 'Kristen Stewart Oscars dress' and 'vegetable recipe cauliflower beetroot'.

Oh, Sarah, Paul thinks when he reads it.

He scans down the list:

'cost fertility treatment manchester'

and

'chances of conception 35'

and

'ovarian cyst 1 ovary removed as teenager chances of conception'.

Why didn't you feel you could talk to me about this stuff? he asks her in his head.

He deletes the xvideos.com entry, closes the lid of the netbook and looks at his flaccid, spermy penis.

I'm going to become someone better, he thinks. Just you wait.

LAUREN
2005

'I didn't want to worry you,' Anne explained, unable to look Lauren in the eye, her scalp visible through her fluffy, patchy hair.

They were both sitting at the kitchen table with mugs of cold tea and plates of untouched toast, and Michael had taken himself out for a long walk around the village to give them both a bit of time alone, and the kitchen felt huge and icy despite the Aga.

'You should have said,' Lauren said, 'when you first found out.'

It's breast cancer, Stage 3C, which means it's spread.

She was diagnosed four months ago, in December. They'd spoken just twice that month, once on her birthday, Lauren using the payphone in the café and calling England via an international phone card after missing three calls from her mum, and then again, briefly, on Christmas Day. And then, in early January, she'd received a longish email from her mum which was mostly about the garden, and described a new friend she'd made who, a few paragraphs later, was revealed to be a squirrel. It transpired that she'd *still* not told any of her friends or her sister or any other members of their family yet. She'd not told Lauren's dad and said she had no intention of doing so, even though it would be a fantastic way to burst his gleeful little post-divorce bubble.

'I thought,' Anne said, then stopped.

'What?' Lauren croaked.

'I thought I could try and get it all sorted out, before you got home.'

And then she began to cry, which Lauren had only ever seen her do twice before, and both times there had been someone else there to comfort her, too. Lauren lifted herself out of her chair and put her arms gently around her mum as she sobbed, feeling how much thinner and smaller her body was beneath her jumper.

In bed that night, Lauren pleaded with Michael to hold her tighter.

'I don't want to crush you,' he said.

She wanted him to crush her completely.

'I don't know what to say,' he said. 'I'm so sorry, Lauren. It's rubbish, it's a rubbish situation. I'm sorry.'

She felt no comfort from this.

In fact, she felt absolutely nothing towards Michael whatsoever as she sobbed into his T-shirt in the dark. She wiped her nose on it. She pleaded with him to hug her tighter, to hug her as hard as he could. When he asked if she'd got anyone else she could talk to, any other close friends or relatives or anything, she thought of Ian then shook her head.

'Please don't go to sleep,' she pleaded as his breathing began to slow.

'I won't,' he promised, his grip loosening a little on her shoulder.

I don't know who you are, she thought as he began to snore.

IAN
2014

'Okay, are you ready?' I ask.

It's just gone six, and everything is blue and luminous and the roads are almost completely deserted as we drive through the suburbs somewhere outside Stockport. It's so cold inside the car that you can see your breath.

'Go for it,' Carol says.

So I stick the CD in the car's stereo and press play.

There's a long pause as the machine quietly whirrs and then, loud and clear, 'Green Door' by Shakin' Stevens starts up.

Carol's wearing her weird purple driving glasses. She cocks her head and listens closely to the music, unsure what it is at first.

Come on, I think. You can't have forgotten this one.

Then her face breaks out in a grin.

'Oh wow,' she gasps.

On the chorus, we both sing along.

Next comes 'Fire and Rain'. It's only halfway through 'You Can Call Me Al' when I notice a large teardrop sliding out from under her glasses and down her right cheek, followed quickly by a second, then a third.

'He might have been a miserable sod at times,' she says, 'but I still miss him.'

'Me, too,' I say.

At home, Carol parks in the space where Dad's blue Ford Escort used to go. When we knock on the door, Mum opens it almost immediately. She looks really, really old – much older than I remember her. She smiles widely and puts her arms out and hugs us both at the same time.

I walk back out to the car and start carrying our bags into the hall.

'Look at all this,' I say.

The skirting boards are a much brighter white and the carpets are different and there's a fancy-looking cordless phone on the table by the door and, next to it, a brand-new, blinking wireless router.

'I've updated things a bit,' she says. 'I've entered the twenty-first century.'

Carol laughs.

'I'm on the internet now, too. If either of you want to use it. I'll write you down the password for the thingy after tea.'

I carry my things up the stairs to my room, which has transformed into a small, plain guest room at the end of the hall. I dump my bags on the carpet in the middle then walk over to the little window on the far wall and look down at the overgrown back garden and the frost-covered, corrugated iron of the garage roof, which probably still contains that old Triumph that Dad never quite got round to doing up.

I turn round and Mum's standing there, looking at me from the doorway.

'Nice to have you back,' she says.

'Nice to have me back, too,' I say.

'You know you can stay here for as long as you want.'

'I know.'

She heads down the small, creaking staircase and I hear the faint murmur of her and Carol's voices in the living room. In the corner of the room is the single bed I slept on all through my childhood and teenage years, the one I lost my virginity on. I close the door to my room, then lie down on it, still in all my clothes.

After dinner, we move over to the sofas and Mum brings out a big bottle of port and pours us each a large glass. A plate of mince pies appears.

'Happy Christmas,' she says.

'Happy Christmas,' we say.

'What do you need the internet for, anyway?' Carol says.

'You sound like your dad,' Mum says.

'It's a waste of money,' Carol says.

'I've joined a forum,' Mum says. 'It's just a glorified book group, really, except there's people from all over the world on it. I've got friends in Australia now, and, um, America. And there's a man from Birmingham. It's good fun. You should try it.'

'Good for you,' I say.

Carol shakes her head, baffled.

'And there's this website called YouTube. Have you heard of it?'

We both nod, trying to keep the smiles off our faces.

'It's just for funny videos really. Have you seen that one of Fenton? The naughty dog?'

Port tastes much nicer than White Label rum. The gas fire is turned up to full and the curtains are pulled shut and the room quickly becomes so warm and fuzzy that I start to feel myself nodding off occasionally, even though it's not yet ten o'clock.

After a while, I excuse myself and go up the stairs to bed.

In the bathroom, while brushing my teeth, I look at my face in the mirror and think: Tomorrow morning you will throw your e-cig away. You will get a haircut and have a shave and start doing some sort of exercise. You will learn a new language. You will buy an acoustic guitar. You will do twenty sit-ups and twenty press-ups each morning and start reading poetry. You will try to do something that is not just for yourself, like volunteering, maybe.

I wish I'd brought my cardboard box.

I don't need it for a bedside table – there's a proper one here – but it would've been nice to read Andrew's letters again. Because for the first time since he sent them to me, I feel about ready to reply.

PAUL
2014

As Paul steps off the train and walks along the platform, he gets caught in a flood of nostalgia; he remembers his years at university, in particular a time when Lauren met him off the train holding a bit of card with his name written on it. In the departures lounge, he remembers the endless weeks after she'd broken up with him, when he'd come and sat here for hours drinking over-priced coffees at one of the little brass tables, watching the people coming and going, and hoping, ridiculously, that Lauren would be one of them even though he suspected she was at her mum's, then found out she was off to Canada for a year (a mutual friend let it slip in town).

Turning out of the station, he thinks about the shitty

student house in the Meadows that he and Ian and David shared. They each chose a poster for the living room from the sale in the student's union. Paul chose *Nighthawks at the Diner*, and Ian chose *Unknown Pleasures* and David chose *Beer: Helping Ugly People Have Sex Since 1862.*

This will be the first time he's seen any of them in six or seven years.

He wonders if they'll have anything left to say to each other.

He wonders what they'll think of him, touching the smooth skin of his scalp.

Amazon keeps recommending him caffeine shampoo but it's way too late for that.

The best lads past and present assemble at five in the Wetherspoon's opposite the Cookie Club. They sit around a large table and drink weak pints of lager, and at first the conversation is stilted and subdued and mostly about what cars people have. Paul sits at the edge of the table, sipping his Fosters, hoping no one will make him admit that he still can't drive. Luckily, before the question reaches him, someone starts describing a video they saw on the internet.

'It's this fucking dog, right. No, wait, it's this kid. This lad. In America. And he starts getting attacked by this dog, right? This, like, wild dog. And it's dragging him off by the leg 'cause he's only small.'

'I've seen it,' someone interjects.

'And then this fucking *house cat* comes bolting up

out of nowhere, right, and chases the dog away! It's mental.'

Everyone nods.

They've all seen it.

'What about that one of the girl dancing and then she goes upside down and falls through the coffee table?' someone else ventures.

They've all seen that one, too.

'I saw one the other week of this drummer at this wedding, right,' a third voice begins, as Paul remembers a pornographic clip he watched last week, of a naked Japanese woman being molested by an unconvincing sci-fi monster with slimy, penis-like tentacles.

Once they've all described videos to each other for a while, the conversation turns to jobs. Paul shifts uncomfortably in his chair.

'What're you up to these days?' asks a lad called Kareem, who Paul wonders if he's ever even met before.

'I was teaching for a while,' Paul says, 'at the uni. Then I did a bit of . . . promotional stuff. But now it's mostly freelance, writing gigs.'

'Is that right?' Kareem asks, nodding enthusiastically, a lot more interested in this than Paul was hoping.

'It's not that interesting,' Paul says.

But Kareem persists.

'What kind of writing? Magazine stuff?'

'It's more online, really.'

'Not SEO?' Kareem almost shouts.

Paul nods.

'No way! That's what I'm in, too! Not the writing of it, but the back-end stuff.'

'What a coincidence,' Paul says.

He's only been bidding on freelancing websites for keyword-rich article-writing jobs for about a fortnight but already he hates it deeply. He's been doing all the actual writing on Sarah's netbook, too, and its miniature keyboard makes the shitty articles he has to compose seem even *more* trivial and banal and ridiculous than they already are. The absolute worst are the porn ones. Paul's latest assignment (he's still got half left to do when he gets back) is writing the bits of keyword-heavy copy for a group of extreme niche porn sites, all with names like Tentacle Rape and Sneaker Sniffers and Domgirls and Schoolbabe Hentai and The Toonporn Repository.

'This horny tentacle monster is ready to fuck every gaping hole of this screaming nude glistening Japanese babe in this erotic and completely free gallery of 100% free hardcore Japanese tentacle rape movies.'

That's the kind of thing Paul's been writing recently.

And the worst part of all is that it's not even *writing*, not really. No one's actually reading any of it. It's just a way of pushing these websites to the front page of Google for the benefit of a small pocket of tentacle fetishists. Paul's copy doesn't need to be elegant. It doesn't need to make sense. It just needs to be a certain number of words long and stuffed with as many potential search terms as possible:

tentacle porn
tentacle sex
tentacle fuck
tentacle impregnation
tentacle monster
japanese tentacle porn
tentacle videos
tentacle porn videos
live action tentacle porn
tentacle sex videos
tentacle bondage
japanese tentacle sex
live action tentacle attack
tentacle swallowing ecstasy

On top of all that, it pays pennies.

For the porn work, Paul's being paid 0.5 of a cent per word, weekly, into a PayPal account. Which means he needs to write about 3,500 words an *hour*, just to make minimum wage.

'Whose round is it?' someone asks.

Paul decides to take the hit early, while they're still in Wetherspoon's and everyone's just on pints.

'I'll get these,' he says, lifting himself out of his chair.

'I'll give you a hand,' David – the stag – says, and after they've taken everyone's orders (Fosters, Fosters, Fosters top, Fosters, Stella, Fosters), the two wander over to the bar.

'You know Lauren's going to be there, right?' David says.

Paul didn't know this, no. He wonders why she would, then remembers that David met his fiancée, Jenny, through them in the first place. Jenny was one of Lauren's friends from uni. Of course.

'Yeah, I'd heard something,' he says.

He feels embarrassed, even now, of the public mess he made of himself after Lauren broke up with him. He still hates anything at all to do with Canada.

'And where's Ian tonight?' he asks.

'No one knows,' David says. 'I sent him the Facebook invites to this and the reception, but he's not replied to any of them. I don't think anyone's heard from him in months.'

David looks more upset by this than Paul was expecting.

He wonders if it's strange that he doesn't really give that much of a fuck about any of them any more.

'Hey, congratulations, by the way,' he forces himself to say, clapping David on the arm.

'Cheers, mate. What about you? You've been with your bird for quite a while now, right? Think you'll ever tie the knot?'

Paul thinks about it seriously, possibly for the first time ever.

'Yeah, maybe,' he says.

After the curry and a small pub crawl – Paul's had six pints of Fosters now; he's not drunk exactly, just bloated and ready for bed – the lads are meandering back towards the Cookie Club for the indie night. A couple of them are singing football songs. One pissed in a shop doorway, and is just leaving his trousers round his ankles and waddling down the street because he thinks it looks funny. Just before they reach the club, Aiden, a man with big biceps and a Liverpudlian accent, drags them back out of the way of the doormen and down an alley near the Riley's.

'I've got some Mitsubishis here, lads,' he whispers. 'If anyone wants one?'

He gets someone to hold the bottle of Becks he smuggled out of the last bar while he rummages around in his coat, then pulls out a small plastic bag. He puts two small white pills on his tongue, takes the Becks and swigs it. 'Any more for any more?' he grins, offering up the bottle and the little bag.

'What are they?' Paul asks David beneath his breath. 'E?'

Paul's never done ecstasy before. Somehow, the opportunity never really presented itself. It didn't seem to be such a big thing back at university, in 2002, at least not for Paul.

'Yeah,' David nods. 'Having one?'

Paul watches David take a pill and swig it down. All the other lads take one, too.

'Oh, go on then,' Paul says.

In the indie club, one of Paul's favourite songs, 'Cut Your Hair' by Pavement, a song he put on a mixtape for Lauren, comes on, but Paul's too worried about the pill to dance. He imagines it sitting in his stomach, fizzing like an Alka-Seltzer. He thinks about a Dangers of Ecstasy assembly that they called in secondary school, years ago, featuring an overhead projector slide of a photo of a dead teenager. The image of that girl lying there on the floor of her kitchen will stay burned into Paul's brain for as long as he lives.

I should've just done a half, he thinks, and seen how I got on with that.

It's too late now, though.

I don't want to die, Paul thinks.

I don't want someone to take a photo of me bloated and dead on the floor of the Cookie Club.

I don't want my brain to pop out through my ears.

He looks at the lads, who are mostly sat around a large white booth, swigging bottles of lager and alcopops, deep in slurry, heartfelt one-on-one conversations that involve a lot of shouting in each other's ears and slapping each other on the back.

As Paul stands to go to the toilet, he feels a rush. It's not dizziness or drunkenness, though. It's a tingling, chemical feeling, in his fingertips, in his spine, in his skull. It's like a million buzzing electric pinpricks all over his body. He feels his mouth pulling itself involuntarily into a grin.

'Eh? Eh?' David says, catching Paul's attention as he walks past the table, clapping him on the leg. 'Enjoying it now then, are we?'

David's eyes are huge and black and his mouth is splayed in a massive, toothy grin.

'Yeah,' Paul says, feeling a sudden love and nostalgia for David.

We went to *university* together, he thinks. We spent a million nights together in that cramped, shitty living room, smoking joints and watching telly, and we were real friends and we grew up together and now here we are going bald and getting married and all that's actually a pretty big deal.

'Fucking shame Ian couldn't be here,' Paul shouts over the music, which has turned into 'Debaser'.

David nods.

'I love you, mate,' David says, sucking his bottom lip in and out of his mouth as he speaks.

'I love you, too,' Paul says emphatically.

'What?' Sarah says angrily, on the other end of the phone. It's half two in the morning and Paul's in the little roped-off smoking area out the front of the club.

'I just wanted to say,' Paul shouts into the mouthpiece, 'that I love you. I fucking *love* you. And I'm sorry for everything, you know?'

'You're shouting,' Sarah says. 'Why are you shouting?'

'Because I love you,' Paul shouts.

'I'm going back to sleep now. You're drunk.'

'Sarah?' Paul shouts, but she hangs up on him.

Everything's going to be okay after all. Paul just *knows it* as he grinds out his fag with his shoe and turns and goes back into the club, up the glittering stairs, towards the flashing lights and the booming indie, pulsing in waves from the upstairs dance floor. There's a big group of them, all the lads, dancing on the stage at the back with their arms round each other, singing along to 'Animal Nitrate'.

This is fucking *ace*, Paul thinks. I can't believe it's taken me this long to find out how good this feels. I'm going to get some more pills back in Manchester. I'm going to do them all the time. And Sarah will do one with me, and then we'll be fine. I'll take them while I'm writing, too, like the Beats did with amphetamine. Shit. I'm going to write the Great Ecstasy Novel of my generation. It's going to be like Jonathan Franzen meets Irvine Welsh meets . . . Who fucking cares? . . . I feel *fantastic.*

Paul climbs onto the stage and slings his arm round David's sweaty shoulders and starts to sing along.

Late the following afternoon, in the quiet carriage, Paul looks down at his cup of Virgin Trains black coffee, but can't quite bring himself to lift it to his lips. The occasional flashes of sunlight through the windows are painfully bright, but if he closes his eyes then his head starts to pound with apocalyptic booms and he sees skulls: actual melting skulls, like a death metal album cover.

This is not a normal hangover.

He feels shaky and gloomy and cobwebbed.

What the fuck am I doing? he thinks, closing his eyes, opening them again, not sipping his coffee, not writing a novel, not doing whatever it is he's supposed to be doing with his life.

He gets up and makes his way down the carriage, locking himself in the podlike toilet. He uses a square of toilet paper to close the lid, then sits and takes out his phone. He scrolls through to Alison's number. He stands again, unzips his jeans, the phone still clutched in his hand as he scoops his dick and balls out the front of his boxer shorts. He thumbs through to the camera with one hand, while tugging at his flaccid penis with the other, looking at it first in the long, streaky mirror on the wall opposite, then on the screen of his phone. But he can't get hard.

He considers just taking a picture of it *flaccid*, and sending that to Alison instead.

No.

He zips himself away and sits back down on the lid of the toilet, holding his throbbing head in his hands, eyes closed, death metal skulls dripping and swirling as he feels the train slow down, pull into a station, then start up again.

He opens his eyes, and presses call, his heart hammering.

'Hello?' Alison sounds different to usual. She sounds far away and angry.

'It's me,' Paul says.

'What do you want?'

Paul can hear laughter and cars beeping. She must be outside somewhere.

'I don't know. I thought maybe . . .'

'Fuck off, Paul.'

She hangs up.

Paul stands, unlocks the cubicle, and makes his way back down the woozy, rickety carriage to his seat. Oh great. Someone's thrown his coffee away. He sits back down, fiddles with his phone, plugs it in to charge, fiddles with it again. He opens Facebook and scrolls through his newsfeed, looking for a post from Alison, wondering where she was, what she was doing when he called her. He scrolls for a long time without coming across any of her updates – she's usually so frequent – and then he realises. He searches for her name. Opens her profile, which seems weirdly blank, all of her thousands of statuses and photos now missing.

Add Friend, it says.

He finds Sarah in the living room, curled in front of a *Grand Designs* omnibus. What a surprise. It's evening now. It's raining hard, drumming against the windows, and his head is fucking killing him still and he feels very tender and emotional and easily damaged.

'Hi,' he says from the doorway.

'Hi,' Sarah says, not turning round.

He comes and sits next to her on the sofa.

'Can we turn that off for a moment?' he says.

'Can it wait till the adverts?' she says.

'You've seen this one before,' he says quietly, but he doesn't push it any further.

He just presses his knees together, his head throbbing, and waits the seven and a bit minutes for the next ad break, when Sarah finally picks up the remote and mutes the TV and turns to face him.

She looks so tired.

'What? What's so important, then?'

Paul attempts to collect his thoughts.

He closes his eyes, sees melting skulls, opens them again, sees Sarah's tired, blinking face.

'I was wondering . . .' he says, feeling his throat close up with emotion as he says it. 'I was wondering if you'd marry me?'

LAUREN
2005

The plan changed. It was almost the same (Michael, London, uncle, spare room, etc.), only now Lauren would no longer be taking part in it. Instead she promised she'd come and see him – very, *very* soon – kissed him frantically on the doorstep and waved so hard as his taxi backed out of the drive it made her wrist click. Then, as soon as he was gone, she felt a huge, tingling wave of relief.

They were due at the hospital in an hour.

'Want anything to eat?' Anne asked when Lauren looked in on her from the doorway to the living room.

'I should be asking you that,' Lauren said.

* * *

In the study a few minutes later, as the computer dialled and beeped, she paced the room breathlessly, gasping in the dusty air and trying to out-walk the suspicion that she'd not been a good enough daughter, that she was *still* not being a good enough daughter, that she should go back into the living room right now and apologise for the countless times she'd been a moody, stroppy bitch.

There were two new items in her Hotmail inbox: one from Emily (who was now working as a live-in chef at a snowboarding resort in Whistler), and one from a theatre mailing list, which she'd signed up for back in her first year and then never bothered to cancel.

She clicked compose.

Dear Ian, she wrote. *I miss you.*

Pause.

I've had some bad news actually and I really need to talk to someone about it.

Pause.

I'm sorry about what happened. I think I made a mistake with Michael.

Pause.

Please give me a call if you get this, followed by her phone number.

Then she selected all and pressed delete.

In the hospital car park Anne leaned in to pay the taxi driver, then took Lauren's arm and led them both around the side of A&E, where they had gone that time for stitches, what seemed like years ago now, and down a path towards the MacGregor unit. The buildings were painted a bland, municipal cream with sarcastically bright red trim.

They entered a small lobby, and Anne gave her name to the friendly, familiar nurse at reception, then they both took a seat.

Out of all the scattered magazines on the coffee table in the corner, Lauren selected the one least likely to have anything sad in it.

It was for ages 9+, with a bright pink cover, and was called *Princess World.*

She leafed through, trying to find something funny or distracting to point at, past the word search on the back page (*Can you find the words Bad Daughter?*), then just closed the magazine and rolled it in to a tight, hard tube and clutched it in her lap.

'Mrs Cross?' another smiling nurse asked, a short while later.

They both followed her down a long, disinfectant-scented corridor, through a set of double doors, and into a large beige room full of padded chairs, each containing a person hooked up to a softly whirring machine.

The nurse led them to a free chair in the corner, which Anne sat down in, while Lauren dragged a plastic chair over from the far wall. There was a window, facing onto the car park, and hung next to it, an inoffensive, abstract print; just overlapping pastel-coloured triangles on an inoffensive, pastel-coloured background.

First they had to take a blood sample.

The nurse took a sterilised needle from a packet, as Anne began to roll up her sleeve, revealing a forearm as thin as a child's.

Remember when you had that blood test, Lauren?

Remember how dizzy and sick you felt, and how you almost fainted?

Well, what happened next?

That's right.

Your mum held your hand.

Your mum looked after you.

Because now it's your turn.

You must ignore your fluttering stomach and fight the urge to run away, and instead reach across and take your mum's free hand and give it a big old squeeze, just like that.

Anne smiled when she did it, squeezed back.

'Don't worry,' she whispered. 'You can look away if you want. I'll tell you when it's over.'

'No, it's okay,' Lauren said, taking a deep, shivery breath. 'I can handle it.'

IAN
2015

I give myself a final look-over in the full-length mirror in Mum's room. I'm wearing my smart trousers, and my smart shirt, my smart shoes, and a slightly-too-big-for-me blazer that used to be Dad's.

As I walk out of my room and down the stairs, I think again about Lauren's reply. It just said: *Are you going to David and Jenny's wedding?*

She'd not even written hi at the top or her name at the bottom.

I read it again.

Are you going to David and Jenny's wedding?

And then I looked back through all my unread Facebook messages and found amongst them two invites, one to 'Dave-O's Wicked Stag Do!!!' (which I'd already missed, thank god) and one to Dave and Jenny's wedding (just the reception bit).

Maybe, I replied. *Are you?*

I'd wanted to write more, but found myself matching the tone of her email. I didn't sign my name, either.

And then I waited two days, pacing around the house, puffing on my e-cig, before a reply finally arrived which just said: *Maybe.*

That's it.

That's all I have to go on.

I've borrowed another hundred and twenty quid off Carol for my train fare and a night in a Travelodge, and I've been trying not to think about the other people who are almost definitely going to be at the reception, too; who are almost definitely going to ask me where I disappeared off to, and why I'd not replied to any of their calls or messages or emails or anything.

Before I leave, I stick my head in the living room.

'Very nice,' Mum says. 'Very smart.'

She smiles up at me from the sofa, the *Radio Times* open in her lap.

'Go on then, give me a twirl.'

So I go into the middle of the room and turn in a slow circle.

'I look like a dickhead,' I say.

'You look lovely,' she says.

I sit down next to her.

'Do you know someone called Daniel Leicester?' she says.

Daniel Leicester is a person I haven't thought about

in over twenty years; a tall, sporty blond boy from the year above who never really liked me. I guess I never really liked him either.

'Only to say hi to,' I say.

'Carol's gone for a drink with him. Is he nice?'

'Yeah, I think so.'

'I'm worried she's making another mistake.'

I don't know what to say, so I keep my mouth shut.

'You okay?' Mum says. 'You seem . . .'

As I wait for her to finish the sentence, I look down at her lap, at the *Radio Times*, at a picture of a smiling young woman whose name I don't know.

'What are you thinking about?' Mum says.

'I'm okay,' I say.

'I am proud of you, you know. Despite what you think.'

'Why? I've not done anything.'

I want to explain. I want to tell her about Lauren and Dalisay and why I've been acting so quiet since I got here, but I don't know quite how to turn it into words. I'm a bad son. I am not okay. The lady in the *Radio Times* is smiling at me.

'I want to tell you that things get easier,' Mum says. 'But I think you also maybe need to lower your expectations a bit, love. Do you understand what I'm saying?'

She reaches across and squeezes my fingers.

'I'm okay,' I say again.

By the time my taxi drops me off in front of the sports club, it looks like the reception is in full swing. The car park is swarming with people in light grey suits and shiny purple dresses, talking and smoking and texting. I don't recognise anyone, not yet. I feel extremely sober as I weave through them towards the entrance. I follow the sound of a live band doing a ropey cover of 'Club Tropicana', down a long corridor, past trophy cabinets and notice boards for five-a-side football events and then, outside a large set of double-doors, I stop.

I take a deep blast on my e-cig, then push the doors open and step into the dark, noisy hall. There's a crammed bar at one end and a dance floor and stage at the other. The wedding band are dressed in corny white suits and there's flashing purple and pink lights everywhere, and purple and pink tablecloths and flowers. I make my way around the edge of the room, towards the bar. Right at the edge of the scrum, I see Paul. He's hanging back, fiddling with his phone.

I tap him on the shoulder and he looks up, startled, then smiles; a huge, toothy grin which catches me completely off guard.

'Alright, mate!' he says. 'Fucking hell!'

I feel myself smiling, too.

'How's things?'

'Alright,' I say. 'You?'

'Not bad. Not bad. Well, *actually*, they're pretty fucking terrible to be honest. But . . . you know . . . whatever.'

He laughs at this and I try to join in.

There's something funny about his eyes. His pupils

are massive: completely dilated. Which is when I realise. He's fucked. He's battered. He's completely off his head.

'I broke up with Sarah,' he says, as if I should know who Sarah is.

'Right, sorry,' I say.

'Are you married?'

There are bits of froth at the corners of his mouth and the veins are all standing out on his neck.

I shake my head.

I wonder if I should go and get him a glass of water.

'Great to see you, anyway, mate,' he slurs, lurching in to give me a hug, and when he does, he smells strongly of a sharp, chemical sweat.

'You, too,' I say.

'Do you want this?' he says, offering me his half-empty bottle of Grolsch. 'I paid about six quid for it and now I don't even want it.'

'Cheers,' I say.

'I'm just going off to the . . .' he says, pointing at the double doors, his mouth chewing and gurning. 'But I'll see you in a bit, yeah?'

I nod and he stumbles off.

I swig the Grolsch, which has gone warm and flat. I chug it down, as quickly as I can, then I push myself into the crush of men at the bar and let myself get slowly jostled towards the front. When it's eventually my turn to be served, I ask for a shot of dark rum and another bottle of Grolsch and I hand the barman a tenner and get almost nothing back in change. I take another deep blast on my e-cig, neck the rum in one, then elbow my way out of the crowd again.

Come on, I think. Where are you?

I move over to the corner and watch the band, who are approaching the final chorus of 'American Pie' now. And when they finish, everyone cheers and the singer announces that they'll be back in twenty minutes, and the dance floor thins out as people head to the bar and to the car park to smoke.

Which is when I see her, leaning against the opposite wall, talking to a tall red-haired girl in a salmon-pink blazer. She's wearing a dark blue dress, and her hair is piled up on top of her head and it's much darker and shinier than I ever remember it being.

I manage to get almost completely across the hall, just a few feet away, hovering around at the periphery of their conversation, and still she doesn't notice me. Up this close, I can see the tiny little lines and crags that, I imagine, my face also didn't used to have.

'I'm really sorry, Loz,' the red-haired girl is saying in an extremely posh, serious voice, and I wonder if I should perhaps leave them to it, go and get another Grolsch, come back later.

'It was a long time ago,' Lauren says, and then her eye catches mine and her face changes completely. 'Hey,' she says, smiling.

I feel myself begin to smile, too.

The tall red-haired girl turns to look at me.

'Ian, this is Emily,' Lauren says. 'Did you ever actually meet Emily?'

'I don't think so,' I say.

'Emily, Ian.'

'Hello,' I say.

'I'll leave you dudes to it,' Emily says, raising her glass of white wine before turning and heading off across the emptying dance floor.

'So you made it, then?' Lauren says.

'Maybe,' I say, unable to stop grinning.

There's so much to say, I don't know where to start.

'I don't know what to say,' she says.

'Me neither,' I say.

'You look good.'

'Thanks. So do you.'

'Have you seen *Paul*?' she says, leaning in a little and touching my arm, very lightly, up near my shoulder. 'He's completely battered. He tried to ask me out earlier on, to convince me we should give it another go.'

'Oh god,' I say.

'I might be single, but I'm not *that* single.'

'Ha,' I say.

She is touching my arm!

She is single!

My head spins and whirls.

'So,' I say. 'What are you up to now . . . I mean, um . . . what do you . . .'

'I'm working for Cancer Research.'

'Right,' I nod.

'Don't worry. I'm not one of those charity muggers if that's what you're thinking . . .'

It's not what I'm thinking at all.

What I'm thinking is the thing I've been thinking, almost continuously, for the last ten years: *Lauren Cross, I am completely and totally in love with you.*

She seems so calm and grown up.

It's amazing.

'What about you?' she says.

Her hand is still on my arm.

'I'm . . .' I say, trying to think of a way to phrase what I'm about to say, that doesn't just sound like 'I'm living with my mum'.

'I'm living with my mum,' I say.

'Oh god.'

I wait for her hand to move away in disgust, but it doesn't. She squeezes my arm, then rubs it gently, up and down.

'Are you okay?' she says.

I feel someone tapping my shoulder, and I turn round and there's David.

'Mate!' he says, offering his hand. 'Didn't think you were going to make it.'

'Congratulations,' I say.

David's hand is large and hot, and there's a small scar on his nostril where his nose ring used to be.

'Cheers,' he says.

'Where's Jenny?' I say.

'Just nipped out. She wanted to change our status but there's no reception in here.'

'Right,' I say, trying to work out whether he's joking or not.

I look across to Lauren; her eyes are wide and she's trying not to smile.

'I don't suppose you'd like to . . .' he says, nodding at the stage.

'What?' I say.

I honestly have no idea what he means.

'Play a song or two?'

I laugh out loud. The idea's completely ridiculous. But David isn't laughing. Neither is Lauren. They're both just looking at me, eyebrows raised, like I might actually do it.

'Why not?' Lauren says. 'You should go for it.'

'No way,' I say.

'It'd mean a lot, mate,' David says, but I'm not really listening to him. I'm looking at Lauren, over his shoulder.

Please, she mouths.

My heart's pounding, just at the idea of it.

'Alright,' I hear myself say. 'Not right now though, in a mi—'

But David's already turned; he's bounding towards the side of the stage and then climbing up onto it.

'Wait,' I shout, but he doesn't hear me.

'I don't know about this actually,' I say to Lauren, panicking. 'I really don't think I can . . .'

'Shhh,' she says, smiling, putting her hands on both my shoulders now and drawing me towards her, so our faces are only inches away. Her eyes are large and green and shining. 'You'll be great,' she says.

Then she kisses me, just on the cheek.

'Excuse me?' David announces from the stage, tapping the microphone until everyone's stopped talking and turned to look at him.

'I just wanted to say another quick thank you to everyone for coming and making this such a special day for Jenny and me.'

People clap.

'And I also wanted to thank the band for doing such a fantastic job so far.'

More clapping. A few whoops.

'And finally I just wanted to let you all know that, as a special favour, an old mate of mine is going to play us a song or two as well. This is someone I've known since uni, and he's really good, and it really means a lot to me that he's agreed to do this, alright, so I want you all to be nice and give him a big round of applause, okay?'

David starts clapping from the stage, and then everyone else joins in.

As I walk towards the small set of stairs at the side, it feels a bit like an anxiety dream.

I can feel everyone in the room – there must be about two hundred people here – all watching as I begin to climb the steps. I pick up the band's electric guitar, put it on, then switch on the amp. A whistle of feedback. I strum a couple of chords with my thumb, the chords of that song that appeared in my head, and guess what, they sound exactly how I imagined – just as good in real life as they did floating around my skull. Then I pretend to adjust the levels of the amp with my back to the room, but really I'm just buying time, scanning through the old Postcards set for a song I can still remember from start to finish. The acoustic one, I think. The one about talking in your head. The one that made her cry.

I walk up to the microphone.

'Hi, everyone,' I say. 'I'm actually just going to play one song. This is for David and Jenny . . .'

It's not, though.

It's for Lauren.

Acknowledgements

I would like to thank: everyone at Canongate, especially Joanna Dingley and Francis Bickmore for their editorial input, the other two-thirds of Metal Man: Joe Stretch and Socrates Adams, Sian Cummins, Nick Iles, Ben Brooks, Tao Lin, Cathryn Summerhayes, Sam Mills (and anyone else I might have accidentally forgotten) who read an early draft and offered their feedback, John McAuliffe and all the University of Manchester's Centre for New Writing, Katherine Potts for the photo, and all my family and friends, in particular Jessica Treen and my mum, Joan Killen.

Finally, I would like to also dedicate this novel – in loving memory – to my dad, Michael John Killen.